Afterimage

Helen Humphreys

Afterimage

A Phyllis Bruce Book

Harper*Perennial*Canada

HarperCollins*PublishersLtd*

for Mary Louise

www.harpercanada.com
Visit www.harpercanada.ca for
PerennialCanada reading guides,
suitable for group or indivual use.

HarperCollins books may be purchased for
educational, business, or sales promotional
use. For information please write:
Special Markets Department, HarperCollins
Canada, 55 Avenue Road, Suite 2900,
Toronto, Ontario, Canada M5R 3L2

First HarperPerennialCanada ed.
ISBN 0-00-648518-9

Canadian Cataloguing in Publication Data

Humphreys, Helen, 1961–
Afterimage

"A Phyllis Bruce book"
ISBN 0-00-648518-9

I. Title.

PS8565.U558A77 2001 C813'.54 C00-932314-7
PR9199.3.H822A77 2001

01 02 03 04 RRD 5 4 3 2 1

Printed and bound in the United States
Set in Monotype Baskerville

The photograph thus taken has been almost
the embodiment of a prayer.

—Julia Margaret Cameron

Un paysage quelconque est un état de l'âme.
Any sort of landscape is a condition of the soul.

—H. F. Amiel, 31 Oct. 1852

The boy will remember it this way forever. His wings are on fire. He stands against a burning wall. The harder he moves his arms, trying to get free of the leather straps, the faster the flames shudder along the white feathers.

The boy doesn't see her until she's right beside him. It seems as if she has poured out of the smoke, her grey cloak flapping around her like waves on the sea. For a moment they stare at each other. He sees the flicker of fear in her young face, but that is something he thinks later— young face *—much later, when he is a man. Now he thinks only,* Save me, *his throat seared shut. He cannot push the dry burst of words through his parched lips. It doesn't matter. She has grabbed him under the arms, holds him away from her body.* Put your arms out, *she says. He stretches his burning wings so that they stay clear of her clothes and she runs with him like this, down the hallway to Isabelle's bedroom. There is smoke in the room but the window is open. She stands him by the door, rushes to the bed, and drags the mattress off. He sees the sparks sizzling along the trailing edge of her cloak as she tears off the bedding, stuffs the mattress through the window, and it somersaults to the earth below. She has hold of him again, leans with him in her arms over the sill.*

I've got you, *she says.*

And then she lets him go.

The boy falls. He puts both his arms out and for a brief moment his fiery wings stay the air and he floats down. The air pushing against the underside of the wings is the same pressure as when she held him over the sill, the same feeling. The rush of fiery air as he slows above the earth. Her strong and steady hands.

This is him, flying.

England 1865

Guinevere

Annie Phelan hurries along the lane to the Dashell house. The coach from Tunbridge Wells let her off on the main road and she is to walk the last half mile by herself.

It is June. The narrow lane announces its summer inhabitants with Annie's every step. A magpie! A bee! The dry clicks of insects busy in the hedgerow. It is so different from London. There, the clatter of people and carriages was constant, though sometimes, at night, when Annie was walking home from reading classes she would hear the soft, tumbly voice of a nightingale calling in the Square. In London, the horizon was stacked with buildings, and the air was rheumy with coal smoke. Here, the sky is huge and blue, uncluttered.

All the long journey down from London Annie has imagined this walk, has imagined that the lane to the house will be rutted and dusty, that the house will suddenly appear as she rounds a bend, that it will be magnificent and stately. Perhaps a little decrepit. Like Thornfield Hall, she had thought in the coach. She has recently finished *Jane Eyre*, again, and this is how she has imagined a country estate.

And just as she had imagined, the Dashell house becomes visible as Annie rounds a bend in the rutted, dusty lane. She stops walking. There it is, looking much more decrepit than magnificent. Huge and sprawling, but definitely neglected. The bushes out front are straggly and tall, block out some of the downstairs windows with their green, swaying bulk. The stone on the upper storey is crumbly with age. A sign on the gatepost says Middle Road Farm. The last two words are obscured by brambles.

Annie stands there, in the lane, looking at the distant house, feeling apprehensive, wishing really that she could just keep walking down this lane, that the house would just keep appearing around every bend. She needs more time than this to arrive here fully. The moment she enters that house, sees the rooms, meets Mrs. Dashell, all her imaginings of this will stop and what is real will fill that space completely. In a few steps, in a few brief moments, this world will be exchanged for that one.

Cook has a crown of flowers in her hair. Eldon sees it when she leans over to serve him the vegetables.

The slick surface of the table looks watery in the weak window light, slopes away from him to Isabelle, at the other end, reading her book.

"Who are you this time?" he says to Cook.

She reddens. "Abundance, sir."

"Abundance?"

Isabelle looks up from her book. "After the bountiful harvest," she says helpfully.

Eldon bends his head over his plate of underdone turkey, which has been hacked from the bone in rough, stringy wedges. There's the whicker of the clock being wound in the hall. A bract of vines at the window. The cut heads of roses float in a crystal bowl, one turning slowly in the whispery light, bumping against the others, turning like a compass disc towards the thought of *North*.

*

Annie Phelan waits in the drawing room. In her hands she holds the newspaper with the advertisement in it, and the return letter from Isabelle, because she might need these to prove she should be here. In the Dashell house the red velvet curtains are drawn back and tied, fall in heavy, pleated braids to the floor on either side of the window. There are oil paintings on the walls, all portraits except for one over by the piano — cows in a field, hills in the background. The sun behind the hills has swept the grasses gold. On a side table by the door is a porcelain figurine of a naked man. Annie smoothes the front of her good lilac cotton morning dress, plucks at the stray threads of her plaid shawl. Her one shawl. In summers she cuts it through to a single layer. In autumn she sews it back together again.

The door to the drawing room crashes open and Isabelle swoops into the room, the flounces of her long dress brushing the porcelain figurine off the side table and onto the rug. She doesn't bother to pick it up.

Annie Phelan bows her head.

"Oh, don't do that," says Isabelle irritably. "Sit down. You've come a long way. No need to stand."

"I'm fine, ma'am." Annie is used to the measured, careful movements of her former mistress. Mrs. Gilbey would never knock anything off a table. Annie eyes the naked figurine on the floor. It is lying face down on the rug. Should she go over and pick it up? The curve of its back looks like a small, white wing.

"Suit yourself." Isabelle strides across the room to the window, strides back again. Her dress makes a breeze. Her tall body carving cleanly through the still air. Her quick movements unnerve Annie. She has not expected Mrs. Dashell to be as young as this — middle-thirties — and so full of energy. Her dark hair is pulled back, secured untidily in a knot with

9

what look to Annie like hat-pins. It is as though Mrs. Dashell has done her own hair, and done it by grasping it with one hand and stabbing it into submission with the other. "You've come from London?" Isabelle asks, as she strides back towards the window. "Remind me."

"Yes, ma'am. Portman Square. I worked for a Mrs. Gilbey there."

"And why did you leave her employ?"

"She died."

Isabelle stops pacing, stands in front of Annie, and, for the first time, really looks at her. She sees a dark-haired, scared-looking girl of perhaps twenty, in a worn-out grey dress. Her skin still milky with youth. "I'm sorry," she says. She feels exhausted by having to conduct this interview, each useless question she utters wrests precious strength from her body. "It's just that I don't like my day's work to be interrupted."

"But" — Annie waves her evidence of newspaper and letter — "you wanted me to come today. Now. After the noon meal."

"Did I?" Isabelle glances out the window, where her real life is waiting for her return. "How can I be expected to remember what I wanted." She turns back to Annie. "What's your name?"

Annie has two names. In Mrs. Gilbey's house she was called Mary, because Mrs. Gilbey always called her maid Mary, no matter what her given name had been. Those were the rules of Mrs. Gilbey's household. Maids were called Mary. Cooks were called Jane. Annie almost forgot her other name, living with Mrs. Gilbey. Now she is trying it on again, something that used to fit but now feels strange to her.

"Annie," she says.

"Annie what?"

"Annie Phelan."

"Irish?"

Annie hesitates. In the newspaper she holds in her hand are hundreds of advertisements for servants of all types. Some of the notices ask for "No crinolines," because the popular dress style takes up too much space in a room and interferes with a maid's ability to light a fire and sweep out a hearth. Many of the ads specify "No Irish."

"Yes and no," she says finally.

"And what does that mean?" Isabelle feels impatience rising in her again. She doesn't sound Irish at all. In fact, she speaks surprisingly well for a servant.

This is not like *Jane Eyre*, Annie thinks. When Jane first arrived at Thornfield Hall she was welcomed by Mrs. Fairfax in a very generous and hospitable way. Mrs. Fairfax wasn't impatient and snappy. Mrs. Fairfax sat knitting by the fire, a cat curled contentedly at her feet. Jane was treated like a visitor. Jane was offered a sandwich.

"What?" says Isabelle again, waving her hand. Annie is shocked to see that her fingers are all stained a hideous black.

Annie closes her eyes for an instant and tries to pretend that the sharp features of Mrs. Dashell are really the soft, kind features of Mrs. Fairfax. "Born Irish. Raised English," she says slowly. "My family died in the hunger. My parents. My brothers. I was given to the Cullens, who were making the passage over here. They took me because I was small enough to carry, but couldn't keep me because they had children of their own. So they left me in a workhouse and Mrs. Gilbey took me from there when I was nine years old." Annie takes a deep breath. It is the most she has said in days.

Isabelle watches Annie Phelan recount her brief life. There is something in her face that opens when she tells her story, this story that Isabelle has heard so many times before, different versions from different Irish famine victims, but the same story. But what *is* different this time is the face of Annie Phelan as she tells her tale, how the expression shows the emotion so completely. Sadness, fear, shyness — it is all right there, all that feeling at once — and this is something Isabelle has perhaps never seen before. Or only once before, long ago, in another world entirely.

"My parents raised money to help the Irish Relief," Isabelle says. "You have nothing to fear from me there." She walks back over to the window. The noon light is high and harsh. Objects outside the room seem transparent. The tin pail on the flagstone path. The apple tree. "The position is housemaid," says Isabelle. "I can pay you twenty-five pounds per annum, paid quarterly. It is what I pay the other servants. We have a cook, a laundry-maid, and a gardener. You may have an afternoon off every week and a Sunday off every month. You must make your own dresses or have them made, but we will pay for the material." She pauses. The light is flattening the apple tree, she thinks. Stepping on it. "Can you read and write? I already have a cook who can't, and the new laundry-maid seems stupid as a brick. Am I to be completely surrounded by imbeciles?"

"Yes, ma'am," Annie says to Isabelle's back. "No, ma'am. Yes I can read and write." She almost mentions *Jane Eyre*, but stops herself. Perhaps Mrs. Dashell, like Mrs. Gilbey, doesn't approve of novels.

"Oh," says Isabelle. "I really can't do this any more. Come here." She beckons Annie over to the window. "Look," she says, tapping the glass. "There's Wilks, the gardener."

Annie sees a leg poking out from behind a potting shed.

"He doesn't do a stick of work," says Isabelle. "He's a

terrible gardener. Cuts the heads off all the flowers. Hides all day down by the cabbages. Nothing but trouble." She sighs, a long drawn-out fluttering sigh. "I hired him because he has a gorgeous back. All sinew, and broad as this county." She looks hard at Annie Phelan, the grey of her eyes, the slightly down-turned mouth. If I hired you because you are beautiful, she thinks. Would I be sorry?

Annie climbs the narrow stairs to her room at the top of the house. She has never slept up high before. At Mrs. Gilbey's she slept in a narrow room off the kitchen, on a cot. The room was once a broom closet. In the early days, when there was a Jane, Annie would be up and in her morning dress by six a.m. to clean and blacken the kitchen range and grates. Later, when Mrs. Gilbey could no longer afford to keep both a Jane and a Mary, Annie would be up even earlier as she now had to take on all of Cook's responsibilities, in addition to her own.

Annie is to share an attic bedroom with Tess, the new laundry-maid, who started work with the Dashells the week before Annie. The room is large, has two dormer windows. Annie puts her carpetbag down on the bed by the right hand window. The bedroom is at the back of the house, and when Annie looks out the window she can see down into the garden, all the way to the orchard behind the old stone wall. She sees Isabelle hurrying along the path, her arms full of black cloth. She disappears into a glass henhouse near the garden wall and then Annie can see the cloudy shape of her moving about inside. From above, through the glass, Isabelle looks like the dark shift of flame in a hearth.

Annie unpacks her belongings, hangs her other morning

dress and her maid's black afternoon dress in the vast wardrobe, stuffs her underthings into an empty drawer. She picks up her Bible and goes down to the kitchen. Cook is making bread, her hands and forearms are coated with flour.

"You sort yourself out all right?" asks Cook.

"Yes, missus." Annie stands against the larder. The Bible is a box of words she holds against her chest.

Almighty Everlasting Grace

Cook looks up again in a few minutes, surprised. "What are you doing still here?"

"I've come for the afternoon prayers."

"Prayers," Cook snorts. "That's a rich one. Prayers, indeed."

"Did I miss them?" Annie is confused. "Were they earlier?"

Cook rests on her knuckles, leans over the table towards Annie. "There are no prayers here," she says. "It is not allowed. The Dashells are not believers in such foolishness. That's what they call it, 'foolishness.' No going to church. No God. Now, out with you. The Lady wants you to take the afternoon to get acquainted with the house. You'll have no cleaning duties today." Cook pounds a fist into the slab of dough on the table. "And mind," she says. "You are not to go into Mr. Dashell's library and disturb his work. And neither are you to go near the glasshouse in the garden."

Annie climbs slowly back up the staircase to her room. She sits on her bed holding on to the Bible, the hard brick of it solid in her hands. At Mrs. Gilbey's, God was everywhere. There were morning, afternoon, and evening prayers. On Sundays there was church and three evenings a week Annie would copy out Bible verses from memory to practise her handwriting and Mrs. Gilbey would correct her spelling and grammar. It was God who taught Annie to read in the first place. The reverend of the nearby church gave reading and writing lessons to maids, and Mrs. Gilbey had sent Annie there when she was a young girl. There was safety in those words she grew up reading. They could be depended on.

God was the sky. With no words to keep the world together, the sun would burn through, brighten everything to black. The lace of apple trees. The flicker of Isabelle moving inside the glasshouse.

"What are you doing?"

Annie looks up to see a plump, red-faced girl in the doorway. The girl walks over and stands right in front of Annie, glares down at her. There is sweat on her forehead and upper lip. Her hands, on her hips, are bright red. "That's my bed," she says. "That one you're sitting on."

Annie gets up quickly. "I didn't know," she says.

"Well, you should have known." The girl doesn't move, remains solidly in front of Annie.

"Tess?" Annie feels that it is a bit hopeless now to ingratiate herself with her new roommate, but she has to try. "I'm the new housemaid, Annie Phelan. I am pleased to be meeting you."

Tess doesn't alter her stance or expression. "My bed," she says.

Annie retreats to the other bed and carefully puts her Bible under the pillow. "There," she says, because Tess is still watching her suspiciously. "This is my bed. This one. Over here."

The Dashell house is full of rooms attached, each to each, through other rooms, as though the builder needed new space immediately and desperately, had no time for such niceties as hallways. The farther away from the main part of the house, the plainer the rooms become, some are even steps down from the level of the preceding rooms. Annie realizes that some of them were perhaps once even outbuildings.

Annie wanders through the strange, unfolding rooms, each one like a pause in a long, rambling story, a place to draw breath before continuing on. The dark furniture, the lavish velvet drapes, the paintings and rugs all seem vaguely sinful compared to Portman Square.

At the very back of the house, in one of the farthest rooms, Annie finds a collection of baby equipment — carriages, cradles, a trunk full of clothes, a rocking horse. She puts her hand on one of the carriage hoods. The carriage sways in great, squeaky wheezes. When she takes her hand away her flesh is coated with dust. No one has spoken to her of children. She has seen no evidence of them in the house. Why is there this room full of dusty prams and moth-eaten receiving blankets? It feels to Annie as though she has been the only living thing in this room for years and years. She pokes at a doll lying tangled with other dolls in a box on top of a steamer trunk. The doll's eyes snap open and Annie jumps. The eyes flick closed again.

Annie is unlikely ever to have children of her own. She is unlikely, if she remains in service, even to marry. Sometimes it is possible for a maid to take a male servant in the same household as a husband. Annie thinks of Wilks, of the leg poking out from behind the potting shed. She shakes the leg of the doll again and the eyes fall open and stare at her, unblinking, blue as a morning sky.

The rest of the house is not as sinister. Rooms for dining. Rooms for receiving visitors. To the right of the sitting room where Annie first met Mrs. Dashell is a long hallway, a wing that, like everything else, seems to have been built on as a kind of rash afterthought. Annie wanders down the hallway, hands out to touch the cool walls on either side of her. At the end of the passage a door is ajar. Annie pushes it slowly open, enough to peer inside. Books are layered from floor to ceiling. The density of them like strata in a glacial bluff. Annie has never seen so many books in one place. The small library in the reverend's house in Portman Square was no match for this one. Near the end of her time in London, Annie was afraid that she'd have to start again in the reverend's library, start back at the beginning, at the first book she'd borrowed from him.

There is no one in this forbidden library and Annie pushes the door completely open and enters. A huge oak table piled up with sheets of paper dominates the centre of the room. There's a desk near one set of bookshelves, and a free-standing globe, almost as tall as Annie, beside the desk. But it is the books Annie is interested in. She stands in front of the shelves, greedily reading the titles of these volumes she has mostly never seen, or heard of before. *Reliques of Ancient English Poetry. The Last Days of Pompeii.*

At Mrs. Gilbey's, reading was Annie's secret. Mrs. Gilbey wanted Annie to be literate, wanted the convenience of a maid who understood written instruction, but she would not have appreciated Annie's feverish passion for words, would not have tolerated passion of any sort within her household. Annie's reading at Mrs. Gilbey's was always done with the same bursts of clandestine intensity that one would use to pursue an illicit encounter. Hiding a book in a cupboard and reading phrases in between changing the bed linen. Putting a book, open, inside the large silver tureen so that she could read and polish the silver at the same time. Luckily the reverend supported her romance with reading and kept her supplied with books from his personal library. But they were largely books on religious matters, or at least with religious leanings. There was not the range that there was here, in Mr. Dashell's library. Annie runs her hands lightly over the soft leather spines of the books. All those words, just waiting for her.

"Never mind what I told you," says Cook, when Annie appears back in the kitchen. "I need you to take these to the Lady. She's in the glasshouse. Down the garden." Cook thrusts two goose wings at Annie. The feathered wings are fully extended, and very stiff. They have crude leather hoops sewn onto the underside of them, two on each wing.

On the path in the garden that leads to the glasshouse, Annie meets Eldon Dashell. He is tall and thin, with a straggly reddish beard and glasses. Hurrying towards the house, looking down at the pattern of stones and grass between his feet, he doesn't see Annie until he is almost upon her.

"Excuse me."

He looks up, delicately sidesteps her, sees her armload of wings and then her face. "Angels," he says. "You must be the new maid."

"Annie Phelan, sir," says Annie, bowing her head. She has said her name so often this day that it is finally starting to feel as though it does belong to her.

"Well, I'm pleased to meet you, Annie Phelan." Eldon bows his head as well, and smiles. "But don't let me hold you up. The genius doesn't like to be kept waiting." He nods his head again. "Good day." And then he continues walking the path to the house.

Annie stands outside the henhouse. Through the glass she can see the murky shape of Isabelle, floating around like a dark, underwater bird.

Angel

Over the grey, stone wall the apple trees make a puzzle of the sky.

Where does God go to if he can't stay here?

When Annie enters the glasshouse she sees a large wooden box on stick legs at the far end. Isabelle is in front of the box, bending over a small child lying on a bench. The bench is covered in black cloth and black cloth is also hung from the ceiling to create a curtain against the end wall. Another child stands listlessly off to one side of the box. He is naked. The child lying on the bench has a white sheet draped over him.

"Ma'am," says Annie, but no one hears her. She advances into the room. Sunlight makes bright flowers on the stone floor. She can hear muffled birdsong from outside. "Ma'am," she says again, and this time Isabelle turns around.

"Thank God," she says, with such relief in her voice that Annie looks behind her to make sure that there isn't someone else in the room whom Isabelle is addressing.

Isabelle takes the goose wings from Annie and gives them to the standing, naked boy. "Now, Tobias, put these on. Quickly, please." The boy looks at the wings scornfully and slowly starts to thread an arm through the leather straps.

"They're on loan," says Isabelle to Annie. "My cousin's children. Silly little beggars," she says, under her breath, just loud enough for Annie to hear. "There." She looks at Annie in triumph. "I've made you smile. I didn't think you knew how. Oh, Tobias, pick it up." The standing, naked child has dropped one of the wings and is fumbling around trying to grab ahold of it with his feathery arm. Isabelle goes to help him. Annie watches them. The Lady doesn't seem so fearsome here. Her movements are tamer. The light flooding through the glass roof softens the whole scene. Annie feels almost as if she could cup her hands around it and contain it safely there, the gentle push of its heart against her fingers. Beat, it doesn't beat, it drops. It falls to earth, slowly, like a word after it's been said.

Dearly beloved

"Now, Tobias, come and lean over Alfred and look mournful." Isabelle moves behind the box on sticks and looks through a hole in it. The standing, naked boy obediently moves closer to his brother and slumps over Alfred.

"You don't need to smother him," cautions Isabelle.

Tobias looks at her with contempt in his eyes. "I am the Angel of Death," he says.

"But Alfred is already dead," says Isabelle. "You don't need to kill him again. You are only supposed to guide him out of his mortal self."

"His what?" says Tobias. Alfred's arm suddenly drops over the side of the bench and hits the floor.

"Oh, wake him up." Isabelle steps back from the box and rubs her forehead. "Infidels," she says to Annie. "Disaster."

Annie notices, again, the blackness of Isabelle's hands. "Silver nitrate," says Isabelle. "It dyes them black. Permanently." She waves them under Annie's nose. "Blacker than yours after cleaning the grates, aren't they?" Annie feels she is being challenged somehow, that there is something cruel in Isabelle's voice. She looks away, looks at the scene coming undone on the bench.

"Ma'am, why do you have an angel and yet you don't have prayers?"

"Ah." Isabelle glances briefly over at Tobias and Alfred, who are wrestling. "Stop that," she says to them. "Symbolism," she says to Annie. "Religious symbols stand for moral values. The symbols are still useful, even if the religion is not."

Annie shakes her head.

"You don't understand?"

"No, ma'am."

"Come here." Isabelle leads Annie over to the box. "Look." She slides the cover from the small hole in the wood and makes Annie look through it. "See. The Angel of Death is helping the dead boy out of this life. He is a passage between this world and the idea of another world. He is a sense of possibility. A looking up. A wonderment. An angel does not just belong to God. It is a feeling in us. A striving." Isabelle's voice is airy, lifts with her excitement at what she is saying. "When I have made this photograph, I want it to be that feeling of looking up. When I show it to people, that's what I want them to feel — the possibilities that could exist beyond this life." She pauses, puts her hand lightly on Annie's shoulder. "Do you see?" she says.

Isabelle has sent Tobias and Alfred home in a fly with Wilks. Back to their mother's house in Tunbridge Wells. She sits on the bench with the black cloth behind her, poking stray feathers back into the goose wings. Tobias and Alfred. They are not obedient enough because they know her, feel they can play when they come here instead of work, don't understand what it is she is doing. Trying to do, thinks Isabelle, threading the bone of a feather through the weave of the wing. What I am trying to do. It is so frustrating. Her ideas are sound, she is sure of that. What is it that happens between her idea and the finished result? What goes wrong? It is as though the moment she sets up a scene it starts to leak away. The image in her head burns brighter, is true. When she looks through the viewfinder of the camera, she sees her image coming undone, trailing threads of smoke, disappearing. How to make it stay. What will hold it until she is able to render it completely?

Isabelle looks up at the lens of the camera. It is supposed to see what she sees, that is the point. It is supposed to be her eyes.

The afternoon light is beautiful now. It slants into the henhouse, all current and moving lines. The air swims with light. That is the half of it, thinks Isabelle, bending over the white feathers. Light. The rest is shape and shadow. Intent. The raised arm that curves up out of the frame is the heart leaping forward, is the moment before arrival and the quickening of anticipation.

Isabelle puts the wings aside and walks over to the wall of the henhouse. There are still boards against the glass and bits of straw wedged in the steel supports from when the hens were there. Now they have eggs delivered from the farm down the road instead. The branches of the trees through the glass, the trees in the orchard, look like lacing pulling together a corset of sky. Apples. That's what the painters do. Mounds of apples and lemons. A blue jug of wine. Still life. Isabelle puts her hand up to the glass. Now she is a tree against the sky.

The budding apples are higher up the trees than she'd expected. The fallen ones from last year still on the ground, a brown, pulpy mass. Wilks probably hasn't been down here in ages. There isn't a single ladder or climbing aid anywhere. Isabelle manages to haul herself up onto a low branch of one tree and stretching up high into the boughs she is able to get to the apples. They are small, but she finds a nice, round, red one, and another with a couple of leaves still attached to the stem. But what to do with them? She can't throw them out of the tree as they might break or bruise when they hit the ground. Isabelle stands in the apple tree, holding the two apples, her feet on one branch, her body angled into the trunk of the tree. There are twigs probing her, and the bark is rough against her cheek. All around there is the soft hum of bees and the warm smell of last year's apples running to earth.

Isabelle puts the apples down the front of her dress. It is a slow, cautious walk back to the studio to unload her cargo on the black bench. The apples are warm from having been next to her skin. She curls a white sheet around them and goes to look through the camera lens. What she sees are apples. A mound of apples with a white sheet coiled around them. The fold in the sheet as it holds the shapes of them is pleasing, but the apples themselves are just apples. They aren't hopeful or faithless or awakening from a feverish dream in which they have glimpsed the afterlife. They are apples only, round and red, flecked with sun. What is so beautiful about apples? What human truth could rise out of this pile of fruit?

Isabelle leans her forehead against the wooden box of the camera. The sullen apples squat on the black cloth. Nothing moves. Still life.

"Beautiful!"

Isabelle turns to see Robert Hill in the doorway of the henhouse. He strides across the floor towards the apples on the bench, waving his arms as though he is conducting an orchestra. "Lovely composition! Look how the sun rolls off the fruit."

Isabelle instantly feels guilty for doubting her apples. If Robert Hill, acclaimed painter and peer of the realm, thinks her composition lovely, then what right has she to complain? "Do you approve of the suggestiveness of the drapery?" she asks her neighbour, trying, really trying, to believe in the apples, but they still stare balefully at her from their seat on the bench, like so many red, angry eyes.

"Oh, wholeheartedly. I most definitely approve." Robert Hill moves behind the apples and bends to tuck the sheet a little closer to the form. "But I think it could benefit from a little shaping." He fusses with the sheet and Isabelle watches him. The sunlight runs through his white beard like water. His long fingers stroke the folds of the sheet to his bidding.

Time, she thinks. Time persuading Beauty to decay.

Robert Hill would not agree to be her subject. He is famous, would consider it demeaning to sit for a portrait. And for all his bluff encouragement, he does not take Isabelle seriously. He does not believe her to be an artist. She is a woman. And she is a photographer. Women do not have the proper souls to be artists, and photographers are only useful to produce a likeness of something. A photograph cannot be a work of art. A year ago, when Isabelle first started taking photographs, she would argue with Robert Hill about his strict opinions on the subjects of women and photography. She had expected greater tolerance from a respected artist. Now, although she still admires his work, she no longer heeds his words. "I was attempting something new," she says. The apples don't glare at her quite so strongly after she has said this. "I'm not sure that I've succeeded."

"Oh, my dear. Beyond your dreams." Robert Hill waves his arms again over the pile of fruit as though he's offering a blessing upon it. "This is so much more worthy of you than those odd scenes. This is" — he searches for the correct words, doesn't have to look far — "so much more, *domestic*." He looks right at Isabelle, his eyes cold and watery.

There are days when Isabelle will parry with Robert, deflect his blows with a casual comment or a laugh. Today she can't find the strength to counter him. "Eldon's in the library," she says instead. "I'm sure he's expecting you."

*

"It is good to see that Isabelle has finally succumbed to more suitable subjects," says Robert, seated in Eldon's most comfortable chair, the black leather wing chair by the library window.

Eldon is standing over a long table, looking down at large sheets of paper. "Angels," he says. "The ascension of the spirit."

"No, no. Apples."

"What?" Eldon looks up.

"Still life." Robert pushes the word "life" off his tongue so that it stretches out into the room, and then snaps shut. "That is much more appropriate for a Lady than live models."

"I wouldn't get too jubilant." Eldon knows his wife, knows that she doesn't think much of photographing the static world. "I'm sure it's just a temporary setback in her pursuit of artistic excellence."

"Artistic excellence," says Robert drily. "Ah, but you believe women have souls and that public education will bring about social reform. And that social reform is desirable."

"Yes, well, my utilitarian ideals have not helped me much lately." Eldon taps the topmost sheet of paper. "A theme map. Dunstan wants me to make a theme map. All the work I've done on the atlases. This was to be my vision. A map of the world. *My* map of the world. And instead they want me to show mineral deposits and native trees. They think that maps are starting to repeat themselves, that there is nothing left to show of the world. Nothing new." Eldon looks at the map in front of him, the carefully delineated boundaries between the countries, the blue of the oceans. How can Dunstan think that all has been shown that is worth showing when the top of the map is still thick with white space? Not much detail. The descriptor of *Arctic Icy Ocean* looping through its empty rooms.

Robert is half bored by Eldon's indignation. He turns to the

bright world outside the window and sees Annie Phelan walking tentatively past the rose bushes.

"Who is that?"

Eldon sighs, looks up at Robert and then out the window.
"The new maid," he says.

"Lovely." Robert presses his hands together in excitement.
"She looks lost."

"She probably is."

"She needs saving," says Robert. "We should save her."

Eldon looks down at the map again. "All she needs," he
says. "All any of them need, is a proper education."

Robert knows what comes next, the long speech about the
benefits of education for the lower orders. "Oh, please," he
says. He runs a finger over his thin lips as Annie trails from
view. "Spare me."

The road is hard earth. It twists ahead of Annie. It twists out
of sight behind her. The bit she stands on is cracked from the
heat of the summer sun. All around her the air swims with
dust from the pickaxes swinging into the hard rind of road,
swinging clear. The arc of the bodies as they heave the axes
through the air looks like a kind of dance.

None of the workers on the road faces towards Annie. What
she sees from where she stands are the backs of the men and
women, the sharp start of the axes at the top of their arc, the
surge downwards to earth. Annie is the only one on the road
who is not working. She looks around for her axe, thinking
she may have left it on the grass at the edge of the road, that
she must have put it down for just a moment. But, no, it is not
at the side of the road. It is not anywhere.

The dust rises like smoke above the heads of the workers. Roils like water. Rises into clouds and muscles away into the far blue of the sky.

Annie touches the shoulder of the woman nearest to her. Perhaps she will know where Annie's axe has got to. The woman turns towards her, and in that moment the whole crew of road workers also turns and Annie sees, to her horror, that all of them, men and women alike, have her face. All of these people are her.

Annie wakes, lies in her bed, listening to the dark. Her breath stoppered in her throat. At Portman Square the noises were all above her basement-kitchen room. Lying in her cot there she heard the house creaking and shuddering over her, Mrs. Gilbey walking among the rooms with tiny, sharp steps, like the sound of tacks being hammered in. At the Dashells', Annie is as high as sound can go. Above her is the roof, above that the night sky. Her thoughts can leave her head and rise right up into the trees, into the dark clouds covering the moon. There is nothing to net them.

This new house is noisier than Mrs. Gilbey's. It is bigger, sprawls out, isn't straight up and contained like the brick town house in Portman Square. Someone always seems to be going up and down the staircase. A window shuts. A window opens.

"Tess," whispers Annie. She wants to be reassured that this is the real world. She wants to know that Tess, curled up on her side in her bed across the room, doesn't have Annie's face, too. But Tess is asleep. Annie can hear the deep shaking of her breathing.

When she lived with Mrs. Gilbey there would sometimes be days when Annie never spoke a word. Mrs. Gilbey wanted her Marys to do only what was required. She never asked Annie anything, or engaged her in conversation. Sometimes, when she hadn't used her voice for a while and was suddenly required to, it would come out all hoarse and ghostly and not like hers at all.

"Lord," she whispers into the darkness. "Take this dream away from me." Annie closes her eyes, opens them again. The room ripples with her words, each one eddying gently around her. If she twists her neck towards the window, she can just see the bright thorns of stars in the sky. If she closes her eyes, she can see the road and the flail of axes, like swimmers crawling through the dusty air.

At the beginning of Annie's first work-day she gets up at 6:30, says a few furtive prayers as she washes her face, and then goes down to the kitchen. Cook has already cleaned, black-leaded, and lit the range, gives Annie a cup of tea before she sends her off to sweep the front hall. At Mrs. Gilbey's, Annie was forbidden to drink tea because it had been rationed once years before and that had made Mrs. Gilbey consider it too valuable to be wasted on a maid.

Mr. Dashell rises early to get work done before breakfast, so there is no need to wake him. At 7:30, Annie is sent up with hot water and tea for Isabelle. She knocks on the door. No response. She knocks again. Finally she puts her tray down, opens the door, and enters the room. Isabelle is asleep, lying on her side, curled up in a ball under the covers. Annie sloshes the hot water into the basin. She bumps the jug against the basin, pours the tea, and sets the teapot down on the bedside table. Nothing. She picks up the teapot and sets it down again. Louder.

"Oh, hello, Annie." Isabelle struggles to a sitting position, her hair loose and wild. She waves her hands around as if she's trying to haul herself up out of the sleeping world. "Is it morning already?"

"It is, ma'am." Annie gathers up the water jug and teapot. She can feel Mrs. Dashell watching her. *Mr. Rochester*, she thinks. In this house, it is Mrs. Dashell who is the grumpy and intense master. It is not the polite Mr. Dashell she met on the path yesterday. When she looks up she sees that Mrs. Dashell has slumped down in her bed again. Annie leaves the room quietly.

In the kitchen Tess is at the table, just finishing her breakfast. She slides down the bench to make room for Annie. "There you go," she says. She does not appear to have held a grudge about the beds. Annie is glad of this, sits down for tea and porridge. "Is this right?" says Cook, at the stove, boiling Annie's egg.

Tess looks up. "There won't be a stove, will there?" she says.

"But the attitude," says Cook.

"I don't want to be rude, missus, but it's mostly your backside I'm seeing." Tess stands up from the table, knocks her knife onto the floor. On purpose, Annie thinks.

"Ooooh," says Tess. "Dropped my knife. Looks as if I'll be seeing a strange man before nightfall." She giggles. "Better go and make myself beautiful," she says, and leaves for the laundry, a brick building just off the kitchen in the back garden.

Annie's cleaning duties are such that she does not need to rush between chores, as she had to at Portman Square, but can even lift her head sometimes to listen to a bird outside or watch how the light brushes a painting in the drawing room. Here, there is no need to scrub the stone steps and flags every day, as she did in London. Here, people do not step over her as though she did not exist. When she was on her hands and knees on the staircase, cleaning the rods, Mr. Dashell stepped around her and even said, "Good morning, Annie," as he passed. Here, it does not seem that her work will constantly be found fault with. In fact it is just the opposite, the Lady and Master do not care enough about the household management. They leave all the instructions up to Cook.

After Mr. Dashell has passed by her on the stairs, Annie sits up and arches her spine to stop her back from hurting. "'Why am I always suffering, always browbeaten, always accused, forever condemned?'" she says softly. It is her favourite phrase from *Jane Eyre*. She used to say it to herself at Mrs. Gilbey's. It made her feel better, saying it, there where she was browbeaten, accused, condemned, and always, always suffering.

Annie wipes her forehead. Upstairs she can hear the voices of Eldon and Isabelle. She still feels full from her generous breakfast. The house is warm and comfortable. Perhaps it is time to read *Jane Eyre* again. Perhaps, now, there is a more appropriate phrase for Annie to choose as her own.

Eldon knocks at his wife's bedroom door and then walks in without waiting for a reply. Isabelle is sitting by the window. She is dressed, but her hair is still down.

"Oh," she says when she sees it is Eldon. "I thought you were the new maid."

"She's cleaning the stair rods." Eldon moves into the room, not quite as far as his wife. "Do we need clean stair rods?"

"I'm sure we'd perish without them. I know I would. What do you think of the new maid?"

"She seems a nice girl."

"Beautiful, isn't she?" says Isabelle. "I thought I could

photograph her when I first saw her. But now I'm not sure about any of that. Models. My ideas."

They look at one another.

"I was on the hunt for my spectacles."

"You don't need an excuse to enter my bedroom," says Isabelle.

"But I found them." Eldon waves them feebly at her. "Must have fallen asleep reading in bed last night." He can remember when they were first married how he never wanted to leave his wife's bed. Now, being married has somehow made him feel more alone than if he'd never married at all. The small distance between them whistles with loneliness.

"Why aren't you in the studio?" Eldon comes back to his original thought when he'd walked down the corridor and seen his wife's closed door.

"I'm trying to decide whether or not I'm a failure."

"And?"

"Eldon." Isabelle puts out a hand and he takes it. They are that near to one another. He takes the hand and it is cool and dry. "Will I ever be taken seriously?"

"Robert Hill?" he asks, remembering yesterday's visit from their famous neighbour, who mostly seemed to come and see them when he was bored with his own work.

"They're all Robert Hills," says Isabelle.

Eldon sees the injustice of it as he sees everything, a map before his mind's eye with the country of *Women* made up of the villages *Injustice, Servitude, Inequality, Humility.* "I would stop it," he says wildly. "In my world, there will be opportunity for all."

"But, Eldon," says Isabelle. "There are more Robert Hills than there are your kind in this world." She withdraws her hand from his moist palm. "That is one sad truth. Another is that most people agree with Robert Hill."

From the window Isabelle can see down into the garden. The wind ruffles the leaves on the trees. Tess stands outside the laundry hut, talking to Wilks. Isabelle thinks that Wilks has been hiding all morning in the orchard, thought she saw him earlier, walking over the rusty cobbles of apples.

Eldon would put things to rights if he had the power to do so. Isabelle is certain of that. He has an innate sense of fairness. It is his most dependable, and perhaps most lovable, characteristic. But what he wants to change of the world will never be changed. She is also certain of this, and so his wild outbursts of indignation on her behalf cause her to feel a certain wariness towards him, a politeness, an unfamiliarity with this man who is her husband and has been for thirteen years.

Eldon can see that Isabelle's brief need of him is over. Her pulling away makes him want to proclaim something even more remote and impossible. *I will make you famous. I will be the answer to all your hopes and wishes.* The territory that is himself grows larger, pushes back the salt tides, the broken chains of islands, flung like broken crockery onto the top shelf of the world.

Tess's laughter drifts up from the garden below, light and hopeful as the wind it rides on. Isabelle can't imagine that she has ever sounded as recklessly happy as that.

"I had better go and see about lunch," she says, although this is something she never does and they both know it. She brushes past her husband on her way out of the room and they both, instinctively, flinch.

*

Annie is outside cleaning her dusters. She taps them against the wall of the house and dust rises like smoke from the feathers. It is a warm day. She stands with her back against the wall of the house, feeling the heat weeping onto her skin from the stones.

There is great activity in the glasshouse. Even from this distance Annie can see the fluttering of dark figures in the building. She cannot help herself. She walks over to the henhouse and gently slips in through the door.

Wilks, the gardener, is standing at the far end of the studio. He is dressed in what looks like a tablecloth, pinned at his throat so that it becomes a cape. On his head is a rough sort of crown fashioned from painted cardboard. On his legs, breeches. On his feet, boots. Tess is lying on her stomach on the floor in front of him, clutching on to his ankle. Her hair is loose and washes out from her head like seaweed, matted and wild. She is wrapped in a sheet.

"You're not trying to trip him up," says Isabelle, circling them madly. "You're begging him for forgiveness, begging him to take you back."

"I don't need to be forgiven," says Tess. Her voice sounds a bit muffled because she's lying on her face.

"Don't," says Wilks irritably.

"What?" says Isabelle.

"She's cutting off my circulation." Wilks shakes his leg as though Tess is a pesky dog he's trying to dislodge.

"He's the one what should be begging for forgiveness," says Tess.

"You're not Tess," says Isabelle slowly. "This is not now. You have to leave yourself behind."

Even Annie, with her limited acquaintance of her fellow maid, knows that Tess could only ever be Tess. She would have great trouble leaving herself behind.

Wilks flaps his tablecloth cape impatiently.

"Who are they meant to be, ma'am?" Annie asks, stepping forward into the room.

Isabelle looks at Annie for a moment before answering. "Guinevere," she says, pointing to Tess. "King Arthur." She taps Wilks on the shoulder. "Do you know the story?"

Annie shakes her head. She has read mostly novels, is not so familiar with the old tales.

"Guinevere and Arthur are married," says Isabelle quickly. "Guinevere has fallen in love with Lancelot, one of her husband's knights. They are discovered. Lancelot is banished. Guinevere is forced to beg forgiveness from her husband."

"And is she truly sorry, ma'am?"

"No." Isabelle thinks of Robert Hill, thinks that it is herself on the floor grabbing on to his ankle, begging to be accepted into the society of the gentlemen painters. "No, she is more sorry that she was found out and that her husband banished her love."

Annie feels banished, cast out from the life she has known, washed up on the unfamiliar shores of this world. "Let me try," she says. They stare at each other across the sun-streaked room.

Isabelle is surprised at Annie's request. Certainly anyone, or indeed anything, will be better than the idiot laundry-maid. "All right," she says.

"Thank the Lord," says Tess. She struggles to her feet, ripping the sheet from her body in a gesture of glorious relief. "May I be excused now, ma'am?"

"Yes, yes." Isabelle rescues the sheet and winds it around Annie. Tess leaves without a backwards glance. Wilks watches her go.

Isabelle reaches up and removes the pins from Annie's hair. She loosens the hair from its tight nest with the same impatient, careless motion that Annie had used to ruffle the feather dusters against the house wall. She lets one hand linger on her maid's head for an instant. "Are you sure?" she says. "Do you understand?"

"Yes. I think so." But the moment she says this Annie also thinks, What do I understand? She has been swayed by the story, by words like *banished* and *forgiveness*. She hasn't had a book to read lately and that feeling of story rushes through her like a swoon.

Wilks stands up straight, flicks his tablecloth so it hangs properly from his shoulders. Annie arranges herself at his feet. The stone floor is cold and hard. When she reaches out for Wilks's ankle it is a relief to find it warm, to feel the heat of him through his boots.

"All right, Wilks," says Isabelle, moving back beside her camera. "Look down at Guinevere. A little scorn, a little pity," she says, as though she's reciting a cake recipe. "Some anger. Some hurt. A little love. And, Annie. You hate him but you need him to let you in, I mean, take you back. You need him to forgive you."

Forgive me my trespasses

Annie is lonely for Jesus. She wants him back, wants him here. She reaches out with everything inside her and holds on to him for that moment before he will notice and pull away.

Then Annie remembers Isabelle, raises her head from the floor and turns it so she can see the Lady over her shoulder, all the while holding tightly to Jesus' ankle.

Is this what you want from me?

Isabelle has never seen a gaze so sublimely sorrowful as Annie Phelan's. It is perfect. That searching sadness just right, so too that she would be looking backwards. Of course what matters is what's gone, not what is there. Guinevere is looking back at her love for Lancelot, not up in humility at her husband. She has not forgotten the true nature of her heart. She looks back fully aware of what it is she had and what it is she has lost. She looks back out of love, out of witness, out of remembrance. She looks back out of faith.

Isabelle can't take her eyes off Annie for fear that look will drain out of her. "Don't move," she says, and rushes quickly to the table with the prepared glass plate and the bottle of collodion. "Don't move," she mutters to herself, over and over again, as she pours the collodion onto the plate and tilts the excess back into the bottle, as she waits a moment for the plate to become sticky and then plunges it into the silver-nitrate bath.

Annie has not moved. Her gaze is as direct and mournful as when Isabelle left her to attend to the plate. Isabelle inserts the wooden holder into the camera. "Don't move," she says, one final time, and lifts the cover off the lens.

Annie's neck hurts and her eyes are starting to ache from staring so intently at Isabelle.

Let me in, thinks Isabelle, for Annie, for herself, and the Robert Hills of the world.

O Lord, thinks Annie. Don't leave me. I cannot bear for you to go.

The light carves them out of air. The folds of King Arthur's cape, the darkness of his hair. Light cuts around them, holds them as silhouettes. The long shape of Annie on the stone floor of the studio, pitched forward, looking back.

Isabelle leads Annie down the narrow stone steps into the old coal cellar, which is far from the house, out near the middle of the garden. A new, larger cellar has been recently attached onto the kitchen. Isabelle carries the wet glass plate in its holder with one hand, grasps Annie's sleeve with the other.

"My darkroom," she says, pushing forward with her feet until she feels the metal basin of developer. She bends down, dragging Annie with her.

The cellar still smells of coal, the dusky bloom of it flowering in the bricks, in the air.

Isabelle and Annie kneel by the tub while Isabelle pours developer into it and then immerses the glass plate. It is as big as a book, and she has to be careful that she has covered all of it. She counts the developing time off under her breath. She has brought Annie with her because she can't let her go yet, can't let her move beyond this moment, this photograph.

Annie can smell the coal. She can hear the quick sounds of Isabelle breathing beside her, and over that the slide of liquid pouring over the negative plate. Crouched in the dark in this small hole of a room they are like animals, hiding. She feels both panicky and calm.

Isabelle fumbles around in the dark, bumping her hands through the developer basin until she finds the treated glass plate.

"Done," she says, and hauls Annie to her feet, back up the stairs and outside.

After Isabelle has clipped the photographic paper into the developing frame and laid the whole contraption down on a flagstone in the sun, she sits on a bench at the side of the path and motions for Annie to join her.

"But, ma'am," says Annie. "I still have work to do." It is getting late and she is now behind in her duties for the day.

Isabelle waves her hand. "There'll always be time for cleaning," she says.

Whose time? thinks Annie. The Lady is much too cavalier on the subject of cleanliness. How would she feel if her chamber pot wasn't emptied every morning, or her bed sheets changed? But Annie doesn't protest again. It feels nice to sit in the sun on the bench in the middle of the day. It feels slightly wicked, in fact.

Isabelle can barely keep still, keeps hopping up to check the exposure, unclamping the frame, and peeling back a corner of the photograph.

"Almost," she keeps saying. "Almost." She seems very much like Mr. Rochester in her impatience.

When you just sit somewhere and don't move, the whole world comes to you. Annie sees things she has never noticed before. Birds and insects circle in the trees above her. Flowers tilt their heavy heads towards the soft-grass ground. The smells of the summer are wide. She looks up at the sun strained through a mass of cloud. How is it then that she sometimes misses Mrs. Gilbey and Portman Square? Is it only because it has been familiar to her? Is that all it is about? The small basement kitchen. The fifty stairs from there to the top of the house. The small darkness of her room, not unlike the coal cellar that she'd crouched in with the Lady Isabelle. The Lady's breathing in the dark next to her, a hoarse, hollow sound.

Isabelle is up off the bench again, peeling back the corner of the photograph with one of her blackened hands. "Look," she says. "It's starting to appear."

Annie slips off the bench and goes over to Isabelle.

Isabelle peels some more of the photo back. It is exactly right, that look in Annie's eyes. It has survived the process of the photograph. It is strong and unwavering and grief-stricken. It is the vision Isabelle had, made flesh. It is a work of art, her art. It is a miracle.

The exposure is still too light and the photograph will need to be fixed, washed, and toned to bring out the shadow areas, but Isabelle knows already that it is a success.

Annie, who has never really looked at herself before, sees the image on the paper and doesn't identify it with herself. A girl holding on to the ankle of a man. Guinevere and Arthur. She can believe that. She can believe that it is true, that she and Isabelle have made that story come true.

"Look at you, Annie Phelan," says Isabelle. "You are made from light."

Ophelia

Isabelle rushes to Eldon's library, the still-damp print pinched between thumb and forefinger. It twists and flutters before her as she runs. With her other hand Isabelle gathers up her long skirts so she can move swiftly over the stones on the path. When she bursts through the door into the library, she is breathless.

Eldon looks up at the sound of the door opening. His wife looks crazed, wild and crazed, as if she has been living for weeks in the woods in the company of faeries and spirits. Some of her hair has come loose from its pins. She is panting. Her dress is crooked. Her appearance both attracts and repels him. He approves of the wantonness and disapproves of the madness.

"Watch the maps," he says, which really isn't what he meant to say at all, but he is panicked about her touching the old sheets of paper with her stained hands.

His warning makes Isabelle hesitate, but only for an instant. She waves the print in front of his face. "My first success, Eldon," she says. "My first real success."

He takes the print and holds it carefully in his hands, although there's no need as Isabelle has smudged it from handling it so much already. It's a picture of the new maid and the gardener, Wilks, whom he has never properly approved of. They are costumed in bed and table linen, acting out some dramatic operatic tableau. It is not unlike her other photographic efforts, but Eldon can see what Isabelle wants him to see. There is an intensity to the maid's expression, a look so clear and true that he could draw a direct line between it and his own eyes as he looks at the photograph. There is nothing between them. It is quite remarkable.

"Yes," he says. "I do see what you mean. She looks so..." He wants to say *beautiful*, but that really isn't the right word for how she looks. He thinks of the bird's-eye-view perspective on early maps, where you look down at the shape of the land-scape and can get a sense of what it feels like to be there. Something felt in what is seen.

"Right," says Isabelle. "She looks so perfectly, absolutely right. I cannot believe it. It feels miraculous. I had to come immediately and show you."

Eldon is touched by this. Isabelle has a generous spirit, he thinks. She is so different from him. When he discovers some-thing marvellous he prefers to hoard the knowledge, keeps it to himself, treats it as fuel to stoke a fire. If he opens the window on it, he will lose some of the heat. "I am very pleased for you, my dear," he says, and he is. He sets the photograph carefully on a corner of his library table. They both look down at it between them.

Isabelle can't keep still. It's as though the energy she feels rippling out from the photograph eddies her around the room. The library is not a place to rush about in. There are rules in this room. Don't touch the maps. Don't careen around disturbing the staid antiquity of the documents, of the atmos-phere. As pleasant as it has been to hurry along here and show Eldon the photograph, Isabelle feels that to stay would just lower her spirits. Her living piece of art would be dragged down by all these dusty old maps.

"You keep it," she says to her husband. "I've mostly ruined

this one anyway. I'll go and make another." She shoots past him and disappears through the door. The air trembles in her wake.

Eldon looks down at the photograph on the table. Those eyes seem to be watching him. The tenor of their gaze is such that you wouldn't want to be feeling unsure of yourself when they looked at you. Those eyes would find you out, would detect weakness and cowardice. This photograph is a place that has found him, not, as it usually is, the other way around. Eldon puts his hand out and very carefully, very gently, traces around the figures in the picture, feels his way along the lines of Annie Phelan — those ragged as a coastline, those smooth as a worn hillside.

Eldon runs the flat of his hand over the piece of paper in front of him. *Cosmographia Universalis.* A map of the world. This is what he wanted for himself, what he thought fifteen years of working on *Dunstan's Library Atlas* would make possible, all the years of his employment, from his youthful self to the forty-year-old man he has somehow become. To create a map of the world is to include everything known to human existence. It is to sort through all the various renderings of the earth and choose from the shapes and sizes of the land masses, settling on those that seem the most accurate. It is to read the diaries and logs of explorers and sailors who are journeying into the still-unmapped places of the world — the Far North, the Antarctic, the jungles and deserts and mountains, the remote reaches of humanity. To make a map of the world is to believe in the dotted line that shows the voyage from Portugal to Newfoundland. It is to go through the evidence and make a case for the world appearing a particular way. One of the earliest surviving maps of the British Isles was plotted by a man named Lawrence Nowell. He made no attempt to obtain proper bearings or to include an accurate scale. His map is drawn as if he had just sailed along the coast of England and put down what he saw. The map, drawn on a narrow strip of paper, is over twenty-five feet in length. Eldon imagines Lawrence Nowell, bobbing up and down in a small boat, perhaps rowed or sailed by a friend or family member. Lawrence sitting on the bilge boards, to minimize the motion, looking up at the rocks and bays, the gulls circling, looking down at his shaky line on the wind-blown paper. Did he see England differently, now that he was recording it? Was he confident that he was getting it right? Did what he ended up with on the paper resemble what he saw from the boat?

There is something comforting to Eldon in those early maps. The lack of perspective. The seeming casualness to the lines. The fidelity to the original shape of a mountain or lake. The concentration on the four elements that were of the most importance to the cartographer in his daily life — towns, the sea, mountains, and forests. The simple purity of the act of making the map, so that the map-maker would find his way back to where he was, so that others could find their way there.

For Eldon to do as Dunstan wants and make a theme map of the world is to go against all those early map-makers, to go against what they believed in. It is as if Lawrence Nowell sat in his small creaky boat only marking on his map the composition of the rocks on the shore, not looking for anything else, not trying to include all that he saw. To mark down the mineral deposits in South America relegates the map to a mere guide. Exploration loses its edge of curiosity and becomes only a reason for exploitation. Eldon can believe in

Lawrence Nowell's desire to make his map as something exalted and noble, unselfish. Who will see Eldon Dashell's map of the world's mineral resources as a testament to his vision of the limits of human endeavour?

Eldon looks down at the map in front of him. *Trust me.* That's what maps are saying. *Trust me.* Never mind that early metal globes were cut in half and used for pots by hungry sailors. Never mind that all forests and mountains on maps throw their shadows to the east, because draughtsmen usually work with the light on their left, which means that on a map it is always a sunny afternoon. Where you find yourself is always afternoon. Never mind that the most common method for projecting the world, the Mercator projection, flattens the round earth and alters the spatial perspective, thus making Greenland nine to twenty-two times its actual size. Europe becomes the centre of the world. Africa is smaller, so too South America, slipping down the side. Making something round into something flat, to sail off the edge of the world, again.

Distance. Position. How to find your way back when where you are depends on where everything else is. Here we are. Here is everything else. A compass of the human body — head as North, feet South, right arm East, left arm West. North as up. The top of the page. Up more important than down. Look up. Stars, the dark night sky screening eternity.

This is where you are. This is what it looks like. Never mind that you don't recognize anything.

Trust me.

Eldon finds the new maid behind the potting shed. She is sitting on the small stone step with her back up against the door.

"Hello, Annie," he says. She turns her face towards him and he sees that she doesn't look at all like Isabelle's photograph. Eldon is glad of that. "What are you doing?" he asks.

Annie feels embarassed to tell Mr. Dashell the truth. "It's my afternoon off," she says.

"And?"

She won't tell him how long she has been sitting on the step of the potting shed. ÚAnd I don't think I know what to do with an afternoon off. I've never had a proper one before."

Eldon feels pity for her as a physical pain in his chest. It makes him angry and sad and eager to come to her defence, all at the same time. "Well," he says. "If you had family nearby, you could go and visit them."

"I have no family, sir."

"You could take a fly into town."

"I have nothing to buy in town," says Annie. And nothing to buy it with. She doesn't want Mr. Dashell to know that she is penniless. Mrs. Gilbey died without paying Annie her quarterly wage and the solicitor who settled the estate refused to believe this was the case, thought that Annie was trying to cheat him when she mentioned it.

"Well," says Eldon. "I am going for a walk to clear my head. You could walk with me. I will show you over some of the countryside."

Annie can't think of a persuasive reason why she should not walk with Mr. Dashell. She is sure it is not proper to do so, but all the rules are different here, and she is tired of sitting on the step trying to think up something to do with the afternoon. One can only explore the house and grounds so many times. "I would be pleased to walk with you, sir," she says.

They trudge along in silence for a while. Eldon occasionally points out meadowlarks or berries in the hedgerow with an easy authority. The sun is shining, making the countryside soft and hazy. Annie has never seen so much land. There are fields and copses. Seams of sheep, ragged across the green. In the distance the small cottages of the tenant farmers. The wideness of it all makes her want to put her arms out from her sides and fly down the dirt laneway. The sun on her back, like a warm hand, guiding her along.

"Annie?"

It takes her a full breathing moment to realize that Mr. Dashell has just said something to her and she hasn't been paying attention.

"Sorry, sir. What were you saying?"

"Earlier," says Eldon. "Back at the house. You said you had no family."

"My family were Irish, sir. They died in the hunger."

"How was it then that you escaped that fate?"

Annie stops walking. The narrow road stretches ahead of them, twists to the right around a corner. The earth is hard and rutted from carriage wheels.

"I had two brothers," she says. In her dreams it is her brothers she most often glimpses, not her parents. Her mother, her father, she senses in an anxious, ghostly way, but it is her brothers—Connor and Michael—she sees. She is small, too small to move on her own, wrapped tightly and laid at the side of the road. There are no birds opening windows of song in the summer sky, only the sharp noise of steel hitting rock and the heavy sound of stone against stone. Over that, close by, is another noise, as rhythmic as the digging. It is the sound of one of her brothers, coughing.

"I had two brothers, sir," she says again. They have stopped walking. She can hear her words strike as clearly as the shovels of her parents on the road. "Their names were Connor and

Michael. They worked with my parents on the road." This is the truth as she has been told it, but in her dreams they are never working, are always beside her. They smell like grass. One of them coughs. They sometimes rock forward into their knees and sing soft songs to match the hammer of the road noise. They smell like earth. Their skin is warm from where they sit beside her, sometimes touching against her swaddled body with an arm or leg. She can lie there and they are huge above her, guarding her. She is safe with them, her brothers.

"What road?" asks Eldon.

Annie knows so little about where it is she comes from. She only has what Mrs. Cullen told her. She was born some time in 1845 in County Clare. In the summer of the next year the blight spread throughout Ireland and the potato crops blackened and rotted in the fields. The stench was apparently so great that one could smell the rot well before seeing it. In the fall of that year the English government implemented relief schemes. Public work relief schemes. Her parents and brothers worked building a road. In January her father died on the road. Her brothers were sick now, with fever, and Annie's mother wanted the Cullens to take all her children with them when they went to England, but they wouldn't take the boys because they were sick and couldn't travel easily. Annie's mother gave the Cullens what little of worth she had to pay for Annie's keep. A silver locket belonging to her mother. Her wedding ring. I had to sell them, Mrs. Cullen told Annie, several times over the years. For our survival. Annie does not blame Mrs. Cullen. Each time she was told of the locket and the ring, it was as if the telling itself was solid, was something she could turn over in her hands, hold up to the light to see it shine.

"Public works," says Annie. "Relief. At first the roads were necessary ones. Ones that needed repair. New ones to connect places up. But there were too many people working and so they started to make other roads. My parents worked on a road that went nowhere. It was not for anything, did not tie this place to that. No one could ever walk down it expecting to get to the next village." She looks ahead, at the road they're on, how it turns the corner, funnelling ahead with great purpose, with the momentum of those who travelled upon it carrying it forward. "My father died on that road. I was sent to England with a family who were leaving for there. My brothers were sick with fever and I expect they died soon after I left. When we reached England the family sent word to my mother that we'd arrived, but she was already gone."

"Gone?"

"Dead, sir. God took her."

Annie's mother is a story. Her mother is a far-off feeling that she sometimes falls out of when she wakes. She has nothing real left to her from that life. Only stories and the dream of her two brothers hovering above her like spent breath.

"I dream about the road," she says. "It is torn up and noisy with people and carts and the hauling of stones. I never see my parents, don't know what it is they would have looked like. But I do see the road. And when I dream about it, the road, it doesn't look like this one. It doesn't look like anything of this world."

They continue walking. Annie cannot speak. She has told no one of her dreams before. She feels the words gone from her body. With the lightness of moths they fluttered out of her mouth and now they are lifted on the breeze, away from her. What she has said won't come back to her, and be hers alone.

Eldon cannot speak. He feels the gravity of Annie's words pushing him to ground. Any sympathetic response he might utter is not strong enough to stay her words. He cannot do anything except walk beside her along this road that will now, forever, be for him a road that has merged with the one of Annie's dreams, a road that disappears into the past.

"If we were different people," says Eldon, "I could take you for a meal."

They have come to an inn. Beyond them is a small village, the sudden noise of people and horses.

Annie's first thought is that he means she is Irish and he is English, that is the difference between them. She looks around at the dozen or so people sitting at the tables outside the inn. Coach drivers. Farmhands. No one so obviously gentry as Mr. Dashell. No one so obviously a servant as herself. Certainly never those two types of people together.

Annie has not been to a public house in a long time. She used to go sometimes with one of the Janes from Portman Square. One of the kind Janes. Annie divided the many cooks who passed through Mrs. Gilbey's kitchen into kind Janes and mean Janes. Mean Janes seemed to stay longer. This kind Jane took Annie out several times. Her name was really Mary Ann. One night she drank too much and stood on a chair by the bar and sang a song about her underthings. Everyone had applauded and they were each given a free drink.

Mary Ann hadn't lasted long at Mrs. Gilbey's, and Annie missed her more than she ever would have suspected. She missed the unexpectedness of her, how Mary Ann could climb onto a chair in a crowd of loud, drinking patrons, and sing a bawdy song. Annie could be so shocked by Mary Ann that for one cool, delicious moment she would forget to judge her actions according to the higher authorities of Mrs. Gilbey and God.

"If we were different people, sir," says Annie, "who is it we would be?" She has often thought how accidental her life has been in some regards. If Mrs. Gilbey hadn't plucked her from the workhouse when she was a child, if she hadn't been converted into a servant, would she have gone to work in the coal yards or in a factory? Would she perhaps have been working in a public house? If some woman had stood on a chair in the bar where she worked, and sung about her underthings in a voice loud with beer, would Annie have laughed along with the others? Would Annie have been the one to offer her a free drink?

Eldon looks at the patrons of the public house. The working men. What he wishes at this moment is that he were one of them, not that Annie was well born like himself, but that he was her equal. "Let's go back," he says. "I should return to work."

They walk back along the road. Around them the noise of summer, thin and insistent, like a whisper. Neither speaks.

"Thank you for venturing out with me," says Eldon finally. "It is nice to have company on my afternoon outing."

"Mrs. Dashell never walks with you?" asks Annie.

"Isabelle? No, she is too busy with her photography. She doesn't like to break her day into pieces with other activities. I used to walk a lot more," he tells Annie. "In my younger days. For my health. I had wanted to be a great adventurer." He tries to say this lightly, as though it is silly, trivial, absurd even, but his voice falls and stumbles. "Not to be," he says. "I was a sickly boy and a sickly young man. I couldn't even lift a basket of apples, how would I have been at sea, or climbing some mountain? How would I have been tramping through the icy Arctic?" For this is where he had wanted to go. To the top of the world. To stand in the white bowl of heaven. He can remember, easily, how he wanted this, feel it as though it is an icy shard of grief sliding through him, slick and clean and all the way in. "That is the story of *my* life," he says.

"Not all of it, sir," says Annie.

"No. Not all of it." Eldon already feels as though he's said too much because he has told this stranger a truth about himself. But she is right. "Isabelle," he says. He looks down at the ground, down at his hands. They are not the thick knotted hands of a climber or sailor. They are the clean, thin, weak hands of a man who reads books, a man who never had to work with his hands. "You have wondered why it is that we have no children?" Don't say this, he thinks, but he is already saying it.

Annie guiltily remembers the room with the cradles and prams, the dusty stillness of it. "You have such a large house," she says.

"Yes. A house large enough to be full of children." Eldon looks over at her. There's a steadiness to her gaze that soothes him. It is as though she has laid a cool hand on his burning skin. "It's my wife's house, you know. Her father was a Lord. He gave it to us when we married."

"It is a fine house."

"Yes, it is. A fine house." Eldon thinks of his library, the cosiness of that room full of his books and maps. When it is cold outside and there is a roaring fire in the grate, he can think of no better place to be. "Isabelle," he says again. "I gave her the camera. It was my idea. She has always been possessed of an artistic nature. She tried painting but the results did not satisfy her. I gave her the camera after the third."

"The third?"

"The third baby." Eldon spreads his fingers as though he is searching for a handhold in an outcrop of rock. "The third dead baby. Stillborn. All of them. Two boys and a girl. The first one, it was a girl. I never even held them."

Two boys, Annie thinks, Connor and Michael. The merciful Lord will take care of them, she wants to say, to him, to herself, but she remembers, just in time, that Mr. Dashell doesn't see the world her way. No God. Foolishness, Cook had called it. Annie looks down at Eldon's hands, fingers spread. They are smooth and white, gentleman's hands. Annie looks at her own hands. They are thick and red and the skin is cracked and rough as tree bark. They are working hands, the hands of a maid. How can she possibly know anything of his loss? His children are not the same as her brothers. His world is not the same as hers at all.

Annie and Tess lie in their narrow beds at the top of the Dashell house. There is a wind tonight. A tree creaks outside their window, its thin upper branches brushing the glass, sounding like the scratch of a broom sweeping flagstones.

Annie lies on her back, listening to the wind. So quickly, she thinks, she has become used to having a room in the treetops. She wriggles down further under the covers, feels something sharp against the back of her head. Her Bible. She traces the contours of it with her fingers, hoping the words will leak out, swim into her body. What would Mrs. Gilbey say about the state of her soul?

Pray for your sinning ways, Mary. The enormity of this imagined rebuke brings the first sharp stars of tears to her eyes.

"Annie," Tess calls out from the other side of the room. "Are you still awake?"

"Yes." Annie takes her hand out quickly, guiltily, from under her pillow. What has happened to her, she thinks, that she is now ashamed of the Lord?

"What do you think," says Tess, "of Robert and Betsy?"

"Who?"

"Lord Robert Montagu," says Tess. "The one what married his housemaid, Betsy. Did you not hear of them?"

"No. I led a quiet life in London." Annie says this and, as she says it, thinks that it sounds as though she was convalescing from a serious illness. "I was not allowed out much," she says, which sounds even worse.

"You poor wretch," says Tess, who cannot conceive of a life spent in forced solitude.

Annie feels impatient with Tess's pity. "What about Robert and Betsy?" she says.

"Well..." Tess stretches her body out, liking the feel of it pulling tight. This is her favourite game now: supposing. It feels delicious to lie in the warm dark and send her questions out across the room, floating away from her like big, coloured balloons. "He saw her washing steps and was so taken with her looks that he had to have her. Betsy already had a sweetheart, but she married Lord Robert without a thought to that. Would you do that, Annie? Would you toss your sweetheart for Robert?"

Annie knows how this game works. Tess is really asking the question of herself. Annie is only a way for Tess to think about the situation out loud. Still, there is pleasure in being included, and Annie, who has never really thought of such things before, tries to imagine both a sweetheart and an amorous Lord. "I don't know," she says. The thought of too much attention makes her feel uneasy. Having a sweetheart would be like the Lady Isabelle looking at her when she took that photograph. It would be that close, the scrutiny. She is not sure she wants this. In Mrs. Gilbey's house she often felt invisible, and this, she thinks now, is sometimes a better thing.

"Well, I would," says Tess, getting tired of waiting for a satisfactory answer from Annie. "I would get rid of my sweetheart quick as anything." She says it with such force that Annie can almost believe it will happen, that Lord Montagu will swoop down out of nowhere and carry Tess off, away from the laundry and the Dashell household. Away from this night, from Annie and the whispery trees outside this window.

"Tess," says Annie. "What are the Dashells like to work for? To live with?"

"They're mad, aren't they?" says Tess. "Mrs. Dashell dressing us up in bed sheets, making us stand around in that draughty henhouse. The Master and his mouldy old maps."

"Mr. Dashell," says Annie carefully. "He's not interested in servants, is he?" She thinks of her walk with Eldon, how both wrong and pleasant it felt.

Tess is quiet for a moment. "Oh," she says at last. "Has he been after me for a kiss? Is that what you mean?"

"Yes."

"They're mad," says Tess, "but I think they're harmless. But then I haven't been here that long myself. Just got here before you." She's quiet for a moment. Annie can almost hear the slow tick of her thinking. "They aren't out to bother us," says Tess finally. "The Lady isn't wanting to catch us up. The Master isn't chasing after us. Not like my last position." There's the shuffling noise of Tess turning in her bed. "Shall I tell you about that?" she says.

"No," says Annie quickly.

"Well," says Tess, "you'll know soon enough."

"Why?"

"Thought you weren't interested?"

"I just..." How to explain that listening to Tess's story would make Annie judge her and that this is something Annie wants to avoid. "I'm not interested," she says, and goes back to listening to the wind searching the trees outside the window.

Soon there is the shuddering noise of Tess's sleep from across the room. Annie lies in the dark. She is afraid to fall asleep, afraid to fall into her dream of the road. The sound of the shovels and axes chipping at the hard ground is already playing in her head, a rattling, sombre tattoo, like the sound of bones knocking together.

Tess is a sound sleeper, doesn't wake when Annie rises and leaves the room. The stairs creak as Annie walks slowly down to the front hall, her candle flickering in the draughty night air of the house.

Eldon's library is as she remembered from that first day. Annie shuts the door carefully once she is safely inside. The candlelight stutters along the shelves. *Cartography. Geology.* Annie slides Richard Hakluyt's *Voyages, Traffiques, and Discoveries of the New World* from its seat on the shelf, tucks it against her chest, and goes back upstairs to her bedroom.

Sitting up in bed, reading about perilous ocean voyages, Annie is able to stop imagining her family on that road in Ireland. The words of the book cover her as comfortably as a blanket on a cold night. She can wrap herself in the warmth of them. She can rest here. The noise of the shovels and axes is replaced with the sweet drop of words falling from her mind into the empty chamber of her heart.

At breakfast the next morning, when Tess and Annie are hurrying through their cups of tea at the table, Cook suddenly bursts through the kitchen door with a kettle of water in either hand. "Would this do?" she says.

Tess looks up, looks down again. "Why is that interesting?" she says.

"It's my work."

"One chore, out of all the work you do. Is that how you want to be? Forever?" Tess looks over at Annie. "Am I right?" she says.

Annie has no idea what is happening, why Cook has turned into a water-bearing statue on the kitchen stoop, why Tess's opinion is required on this. Mad, she thinks. They're all mad here. Every last one of them.

"Annie!"

Annie looks back, stops hurrying along the path to the glasshouse, and waits for Tess to catch her up.

"Where are you going?" Tess is puffing, bends forward to catch her breath. Her face, when she looks up, is red from being in the laundry all morning and from sprinting up the path after Annie.

"Mrs. Dashell wants me to model for her again today."

"You haven't stripped the beds." Tess stands up straight.

"I know."

"I'm supposed to wash those sheets today. Now."

"I'll do it when I get back." Annie glances down the path to the glasshouse. She doesn't want to keep Isabelle waiting. "Just leave them."

"I can't do that." Tess works to a strict schedule. Monday, Tuesday, and Wednesday are for washing and rinsing. Thursdays and Fridays are for mangling, starching, and ironing. She washes linen on Mondays, muslin, coloured cottons, and woollens on Tuesdays, bed sheets and kitchen cloths on Wednesdays. Today is Wednesday. If something isn't washed on the correct day, it changes the entire week's schedule and throws the household management into confusion. "I'll have to do it myself, then," she says, waiting for Annie to change her mind. Annie says nothing. "Well, then," says Tess. "I'll do it myself, but I'm none too happy about it." She turns and stomps back down the path towards the house. Annie watches her go, feeling regretful. Tess has enough work of her own to do without taking on extra. They have been getting along so well together, too. Annie enjoys the companionship at night in their attic room, how they talk to each other when the lamps are blown out, lying in their beds, calling softly across the dark. Stories of Mrs. Gilbey's meanness, of Tess's family struggles in the north of England.

Annie resumes her journey to the glasshouse. She needs to speak to the Lady about how she is to do her duties and do this modelling, too. Annie has only been here a few weeks. She cannot let Tess do work for her again. It is not fair.

But when Annie gets to the glasshouse, there is no talking to Isabelle about her maid-work. Isabelle is fussing around, all quick and cranky.

"What took you so long?" she says, when Annie hurries into the studio. "I sent for you ages ago. We're losing the good light. Here." She shoves a wooden box into Annie's arms. "Carry this. And follow me." She has folded up the legs of the box camera, clasps the length of it to her bosom, and pushes through the door of the glasshouse, out into the afternoon sun.

Annie struggles to catch up as Isabelle strides through the orchard. "Where are we going?"

"To drown you," says Isabelle. She doesn't sound as though she's joking and Annie has to tell herself that it can't really be the truth. Maids are useful. They aren't just casually disposed of by murder. Still, she has never found out what had happened to the last housemaid, the one whose place she has taken.

They walk through the orchard, across a field, and down a wooded slope. There, at the bottom of the slope, flows a small brook, pale with sunlight.

"All right," says Isabelle. "This will do." She lays her camera gently on the bank. "This is a good spot to drown you." She takes the box from Annie, smiles when she sees the look on her face. "Ha! You're frightened. You think I'm serious."

"No, ma'am." Annie can feel herself blush.

"You're lying," says Isabelle.

Annie is lying. She feels a fool. "Well," she says defensively, "I thought that you wouldn't. But I felt that you might."

Isabelle laughs. "Good girl," she says. "Now go and sit on those rocks over there and look distraught."

Annie obediently squats on a narrow shelf of stone by the water's edge. She squints up at the sun, watches Isabelle arrange the camera on the bank.

"Field darkroom today," says Isabelle, attaching a black cloth hood to the back of the camera. "Doesn't always work, but never mind." She fusses around in the wooden box, laying things out beside it. She hums, seems to have forgotten about telling Annie to sit on the rocks.

"Ma'am," says Annie, after a while. "Is this right?"

Isabelle looks over. "No," she says cheerfully. "All wrong. Just a moment and I'll be right there." She pushes at her camera to make sure that the legs have embedded properly into the ground of the bank and that it's stable. "Good," she says, and stepping carefully over the paraphernalia she has laid out on the bank, makes her way to Annie. "Loosen your collar." Annie tentatively undoes a few buttons at her neck and Isabelle impatiently reaches down and undoes a few more. She pulls one side of Annie's dress away from her neck. "I need this line," she says, and touches Annie's collarbone.

Even though Mrs. Dashell's touch is brazen and careless, Annie shivers at it. She has not been touched by anyone in so long that she is startled by the feeling of Isabelle's fingers trolling her collarbone. Isabelle doesn't notice Annie's reaction. "Those rocks are a catastrophe," she says. "You must be lower down than that." She scans the bank and, finding nothing to her liking, bends down and scrabbles through the dirt herself, rearranging the stones until they suit her.

Annie takes her seat on the new rocks. She is closer to the water now, can almost feel the jump and tumble of it beside her as it shoulders through the narrow streambed, rolling from hollows, dodging rocks.

"Your hair," says Isabelle, and Annie reaches up and takes out the pins that hold it up in its neat bun. She shakes it briskly, like a dog that has just stepped out of the water. She remembers, from last time, how the Lady prefers her hair to be loose and unruly. She shakes her head again, and Isabelle absent-mindedly reaches down and touches it with her fingers. "Good," she says.

"Who am I?" asks Annie.

Isabelle crouches down beside her. "Ophelia," she says. "Do you know the story?"

Annie shakes her head.

Isabelle's voice is soft. "You are Ophelia," she says. "You're in love with Hamlet, but he doesn't love you back. Your father and brother have advised you poorly on this matter. Hamlet is preoccupied with his own demons. He doesn't even notice you, certainly doesn't guess that you love him."

Annie can feel the warmth of the summer sun on her bare throat. The whispery voice of Isabelle beside her sounds like the wind in the tops of the trees outside of her window last night. She puts a hand out and lets the cold water of the stream spool through her open fingers. She can guess the rest of the story. "I drown myself," she says.

"Yes. You drown yourself."

"Am I always to be full of sorrow, ma'am?" Annie thinks back to Guinevere, to how it felt lying on the stone floor, clutching Arthur's ankle. After that photograph, she had been shaky most of the day, as though she'd suffered a bad fright.

Isabelle looks carefully at Annie. She is clever, this house-maid, certainly more observant than any of the others. "I know," Isabelle says. "I know what you mean. They are tragedies, but they are also the stories we have, the ones available to us. And I like to work with the stories that people know." She says this, and at the same time as she says it, she stops believing that it is true, that it has to be true. "Just because these women are tragic," says Isabelle, "doesn't mean that they aren't strong."

"But how strong am I if I drown myself?" asks Annie. "If I drown myself at the first hint of trouble?"

"It's more than a hint of trouble," says Isabelle. "It's loving someone and having them completely ignore your love." But Isabelle feels less convinced. She thinks of the stories she is drawn to, the heroines she has portrayed in her photographs — Guinevere, Beatrice. Is she attracted to these stories partially because she has seen them depicted so many times by male artists, by people like Robert Hill? Maybe, as a woman, she should resist these stories, not embrace them?

"Ophelia," says Annie.

"Ophelia," says Isabelle, standing up. She no longer wants Ophelia to drown. She wants her to not care a whit about Hamlet, not bother about his love. Why does she need to drown herself anyway? Why can't she just love someone more appropriate?

The sun has made runnels of light on the water, coming down from the green boughs above. There is a patch of light at Annie's throat, like a word lying on her skin. The delicate line of collarbone looks as frail and solid as a bird's wing.

"What do you want me to do?" asks Annie.

"Ophelia," says Isabelle again. "Maybe you're not going to drown yourself."

"But what about the spurned love?"

"Well, maybe this time you're just going to think about drowning yourself over Hamlet. Consider it." Isabelle moves back to her camera, back to get perspective on Annie and the stream. "Besides, this stream isn't really deep enough to drown in. You would have to make a tremendous effort to die here. I think we'll just offer it up as a possibility." Isabelle plucks a wild orchid from the stream bank, tucks it into the turned-down collar of Annie's dress. The flower droops towards Annie's throat. Something young and natural, considering defeat. "Put your hand in the water again."

Annie trails her hand in the stream, playing scales of watery notes with her fingers. She is glad that Isabelle has decided to let Ophelia live. Ophelia wouldn't want to drown herself on such a fine sunny day, Annie is sure of that. No matter how much she loved Hamlet. And really, wouldn't Ophelia have thoughts and feelings that had nothing to do with Hamlet at all? Annie tilts her head up to Isabelle. I am alive, she says to herself. She can feel the pulse of the water playing against her hand. I am alive, and I am everything.

"Perfect," says Isabelle, from behind the camera. "Don't move."

*

Eldon cannot stop thinking about Annie Phelan and the story she told him that afternoon when they walked out together. Her story seems more clear to him every day that passes. He remembers the angle of the sun on the fields, the sounds in the hedgerows. How when she started talking, telling him about her brothers and parents, the outside world thinned to nothing and all he could hear was her voice, all he could see was the road she described her parents working on. A famine road. Eldon has heard various stories of the Irish plight during the famine. The famine seems recent because there are still so many Irish people living in England. A lot of them brought the hunger sickness with them. Eldon has memories of walking with his father in London twenty years ago and seeing entire families huddled against brick walls, too sick to stand or talk, their hands out for money, their eyes dark and blank. He remembers seeing an Irish woman walking the streets with a basket. She was a "pure-finder," collecting up dog excrement to sell to the tanyards. Poor wretch, said his father. That must be the only work she is able to get.

And now, this summer, Eldon is reminded of the famine again because of the cattle plague that has descended on England. A mysterious swift-moving disease, the "rinderpest" has devastated the dairy herds. On almost every farm now there are massive graves dug for the carcasses. In Ireland, twenty years ago, Eldon knows there were similar mass graves for the victims of the famine. Often, at the side of these vast pits would be a coffin with a sliding bottom so that a body could be dropped into the pit by drawing out the bottom. The coffin could then be used again. The famine. The blight. *Blight* was such an inappropriate word for what had happened. Blight—a brief stumble into light. The right word would be heavy, drawn to earth, leeching down into darkness.

Eldon has thought about the famine a great deal. The injustice of it. The way it is still being blamed on the Irish themselves. He has thought about it, but he has never imagined it so vividly as he did when Annie told him about the famine road. All of his life he has believed in connecting things, in filling in the spaces on the map. A connecting line is a bridge that makes two worlds accessible, whether it is just the joining of two villages or the joining of two huge continents with a transatlantic telegraph cable. It is a way over, a way through, a way for people to believe in something beyond the limits of their known world.

Now Annie Phelan has drawn a line in his mind, each end of it falling away into nothingness. Her parents, the Phelans, used the last of their strength to build a road that would never carry the weight of horse and cart, never carry a man into town for supplies, a family to market. A hundred years from now that road will be invisible, will perhaps be a line in a forest where the vegetation does not grow as high as elsewhere. And to work on a road like that, surely it would make you die faster? The road would end where you ended and the road ending meant that you would die. The whole enterprise was a gesture of hopelessness.

Eldon stands in his library, before his large oak table. There is a map spread out on it, but he is not seeing it. Over and over he sees the famine road. He feels the weight of the shovels, feels the futility in the bones of the men and women, the children. It would taste like metal on their tongues, he thinks, that futility.

It is so much stronger, this discontinuous line, stronger than the careful, ordered lines on a map. It is a dash, a pencil skidding by accident across a fresh sheet of paper.

Perhaps those early explorers were right to fill their maps equally with what they knew to be there and what they imagined to be there. All the sea monsters, the winds with angels' faces. Perhaps what can be imagined is somehow a stronger truth because it inhabits you, is you, becomes you. It happens from the inside out.

Eldon does not want to show the mineral deposits of the world. He wants to go back, to include the imaginings of the early map-makers. Mountains like braided rope. The early compass roses with a holy cross marking the east, where the sun came up. He wants to combine the old ways of imagining the world with new ones. Even to have a system of measurement that was different from miles and nautical miles, something more humanly tangible than latitude and longitude. There was a map he saw once, made by French Jesuits in 1671. They had charted Lake Superior in Canada and used the canoe stroke as their unit of measure. Their map was not surpassed in accuracy for a hundred years. That is how distance is felt, the simple rhythmic act of pulling a paddle up, pushing it through water. Miles becoming a turn of the back, the ache in a forearm.

Eldon thinks that he will travel up to London. He will go and see his publisher, Dunstan, and explain what he feels about his map of the world. Surely he can plead his case, can make Dunstan see that a less accurate map would, in fact, be the most accurate map he could make. He will offer examples, make a case for himself. There is the Apian map of the world, for one. Peter Apian's world map of 1530 was unique because it was in the shape of a heart. It joined the inner and outer universes together. Who, standing before Apian's heart-shaped map, could not believe that this was where he lived? Eldon, seeing it for the first time, was overwhelmed by its power. The world seemed both infinite and fragile. The boundless elliptical oceans. The blood stuttering in his chest.

*

Annie continues to borrow books from Eldon's library. At night, creeping along the passageway with a candle. She is always careful to replace the previous volume before taking another from the shelf. She does not want to be caught, so she doesn't leave the books in her bedroom in case Tess will find them there and she will have to explain herself. Lie, she will have to lie, and she does not want to do this. Instead she takes the books into the room with all the baby things, a room she is certain no one ever goes into. She sits on the floor, wedged in between the carriages and cradles, and reads. She leaves whatever book she is currently perusing stuffed under the straw mattress of the big perambulator. Sometimes she is able to sneak into the room during the day, when there is a break in her chores, but mostly she comes here at night. It is better to read than to try and sleep because sleep offers only the dream of her family on that road, the hollow achy feeling that follows upon waking.

Annie has not tried to pattern her reading, or impose a certain kind of discipline on it. Mr. Dashell's library is so much broader in range than the library of the reverend in Portman Square and Annie wants to take advantage of this. She wants to read as widely as she can.

Sometimes the contents of the library sadden her. She thinks of their talk that afternoon on the road, how Mr. Dashell had confessed his desire to have been an explorer. All these books that explain something of the world, so that he could know what to expect when he journeyed out of England. A whole wall of words in readiness for a pursuit that never happened.

Tonight, wedged down against the wheels of a carriage, Annie is reading Samuel Johnson's dictionary. It is a large book, comes in four volumes. She has skimmed the first one and is now reading the second.

She opens the book, the weight of it heavy as a stone across her knees. The candle on the floor beside her breathes in the dusty air in this room, breathes out as this sputter of flame. In all her reading Annie is not sure if she is stopping something or bringing something back. Reading blocks the dreams, but reading also gives words to that experience she was not old enough to remember, being on that road in Ireland. What is to be believed? Is the true story the story that is made or the story that is forgotten?

Annie opens Samuel Johnson's dictionary to the entry "heart." "The chief part; the vital part; the vigorous or efficacious part." And then further down the page it says, "The inner part of any thing."

Eldon is having a drink with Robert Hill at Robert's London club. Tomorrow Eldon is to see Dunstan and he has been walking through the streets nervously rehearsing the imagined conversation. He is having a drink with Robert to practise his arguments.

"Nonsense," says Robert, sipping his brandy, his feet extended towards the fire which has been extravagantly lit on this dreary summer's day. So far he has disagreed with everything that Eldon has proposed.

"But it is," says Eldon. "Can't you see? It's all the fault of Crystal Palace."

"Nonsense," says Robert again. "Crystal Palace was a triumph."

"Well," says Eldon, slightly hurt by his friend's differing opinions. "I don't see why something can't be both a triumph and a disaster."

It was Eldon's feeling that the Great Exhibition first held at Hyde Park in 1851, and repeated each year at Crystal Palace in south London, was responsible for Dunstan's desire for a themed map of the world. "The commodities of the world became desirable to the average man and woman," says Eldon. "Who, after seeing the finest Chinese silk, will not want some?"

"It was just a market," says Robert. "On a grander scale than usual."

"No." Eldon will not be convinced otherwise. "It was something more. Many of those products were items never seen by Englishmen before, from places they had no knowledge of." He remembers the beautiful iron-and-glass building, the rooms and rooms of furniture and jewellery, textiles, and sculpture — Turkish carpets, jade vases from the Orient, ornate Austrian bedsteads made of dark zebra wood. "It made the world seem small, Robert," he says. "It made the world seem ours."

Robert Hill, who finds nothing wrong with this notion, wriggles his toes and swishes his brandy around the inside of his glass. He has exhibited paintings at Crystal Palace. He thinks of his art hanging in those magnificent sunlit rooms and experiences a rush of pleasure. "I do know that it is hard to perform work you have no interest in," he says. It is all he can think of to say to Eldon that is sympathetic. His young friend is obviously in distress over his meeting with his publisher, but Robert is comfortable in his chair by the fire, comfortable drinking brandy and remembering his triumph at Crystal Palace. He cannot move far from that comfort to provide a different sort of comfort to his friend. What Eldon wants is always so moral and heightened with emotion, as though he constantly suffers from a kind of fever of the soul. Robert sighs. Why can't Eldon just enjoy what is in the world?

Eldon looks into the fire. It is not making him feel better, being here in Robert's club. He would be better off striding down Cheapside, thinking up reasons to convince Dunstan that a map of the heart was a better idea than a map of gold mines. Eldon studies the fine profile of his friend. Robert's wealth shows in his fine grooming, his shiny new leather boots, his baggy linen suit which is neat and well tailored. A dandy, thinks Eldon, unkindly. An aging dandy. He wishes he was talking this over with Isabelle. No. Eldon watches the flames shift and send a shower of sparks, like applause, into the air. He wishes that he was telling this to Annie Phelan.

Eldon is with Robert Hill at the Royal Academy. Robert's new show is being hung and he is flitting around the gallery, ordering people about who know perfectly well what they are doing.

Eldon stays down at the calm end of the room, surveying the paintings already satisfactorily attached to their designated places on the wall. It has been a while since he has seen a body of his neighbour's work and he realizes, again, both how brilliant and how offensive it is.

Robert Hill depends upon a muse. The muse is invariably a young, good-looking woman. He finds her, paints her, beds her, and then rids himself of her. Sometimes he seeks to paint a particular young woman as an act of wooing her, hoping the attention she receives as his model will move her feelings towards him.

The three paintings Eldon stands in front of show the history of one of Robert's recent muses. In the first painting she is Helen of Troy, her bosom straining at the loose fabric of her dress, nipples visible through the organdie sheer. Her red hair is loose around her shoulders. Her gaze demurely lowered to the apple on the table before her. The apple is red and luscious, almost glows with indiscretion.

In the second painting this model is now Medusa. She looks towards Eldon, a startled expression on her face, as if she can't quite believe that Robert would really paint snakes in her hair, that he would want her to look crazed and monstrous, that this is how he has come to see her, as he tires of her attentions.

Eldon looks at the snarl of reptilian flesh in the girl's hair. The snakes look alive, Robert's rendering is that good, his lines so clean and acute. It makes Eldon want to stand well back from the painting, in case one of them strikes out at him.

In the third painting it is obvious that Robert has wearied of his muse, and has probably already, at the time of painting the picture, moved on to another. In this painting the model is dead, floats beneath the surface of the water she has drowned in, her eyes shut tight, her face pallid as the moon. Ophelia. The faint colours of her dress are visible from where she lies, on her back, in the shallows. On the banks of the stream the vibrant colours of flowers mock her pale failure at life. Once she was as bright and necessary to the painter as they were. Now she is over. This dead heart. This unnecessary girl.

Sappho

Annie is having a late supper in the kitchen. She has been cleaning all day and is tired. She has swept, dusted, and tidied the bedrooms, the landings, and the sitting room. She has polished the drawing-room silver. She has cleaned the lavatory. Because Mr. Dashell is in London and Mrs. Dashell has gone out to supper, there has been no meal to help prepare and serve, and so Annie has worked right through, scrubbed the flags and swept out all the hearths. She is trying to make up for being neglectful of her duties when Mrs. Dashell has required her to model. She wants to show Tess that she will never have to take up any extra work on Annie's behalf, but it is Tess's afternoon off and she isn't back yet, has not been witness to Annie's industry.

Annie sits at the kitchen table and eats her plate of cold chicken, potatoes, and carrots. Since the cattle have started dying they have been eating a lot of chicken. Annie rushes through her meal, not looking up from her plate until she is finished. It is warm in the kitchen. Cook is moving about, wiping down the range, putting water on for tea. She keeps stopping, freezing into position. A statue of Cook reaching up to the shelf above the range for the teapot. A statue of Cook setting the kettle on the burner. Annie watches Cook as she acts out, in a slow sort of mime, the process of making them tea.

"You should leave soon," says Cook, handing Annie a mug of tea and sitting down opposite with hers. "Mrs. Dashell said nine o'clock. She isn't one to be kept waiting."

Annie knows this, knows how impatient the Lady can be when she is made to wait even a few moments for someone whom she feels should be attending to her that very instant. "Don't worry," she says. "I have no desire to keep the Lady waiting."

"Don't know why she bothers," Cook says, arching her back into the flat of her hand. "All she does is complain about it afterwards. Used to come down here and pace up and down and tell me how much she hated going over there."

"But she still goes," says Annie.

"Yes, she still goes," agrees Cook. "I guess she's not one to heed her own good advice."

Isabelle is off having supper with her neighbour, Mrs. Robert Hill. She has left instructions for Annie to walk over and fetch her at nine o'clock. This is her way of ensuring an exit if she is not enjoying herself.

"Missus," asks Annie, sipping her tea to try and prolong the comfort of it. "Who was here before me? Who was it that I replaced?"

Cook is now rubbing her shoulders, her eyes closed. "What?" she says, wincing from a particularly painful spot at the back of her neck.

"Who," says Annie, leaning forward over the table, "was the old me?"

"No one, really. We had day-girls mostly. Mrs. Dashell was meant to hire someone and then she didn't, and then she was meant to again, and didn't. This went on for about a year." Cook opens her eyes and smiles at Annie. "And then there was you. And a good thing, too. It was wearing on me, explaining the house always to someone new and only there for a month or so." Cook pours them both more tea. "Would you like to see something?" she says, on her feet before Annie has had a chance to reply. She goes over to the stove, takes a biscuit tin from a shelf, and brings it back to the table. "Scoot over here, love," she says, patting the chair beside hers. Annie obediently changes sides of the table.

Cook removes the lid from the biscuit tin. There, stacked up inside, are piles of small photo cards. *Cartes de visite.* She takes them carefully from the tin, arranging them on the table neatly in rows, the same amount of space between each one.

"Look," says Cook. "My sister had her likeness done." She taps one of the small photo cards in front of her.

Annie leans towards Cook, towards the photograph, sees a stern-looking woman in a dark morning dress and bonnet. She stands facing the camera, her arms stiffly pinned to her sides. *Cartes*, unlike most portrait photography, usually include the whole body of the subject and Cook's sister takes up most of the frame. To the left of her, Annie can see what appears to be the arm of a chair.

"They put her head in a clamp," says Cook. "To keep it straight."

"She looks" — Annie fumbles for a word that isn't a complete lie — "nervous."

"I'm saving up to get mine done," says Cook. "But I don't want to look like that. I've been trying to decide how it is I want to be looking. A book might be good, don't you think?" She glances up at Annie. "If I was sitting in a chair holding a book, I'd look the part of an educated Lady. I can't read, but no one would be knowing that from the likeness, would they?"

Annie studies the photographs laid out so carefully on the table. To be who we think we are. To look to someone else how we feel to ourselves. How hard that is to align. Cook's sister might never have her photograph taken again. For people who don't know her she will only ever be this stiff woman, her body so rigid in the photograph that there is nothing to read into it, into her. There's no crooked elbow to suggest a casual ease with life, no chin tilted upwards to show interest in the world. And yet, who has decided that is what those things mean? If eyes are looking skyward, couldn't it just be that something has caught the model's attention? A bird has flown into the room or a drop of water has filtered through the ceiling plaster.

"I'll show you something, dear," says Cook conspiratorially. She plucks one of the cards from the table and holds it in front of Annie. "What do you see?"

"The Queen." It's a photograph of Queen Victoria before she entered her continuous and continuing mourning period for her husband's death. She's seated on a royal-looking chair, her dress splayed out around her.

"If you look through a magnifying glass," says Cook, "you can see that she has a hair sticking out of her nose. Imagine that! The Queen with a hair hanging from her royal snout."

What Annie can't believe is that Cook would have spent time looking at the *carte* with a magnifying glass. Is such intense scrutiny desirous because this is likely as close as she will ever get to the Queen?

"Do you do that with everyone?" Annie looks over the boxers and actresses, circus performers, heads of state.

"Of course," says Cook. "There are all kinds of things to see if one looks closely. Even in this house." She replaces Queen Victoria into her allotted space on the table. "I think it's such a shame that Mrs. Dashell won't do likenesses. Don't you?"

"Isn't it that a photographer who takes a likeness makes the photograph for the model," says Annie, "and that Mrs. Dashell takes her photographs for herself?" She's not sure what Cook means — *Even in this house*. Have her secret visits to Eldon's library been observed?

"Well," says Cook. "Aren't you the smart one. It would be a lot easier for me if I could walk out to the garden for my likeness instead of taking a horse and fly into town."

Annie doesn't respond to this, keeps looking at the photographs in front of them on the table. It is not the ones of the Queen that interest her, but the pictures of the ordinary working people, like Cook's sister. The men, stiff in their Sunday clothes, eyes wide with apprehension as they stare into the camera that will hold this moment for them forever, will treat it for the first time ever as equal to the moment the Queen settled herself grudgingly down on her royal behind and said, "Well then, let's get this over with."

The Hills live a few miles from the Dashells on the road to Tunbridge Wells. The night sky is a net of stars and the moon gapes open wide enough for Annie not to need a light as she sets off to fetch Isabelle. It is a bit disconcerting at first, walking along the road with everything so quiet and close, but she soon recovers her nerve and begins to enjoy the soft darkness brushing up against her like a cat.

The Dashell house had been an old farmhouse and it still has obvious remnants from those days. The past is close enough to touch. There is the orchard and the several outbuildings, now used for the laundry and the garden, but formerly used for the housing of animals. There is the large farmhouse kitchen and the flat land around the house that would have been pasture. The house itself seems to fit so perfectly into the landscape that it appears to have grown there, as naturally as a tree.

The Hill house is a different matter altogether. The Hills used to live in London, but with Robert's increasing success and the demands of London society, they had decided to choose a quieter country life. They bought a smaller house in town and had a new house built for them in Sussex in the south. Robert wanted it constructed in the style of a town house. The huge brick structure looks as if it has just suddenly dropped out of the sky and landed there accidentally. It has a large circular driveway and massive columns on either side of the great slab of a front door.

Annie stands at the bottom of the front steps. She is a maid and therefore is required to call at the kitchen door. But since she is there to collect the Lady, and the Lady has to enter and exit through the front door, should she be knocking there?

The Hills have a manservant, a butler. He opens the door to Annie's tentative knock. "Yes," he says, looking her up and down and quickly determining her societal position in relation to himself, determining that he need not be deferent to her. "Why are you not calling at the kitchen door?"

"I've come for Mrs. Dashell," says Annie. The hall behind the butler is bright. Beyond that Annie can see the curving banister of a staircase, beside it a cavernous vestibule lit by a chandelier.

"Wilfred?" There's a woman's voice from behind the butler. "Who is it?"

"A maid, ma'am."

"A maid?" A small woman engulfed in an enormous blue crinoline dress peers out from behind Wilfred. The vastness of the dress makes the woman's head look abnormally small, like a tiny flower swaying in a giant vase. "What is a maid doing at my front door at this time of night?"

"I've come for Mrs. Dashell," says Annie again.

"Isabelle!" The crinoline woman's voice echoes shrilly in the hall. "There's a servant here who professes to know you." She speaks of Annie in a tone that makes Annie feel as if she is a piece of soiled linen, held out at arm's length, too distasteful to gaze upon.

"Annie." Isabelle pushes in front of Wilfred, holds out her hands, and pulls Annie into the hall. "She's mine," she says to Mrs. Hill. "Aren't you?" she says to Annie.

"Yes, ma'am." Annie feels relief singing through her bones. "I am."

Mrs. Hill still hasn't recovered from the sight of a maid at her front door. "But, Isabelle," she says. "I would have sent you home in a carriage."

Why am I here? thinks Annie. It is true that Isabelle could have easily gone home by horse and driver. She looks into her mistress's face and sees that Isabelle has blushed slightly. What is it? Why does Mrs. Dashell not have a ready answer?

"There's a situation at home," says Annie slowly, thinking it up as she goes along. "A delicate situation. I have come to collect Mrs. Dashell so that I might have the walk home with her to explain it properly."

There is gratitude in Isabelle's face when she looks at Annie. Something else, too, that Annie can't read. It only takes a moment for Isabelle to recover herself.

"Then there is not a moment to lose," she says. "We must be off. My shawl," she says to Wilfred. "Goodbye, Letitia," she says to Mrs. Hill. "Thank you for a lovely evening."

The butler helps Isabelle with her shawl. Mrs. Hill fusses around, saying her goodbyes with a false sincerity that Annie finds painful. Then the door is closed behind them and Annie and Isabelle stand alone at the top of the stone stairs.

"Thank you," says Isabelle, as they begin their descent. "You saved my lying soul. Although now Letitia will be round tomorrow, trying to find out what was so urgent."

It feels to Annie as if the night has opened its arms to embrace them as they walk from the house. She is glad for each tufted hillock of grass along the road, each broken ache of earth. The world is suddenly lit with sound. The sharp sparks of crickets, glow of owl song from the darkened trees.

"Why did you send for me, ma'am?" she asks. The Lady might have redeemed her lying soul, but Annie still has her own to account for.

"Ah." Isabelle is quiet for a moment. It is dark enough out that Annie cannot see her face properly. "The truth is, Annie Phelan, I wanted you to walk me home. I didn't want to be sent with Wilfred, or have Wilks come for me like a parcel. Is that terrible?"

"No." It seems to Annie that there is something wrong with it, but it also feels pleasant.

In the moonlit darkness Annie Phelan looks enough like Ellen that Isabelle can almost convince herself that it's true, that she and Ellen have met again, at night, secretly, in the woods behind her father's house. Isabelle, the daughter of a Lord. Ellen, the daughter of her parents' cook.

They walk along in silence. In all the rush and excitement Annie has forgotten to fall back a few paces behind Isabelle, as is customary when a maid walks with a Lady. But Isabelle doesn't appear to expect it and tonight Annie does not feel that she is a few paces behind Isabelle. It feels to her that she is exactly where she is, walking along this darkened road with Isabelle Dashell beside her.

"It's so boring," says Isabelle. "All she does is show me all the new things she's bought. Horrid dresses and *objets d'art*. As if I'm interested. As if I'm the same as her."

"You're not the same as her," says Annie.

"Thank God."

"But why do you go, then?"

Isabelle tilts her head back to look at the stars. How wonderful it would be to be able to photograph a night sky. The absolute contrast of light and dark makes both seem so lovely. Heavenly. That is the right word for that. Perhaps if she exposed the plate for as long as possible before the collodion dried. Would there be enough light from the moon to cast even the faintest ghost onto the glass? "Eldon's in London," she says. "And I find it lonely to dine by myself. I expect Letitia asked me to come for supper for that very same reason. Robert's in London. She didn't want to be alone."

Annie thinks how strange it is, loneliness in a house full of people. In the kitchen there are always people — the Dashell servants, neighbouring servants who are visiting Cook, tradesmen. And yet, upstairs, there are only the two of them. How different their sense of being alone must be.

"I was born near here," says Isabelle. She tries to make out familiar objects, trees, but it is all a blur of darkness. "As a child I knew my way over this countryside. All the paths. All the fields. I would stay out from morning till night. My parents despaired of me ever changing from a wild animal into a Lady. But I had to," she says, a tinge bitterly. "My father was a Lord." She thinks of the day when she was ten and her mother told her she must no longer associate with Ellen. No matter that they had grown up together, were inseparable. When Isabelle was ten her world was suddenly divided into upstairs and downstairs. Ellen had to remain in the kitchen, a scullery maid-in-training, daughter of the cook. Isabelle had to stay upstairs and learn how to become a Lady.

She remembers how Ellen would always surprise her, suddenly appearing from behind a tree, always the first one to arrive at their secret meeting place. Often she had something for Isabelle, a gift she'd found on her journey through the woods. Bird feather. Lace of fern. The slow surprise of Ellen suddenly there. The slow surprise into a pure kind of happiness she's sure she has never felt since.

"If you hadn't had to be a Lady," says Annie, "what would you have done?" She likes imagining Isabelle as a wild child, hurtling through a forest with her hair matted with leaves and sticks, her arms and legs scratched and smudged with dirt. She can almost feel the slick rise of the path beneath her bare feet, dirt worn smooth as the leather on an old saddle.

"Oh," says Isabelle. "I wanted to be a great artist of course."

Isabelle, as the only child, was expected to uphold the position she'd been born to. She wasn't supposed to marry a man with few prospects, but she had persisted in spite of her parents' wrath. She certainly wasn't supposed to have been an artist. It was fortunate really that her parents were dead, as they would have very little to say to her now if they were alive.

"But you still could be a great artist," says Annie. It is not as though Isabelle Dashell is old. She seems barely into her middle-thirties.

"Yes." Isabelle looks over at Annie's face, beautiful even in the murky dark, especially beautiful in the murky dark. That dark hair and pale skin. So like Ellen. "I could be. But then I thought it was to be as a painter. I was wrong about that."

Annie thinks of how slow modelling for a painting would be, how each time the brush was lifted Isabelle would have to raise her eyes to check the pose. "What you do is better than painting," she says.

Isabelle takes Annie's arm. "Art is like a light," she says. She almost says, like *Love*. "Isn't it? Always burning with the same brightness, no matter how long we've been gone from the room."

Isabelle's arm is warm against Annie's. Their linked arms are a bridge between them. Light, Isabelle is saying something about light. Annie thinks of her life in Portman Square. How quiet and contained it was. How she worked, and studied the Bible. Her only escape from the dourness of that world was to fall into the comfort of reading. Annie remembers the darkness of Portman Square, how Mrs. Gilbey liked to keep the curtains closed because she said the light from outside hurt her eyes. "My world was always shrinking," she says. As a child she had wanted to play on the street with the other children, but Mrs. Gilbey frightened her with stories of men who would hurt her, steal her away. Always, it seemed, there were things she wasn't aware of, and when she became aware of them it stopped her impulse to participate in anything beyond the confines of the house, beyond the watchful eye of Mrs. Gilbey. It wasn't that she was afraid, but she became cautious out of habit, and that caution shut windows and pulled the curtains tight across them.

"That is the difference between your world and mine," Annie says. "Yours can expand. Mine shrinks." She is probably enjoying the most comfortable part of her life, right now. In a few years the work she does will start to show on her body. Her knees will swell and ache from scrubbing floors. Her hands will grow stiff. What is there to look forward to? The future is more of the same. No, the future is less, and the same.

Isabelle doesn't say anything, and Annie suddenly feels

afraid that she has spoken too freely. "I didn't mean to suggest..." she says.

Isabelle cuts her off. "I spend so much time with people like Letitia Hill," says Isabelle. "I forget that one can speak from the heart." That's how it will be for Ellen, she thinks. Wherever she is, her world is small and getting smaller. She will never be able to equal the freedom she had when she was ten. "What was your last mistress like?" she says. "That one in London."

"She didn't trust anyone," says Annie. She thinks of her one act of defiance in Mrs. Gilbey's house. "She used to try and trap me to see if I was stealing from her."

"How?"

"She would hide coins under the carpet, as though they'd accidentally spilled there. Taking them would not necessarily be stealing, as she did not supposedly know they were there, but it would be an act of dishonesty. It would be a reason for her not to trust in me."

"So you were supposed to go to her with the coins and say, 'Look what I found. You must have lost these?'" says Isabelle. She is always amazed at the time some employers spend trying to trick their servants into behaving badly. Don't they have anything better to do?

"Yes, ma'am."

"And did you do this?"

"All but one time." Annie smiles, remembering the guilty satisfaction she felt from what she had done. "Once I got angry with her for doing this so often. It was like a battle between us. She was trying to force me to take the coins so she could punish me. I kept giving them back to her and giving them back to her, and then once I didn't."

"You took them?" Isabelle is surprised that Annie would be so foolish.

"No. I didn't take them." Annie chuckles out loud, she can't help herself. "I glued them to the floor."

Isabelle puts her head back and hoots with laughter. "Oh," she says. "That is very good."

"And it worked," says Annie. "She couldn't confront me because it would mean she would have to confess to putting them there in the first place. For a couple of weeks they were still there and then she managed to pry them up and they never appeared again."

"I must remember never to try and trick you," says Isabelle. She laughs again, thinking of Letitia Hill as Mrs. Gilbey, kneeling down in a good dress, trying to pry shillings off the floor with a butter knife.

They reach the Dashell house. It is darkened except for a carriage lamp in the drive. The flame like a whisper, a soft voice calling for Isabelle as she runs through the woods to meet the Cook's daughter. She remembers the light hanging in the trees like green lanterns above her head, the rush head-long through stasis, the sound of her heart in her ears like the whirr of a grouse, beating up from the alders.

"Annie?"

"Yes, ma'am."

A reason, Isabelle needs a reason. "I know it's late, but would you bring me up water for a bath?"

"Of course." Annie no longer feels tired. She no longer feels as though she's worked hard all day. "Right away," she says, and, disentangling herself from Isabelle Dashell, she goes round to the kitchen door.

Cook has gone to bed. The kitchen is dark and cool. The range has been shut down for the night. Annie will have to start it up again to heat the bathwater. This means that she will let it burn out and then have to rise before Cook in the morning to get it swept and cleaned again for the day ahead. She takes off her shawl, rolls up her sleeves, and gets to work. She lights an oil lamp, fires up the range, then takes the two largest kettles outside to the pump to fill them with water. The pump is not far from the kitchen door, halfway between the kitchen and the laundry. After a few hauls of the handle, the banging, rusty voice of the metal pump softens and water gushes out from the spout. Annie puts her hand under the cascade. The coolness of the water prickles her skin like nettles.

It is when she is filling the second kettle, stooped over the pump, lost to the sound of the water spilling into the tin, that Annie hears the noise. It is close by, on the other side of the laundry building. A grunting, hurried noise. An animal, she thinks, out there in the darkness. Something enormous. She lets the pump handle rise into its moorings and the remaining water from the vacuum slosh out. Carefully she makes her way over to the laundry, sneaks around the side of the building. Sure enough, there is a dark tangled shape up against the bricks. It takes a moment for her eyes to catalogue and identify the shape. It is not an animal. It is Tess and Wilks. Wilks has his trousers down, his bare arse white in the moonlight. He has Tess pinned up against the wall of the laundry and Annie's first thoughts are that she must rush to Tess's aid, that this is what Mrs. Gilbey was always warning her about. But Tess puts her hands down on Wilks's arse, goading him on. She is obviously not struggling to get away. Annie stands there. She can hear their breathing, the sounds they make. How their breathing overlaps, knits together in rough, raw gasps, their bodies pushing through each other. It seems to Annie that they are so intent on each other that even if she said something or made a noise to show she was there, they would not stop.

They have left themselves, the selves that say "yes, ma'am"

and fetch and carry for Cook. Who they are now is something that belongs only to them. Annie is surprised to find that she envies this. She envies the urgency of these selves they have become.

Annie has never even kissed a man. Once, the butcher's boy at Portman Square asked her to come out with him for a walk, and before Mrs. Gilbey put a stop to it, they walked around the Square at night and he held her hand. His hand had been sweaty, cold as a piece of beef liver, and Annie had been glad he hadn't tried to kiss her. He was too nervous of her to be appealing.

She stands in the shadows, watching Tess and Wilks writhe against each other, and she realizes she has never thought of this. She has known about it, from downstairs talk, but she has never thought of it for herself. There was no one's body she could imagine herself pressing up against with such a fever. Only Jesus, but that is a wrong thing to think, and she does not allow herself to think it often.

Annie starts retreating backwards, carefully trying to put her feet in the exact steps she made when she had crept forward. But her foot rolls on stones, there is the noise of it sliding, and Tess's eyes, which have been closed, snap open. She stares, over Wilks's shoulder, right at Annie, for the moment before Annie shadows around the corner and runs back into the yard to collect her kettles from the pump.

"What's the matter?" asks Isabelle, when Annie comes into her bedroom breathing fast and carrying two steaming kettles. "You look" — she stares hard at Annie — "different somehow."

"They're just heavy, ma'am." Annie empties the kettles into the tin bath which Isabelle has brought out into the room from her dressing area. It is bigger than the hip bath at Portman Square, looks like a big shoe, with the covered-in toe part long enough to stretch one's legs out in. "I'll be right back with more hot water, and the cold," says Annie. She is slightly annoyed that Mrs. Dashell is still in her evening clothes. By the time she has shed them the water will be cold. "You had better get undressed, ma'am," she says.

"Yes, yes." Isabelle was looking at a book when Annie first entered the room. She picks it up again now. "More hot water," she says. "I want it to be a nice, deep bath."

It was a struggle for Annie to clamber up the stairs with the two huge and heavy kettles. More hot water means an additional two trips, as well as having to go back out to the pump to get more water. What if Tess and Wilks are still out there? What will she say to Tess?

"Yes, ma'am," she says, and covers the opening of the bathtub with a towel, to help keep the heat of the water from escaping so quickly.

By the time Annie has brought all the bathwater upstairs she is exhausted. She is sweating and breathing quickly, her arms ache from the heaviness of the kettles. She no longer feels very kindly towards her mistress, wishes only now to go to bed and sleep. As it is, she will have to rise early to see to the kitchen range, and it is already past eleven o'clock.

"Right," says Isabelle, when Annie has emptied all the water into the tub. "Take off your clothes." She snaps her book shut.

"Pardon, ma'am?"

"Take off your clothes. The bath is for you."

"But I would have had a bath in the kitchen. Where I usually have my baths," says Annie, meaning that she would not willingly have hauled water upstairs for her own bath.

"But I want you to have a bath here," says Isabelle. "Undress." She is using her commanding tone. This is not the same voice she had when she was at a loss to explain to Mrs. Hill why Annie Phelan had come to fetch her home.

Annie just stands there. She does not know what to make of this. Her heart is still beating quickly from her labours. She can hear it as though it is in the room beside her.

"Oh," says Isabelle, softer now. "I see. You're bashful. Well, I need to go and fetch something anyhow, so I'll give you your privacy. But when I'm back"—she waves her finger at Annie—"I want to see you in that tub. And," she says from the doorway, "stoke up the fire so it's burning bright. We'll need it."

Annie heaps coal onto the fire, makes sure it is drawing properly. She takes her clothes off slowly, laying each item in a neat pile by the tub. When she is down to her shift she hesitates. Surely Mrs. Dashell didn't mean *all* her clothes? She climbs into the tub with her shift still on. The water is deliciously hot, and as she slides her body down into the comfort of it her bad humour lifts from her skin, like steam. She closes her eyes. A face floats above her. *Mother*, she thinks. The features are hazy. It takes Annie a moment to realize that she has fallen asleep and that it is Isabelle kneeling beside the tub, leaning over her.

"You look lovely when you're asleep," says Isabelle. "No need to blush. It's the truth."

Annie has slid down into the tub, pulls herself up straight and sees that her hair is down, lying on her breasts. Isabelle must have loosened it while Annie slept. As she's sitting up she sees something out of the corner of her eyes, something that wasn't in the room before. The camera, on its legs, standing by the fire.

"You want me to model?" asks Annie. "Now?" Surely Mrs. Dashell can't want to photograph this late at night?

Annie looks down at herself in the tub, at her legs disappearing under the cuff of tin. "Ophelia?" she says.

Isabelle smiles. Her hand on the edge of the tub is inches from Annie's bare skin. "No," she says. She thinks that she was almost happy, watching Annie Phelan sleep, watching her face collapse its sorrows, become peaceful and sweet like a child's face. There could be nothing else to want, Isabelle had thought. If I wasn't who I am. "Not Ophelia," she says. "No more of Ophelia. I've thought about what you said. About all my tragic heroines. We're going to try something different now. From now on, things will be different."

"Who?" asks Annie. Isabelle has sad eyes, she thinks. That is their natural resting state, sadness.

"Sappho." Isabelle takes it for granted that Annie won't know who she is talking about. "A great Greek lyric poet, although what has survived of her writing is mostly fragments. It is said she was a lover of both men and women. Here." Isabelle fetches the book she was looking at from her dressing table. She pulls a chair over to the bathtub and flips through the pages. "Listen," she says, needlessly, as it is only Annie there to listen. Isabelle reads:

> *What my heart most hopes will*
> *happen, make happen...*

She looks up at Annie. The words hang still in the space between them. "You see?" she says.

"No," says Annie. "I don't."

Of course not, thinks Isabelle. Of course Annie isn't Ellen, is only a maid, cannot be expected to understand the higher orders of art and cultural thought. She is not smart like Ellen, schooled with Isabelle until the age of ten because only then would Isabelle try to learn literature and geography. Ellen, matched to Isabelle in a way no one has ever been since. "'A thin flame runs under my skin,'" she says, carelessly now. What does it matter? "'They are only breath, words.'"

That makes Annie think of Tess and Wilks, not of them so much, but how she felt standing in the darkness watching them. The words of the poet slide right into her heart, lodge under her skin. And they will stay there, she thinks, these words, until something urgent and entirely present sets them free. That's what Tess and Wilks were doing, letting the words out, bleeding the words' fever from their bodies. Words like these that had found them somehow and wouldn't let them go.

But it was sin. All of it. Tess and Wilks in the garden, this poet who loved both men and women. Annie knows it is all sin, as surely as she knows anything, but somehow what in her mind is sin has been translated by her body into pleasure. She doesn't know what to do about this.

The water is getting cold around Annie's stomach. The wet shift is sticking to her skin. "Ma'am?" she says. "What about the bath? What use is it?" She doesn't see how her having a bath has to do with Isabelle photographing her as Sappho.

Isabelle closes the book. What has happened to her tonight that she has allowed such sentiment? She leans forward, the book on her knees. What is the truth? she thinks. What is the thing to tell Annie Phelan? The light from the fire behind Annie throws itself out into the room, pulls back again. "I have to feel something to see it," she says. "And, the other way around." She is suddenly doubtful, grips the book hard with both her hands. "Sappho is better than Ophelia, don't you think?"

"Much better," agrees Annie. She is glad not to have to die for love, or be sorrowful for its absence.

"I need to feel the scene I want to fix," says Isabelle. "And this — the bath, the fire, your nakedness — is how I can feel what I want to see."

"Like prophesy," says Annie. She is quiet for a moment. There is no sound from outside this room. The rest of the house sleeps on. "What do you want me to do?" she says.

The moment Annie asks this, Isabelle feels her careful staging of the scene fall away. Sappho wouldn't be so tentative, so shy with her body. Hadn't she told this maid to remove all of her clothes? Why was she still wearing her shift?

"I had a friend once," she says, but it is futile to try and explain anything. She is silent for a moment. "I want you," she says finally, "to take the photograph of me. Can you do that?"

Annie is tired tonight and that makes her less careful. Hearing the words of the poem and seeing Tess and Wilks in the garden have made her feel as though she wants to push against something, and this is what she has to push against — Isabelle, this room soft with firelight, the photograph that will come to hold all this. And then, somewhere underneath it all, she has thought, briefly, of her mother, thought that the one thing above all others that she wants to know about her is what she looked like. This is the one thing she can never know. What her mother looked like, and if Annie looks like her. All she can really imagine of her mother is the work she did. Annie cannot guess what it is her mother would have been thinking on that road in Ireland, or even what she would have been wearing, but Annie does know what the labour would feel like. The roughness of the stone would rub hands raw and bleeding. The stooping and lifting would make a back ache and force the body to move stiffly to accommodate the pain. Looking up would hurt. It was as simple as that. "Yes, I can," she says.

Annie dresses in Isabelle's robe and poses her near the fire, so the light from the coals will be behind her. Isabelle removes her evening dress and corset and sits, on the floor, in her slip. There is something so forlorn in the way she just sits there, looking as though she's waiting for someone to suddenly appear before her. Annie doesn't know how to change this. She asks Isabelle to shake her hair out. "Now look at me, ma'am," she says. She stands beside the camera. She wants Isabelle's defiant gaze, the one she had at Mrs. Hill's when she told Wilfred to fetch her shawl. The look she has when she poses Annie.

"Now you know," says Isabelle, for the third time, "that because this is indoors we're going to have to do a long exposure. Firelight is not the same as sunlight. Four, maybe five minutes."

"I know."

"And make sure the collodion entirely covers the glass plate."

"I know."

"And..."

"Ma'am," says Annie, looking through the camera at Isabelle, "if something goes wrong, you're right here." Trust me. Through the camera lens, Isabelle looks worried, anxious. Annie is not sure she can do this. "Look at me, ma'am," she says again.

Annie fills the frame with Isabelle's head. On the eleven-by-seven negative plate it will be life-size. She holds the focus of the lens only on the eyes, lets the background fall away to smoke. Even Isabelle's hair, at the edges of the frame, is fuzzy and indistinct. It's the eyes Annie wants, the directness of them. And underneath, a tremble of sorrow. "Don't move," she says, and opens the lens.

Isabelle stares into the camera. It is like looking into herself, a strangely disconnected feeling. She has always thought of that wooden box, that lens, as her mind's eye. It belongs to her vision of the world. To be looking at it from this side is to have given over the power of it. She has closed her eyes and has let Annie Phelan guide her through this darkened room.

Let me tell you this: Someone in some future time will think of us.
Ellen.

Now it's just me, thinks Isabelle, thinking of you. No one is thinking of us. We no longer exist to anything in the world. Maybe, in that forest there's a tree that remembers your touch when you stood there, close against it, waiting for me, over twenty years ago. Maybe that patch of bark you laid the flash of your hand on is now farther up the tree than I could reach, right up in the tangle of branches far above my head.

Annie counts off the minutes on Isabelle's pocket watch. She alone moves this future forward, fixes Isabelle's face forever to this moment.

When she finally says, "Done," Isabelle leaps up from her place by the fire, dresses hastily, rushes the plate out of the camera on its way to the darkroom. Annie can hear her running down the stairs and then the bang of the back door as she hurries from the house.

Annie carries the kettles of water from the bath down the hall to the lavatory and throws the water in. Then she scrubs out the tub, dries it, and leans it back against the wall of Mrs. Dashell's dressing room. It is now so late there is almost no point in going to bed. She takes the kettles back to the kitchen and sits at the table, in the dark, waiting for the range to burn down so she can clean it out. She lays her head on her arms. This evening she was not thinking of work she had to be doing. This evening had been different. She had stood in the glow of Isabelle Dashell's room and, although it had felt unnatural and vaguely sinful, she had been in command of four and a half minutes. This world, for that time, had been hers and she had never felt such a sense of possibility for herself, a sense that she was someone apart from what she did, that she was real. She had been trusted. She had been in charge and had not faltered. She had not faltered.

There's a noise in the darkness of the kitchen. Someone coming in through the door, clumsily knocking into a pail and sending it skittering across the floor.

"Ma'am, is that you?" says Annie, thinking that it's Isabelle, back from the darkroom.

"Annie?" says the voice. "It's me."

Tess. She bumps her way over to the table, feels with her hands for Annie's shape, and sits down heavily beside her. Annie can smell the sweet musky bloom of alcohol on her breath.

"Can you see me?" says Tess. She's looking right at Annie.

"Yes."

"You see me. You saw me," says Tess, swaying a little on the bench.

"I did," says Annie. "I saw you."

"Don't say anything. Because I could lose," says Tess, swaying again. "My position."

Annie grabs Tess and holds her firmly by the arm. "You could lose your balance," she says. "Come on. I'll take you up to bed." She loops Tess's arm around her shoulder and stumbles her up the stairs to their room. Tess is asleep before she falls onto her bed. Annie removes Tess's shoes and then pulls the covers snugly over her. It is cool upstairs. Annie sits down on the edge of Tess's bed. A moth thrums against the night window. The soft thump of it hitting the glass, like the beat of someone's heart heard with an ear against her chest. *Are you alive?* What she had asked Mrs. Gilbey as she lay there on the drawing-room floor. The answer was yes. The answer was no.

Are you awake? thinks Isabelle, lying in the close darkness of her bedroom. Are you awake, Annie Phelan? Have I made these feelings happen? Are they mine, or will they disappear tomorrow when the sun pushes the image of Sappho out onto the coated paper?

All day long Isabelle has been imagining Sappho. The fragmented lyrics, brief as roses. All day she has been thinking how it would be to be lover to both men and women. She had fallen easily into it, having Annie Phelan fetch her home, arranging the bath so she could look fully on a woman's body again, without shame. And then, she had been the one who was Sappho. All night Isabelle had been trying to conjure an atmosphere, forgetting that there were character considerations. There was lover and loved. It should have been obvious to her who she was in this scenario. In that old scenario.

Isabelle stretches her arms out from her body, feels the emptiness of her bed, the vastness of it. Has she made her own feelings happen? Has imagining Sappho made her become Sappho, even temporarily? These feelings she still has, the residue in her body, the trailing ends of desire, will they go with morning? Does she wish them gone?

Ellen, do you ever think of me?

And how much of this is due to her husband? How much to the fact that they no longer touch one another. It was not the first one that stopped this, or even the second. It was the third dead baby. It's as though they are lined up on the mattress between her and Eldon, and when she puts her hand out she can't reach him across their stiff, blue bodies. This is what has been made from her and Eldon's love — a love that once seemed as fierce and bright as moving blood — three dead babies.

Tonight, when Annie arranged her by the fire, tilting her head up gently, it was the first time in over a year that anyone had touched Isabelle in an intimate way, that anyone had touched her with feeling, with purpose. To be Sappho is tempting. To love a woman is never to have the product of that love be death. She would never have had to have held them in her arms, their blood-slick bodies, slippery as fish, having swum from their dark ocean out into a light that killed them.

Annie can't sleep. She lights a candle, descends the stairs, walks the familiar passage to Eldon's library. She has travelled this route so often that she doesn't really need a light to guide her. She could walk this, with confidence, through the thickest thicket of dark.

Tonight, for the first time, Annie feels too restless to settle to reading. She runs her hands gently over the books on the shelves, each spine a soft flash under her fingertips. There are no words to calm her here. Not tonight.

Annie leaves Eldon's library without a book, walks the corridor back to the main part of the house. She goes to the room with the old prams and carriages and settles herself on the floor in her usual place. This room no longer seems sinister to her. When she first started coming in here she thought of it as the room of old baby things. Now she thinks of it only as the place she comes to read.

Annie sits on the floor, pulls her knees up to her chin. The evening still flashes around her, like the tiny stings of light from fireflies. The bath. The camera. What is it Isabelle had said about that poet? A lover of both men and women. Annie thinks of Wilks and Tess out by the laundry wall. Then she thinks of herself and Isabelle, of Isabelle pushing her up against the bricks. How that might feel, to have Isabelle's skin on her skin. The thought of this panics her. The thought of this makes her hold her breath. Makes her breathe.

The next day Annie moves slowly through her work. She drags her body around as though it is a heavy sack, not something she lives inside, but something she must haul unwillingly through her day. By the afternoon she is woozy with exhaustion and pleads with Cook to allow her an hour to lie down. She says she isn't feeling well. She isn't.

She sleeps hard and fast, waking to someone's hand on her shoulder and her name spilling out into the room like a stone. The rattle of it in her ears moving her out of sleep.

"Annie." It is Isabelle there, by the side of her bed, shaking her awake. "Annie."

"What is it, ma'am?" Annie struggles up, makes it halfway to sitting, and then falls back against her pillow. She is crossing from sleep to the waking world and is still not sure she isn't dreaming.

Isabelle lays something on Annie's chest. A photograph. Annie picks it up gingerly. The head of Isabelle as Sappho fills the paper. The face softens away from the eyes, sharp as stars.

Isabelle sits on the edge of Annie's bed and Annie shifts over to make room for her there.

"There it is, Annie."

"Do you like it, ma'am?"

"Do you?" Isabelle looks straight at her and Annie looks down at the photograph again. The bigness is right, and the softness. The look is sadder than she'd meant, but it is not wrong. She remembers last night, remembers her thoughts about Isabelle when she was sitting in the carriage room. Her skin flutters hot.

"Yes," she says.

"Art finds us out," says Isabelle.

Annie thinks she must be blushing.

Isabelle puts her hand on Annie's where it holds the photograph. "You have made something of me that has surprised me." And it's a bit too good, she thinks. That has surprised me also. She stands up, leaving the photograph in Annie's hands. "Keep it. It's yours." She goes out of the room.

Annie sits up in bed. She still feels disoriented from her brief nap. She looks at the photograph again. It does not look like the memory of Isabelle posing that she holds in her head. The firelight. The warmth of the room. And yet, there is something of last night there. Here. The way Isabelle looks out. The way she looks out at Annie, almost as if she loves her, almost as if she could.

Annie's dress is twisted from lying in bed. Her hair is falling from its pins. She had better tidy herself before she goes back downstairs. She swings herself out of bed, feet first. Before she stands up she puts the photograph of Isabelle under her pillow, underneath her neglected Bible. For safe keeping.

What is holy to me now?

Before Eldon takes the train home from London he does two things. He goes to a public house and drinks three glasses of whisky, and then he goes next door, to a place he has never before imagined going.

Up the long, shabby flight of stairs from the street to the second floor. His breath catching in his throat from the effort. His sweaty hands out to press against the walls either side of him, to keep him on a straight ascent.

The room is bright. Eldon blinks from the sunlight rushing the windows.

"Whatever you desire," says the woman, and Eldon chooses an object from the curio cabinet in the corner of the room, stands with his hand covetously on the round slur of it.

"Is this what you want?" asks the photographer, from behind the camera. He motions his assistant out of the way and she scuttles off to one side.

Eldon feels the hard surface of the globe beneath his sweaty palm. The pack ice of the Arctic Circle burns against his fingers. "Yes," he says. "This is what I want."

When Eldon bursts into his wife's bedroom, Isabelle is sitting on her bed, head bent over something in her lap. She looks up, startled, when the door flaps back on its hinge, bangs against the wall.

"Eldon," she says, surprised to see him. He stands in the doorway, as though now that he has announced his entrance in such a dramatic fashion he doesn't know what to do next. His suit is crumpled. His beard is unkempt. "What happened?"

Eldon doesn't move from the doorway.

"What happened?" asks Isabelle again.

"No," he says.

"No?"

"No. Dunstan said no. No to my proposal. No to my map. No to me."

Isabelle stretches out her hands and Eldon comes over and sits on the bed beside her. She holds his hand. "Can you not go to another publisher?"

All afternoon, travelling down from London, Eldon has thought of, and dispensed with, every possible avenue of redemption. "Not possible," he says flatly. "My history is all with Dunstan. I don't have the credibility with another publisher." Eldon looks down at the blue patterned carpet, at his shoes floating there. "I thought, all this time, that he respected me, that my work on the atlas was important to him. But he doesn't want to allow me a vision. He wants me to work for him. That is what he thinks I do."

Isabelle squeezes his hand.

"There's still the theme map," says Eldon bitterly. "I could redeem my good name by pointing the way to rubies and emeralds in Africa." He feels frustration climbing through his blood again. His wife's hand in his is an irritation, not a comfort. He shakes it off, sees the photograph she has lying on her lap. "What is that?"

Isabelle passes the photograph over without a word.

"A self-portrait?" Eldon has never known his wife to photograph herself. She is always constructing some vignette, some allegorical scene. "This is something new."

"No," says Isabelle. "It's not a self-portrait."

Eldon looks closely at the photograph. It is Isabelle as he has never seen her. The expression in her eyes is so private it makes him want to turn away. If she hasn't taken the photograph herself, then where is this look directed? "Who took this?" he says.

"Annie Phelan," says Isabelle. "Under my instruction, of

course. Look how complex it is. My new technique is quite effective for portraiture. The life-size head. The focus only on the eyes — that's one story. How the face and the background soften and disappear, are blurred to a kind of smokiness — that's another story."

"Annie Phelan?" Eldon looks down at the photograph again, at his wife's face full of gentle feeling. "The maid took this photograph?" Isabelle has never let him near the camera. Once, when he suggested he take some photographs of her, she refused, shrugged him off. She has never allowed him to see her in this way. And the few times she has photographed him, before he protested too often that he was too busy to be King Arthur or the North Wind, she had never looked at him with that much intensity. Eldon feels his body go cold, flash with heat, go cold again. When his meeting with Dunstan was failing, when he felt that he was losing his hold on the argument, slipping down the side of that cliff, he had remembered the story of Annie Phelan, the story she had told him on the afternoon they had walked out together. This had made him feel better, had strengthened him. Now the warm thoughts of her have been dissolved by this evidence of feeling between her and his wife. She had been his secret, and now he fears she belongs, as does everything else in this house, to Isabelle. All the disappointment he has held back from his meeting with Dunstan spills out now. He is reckless with feeling. "She's a maid," he says. "She should not be taking photographs. And especially not of you."

"Yes, well, you know I've never been good at that sort of thing," says Isabelle, a little guiltily. "Servants." She and Ellen had been found out, had been discovered one evening walking down the lane by her father on his return from town. The next day Ellen and her mother had been sent away. There had not even been time to say goodbye. Isabelle hadn't known it was happening until after it had happened.

"I'm just not very strong on the whole servant business," says Isabelle. "Sometimes I don't have the heart for any of it."

"Grow up, Isabelle," says Eldon harshly. "You are the mistress of this house. Act like it. Keep the maid in the position she belongs. Maids are maids." He stands up, the photograph in his hand. "They are not artists. Or friends." Methodically, and without looking at Isabelle once, he tears the photograph slowly into bits, tosses the torn photograph up into the air, and marches from the room.

The pieces of photograph flutter down. Isabelle puts her hand out and a few land in her open palm. Like broken stars come to earth. Like snow falling from heaven, bright and turning in the shaft of window light, drifting down on wings of air. The breath that has left her body.

Grace, Humility, Faith

Eldon sees Annie Phelan from his library window. She is hurrying along the path from the glasshouse, back towards the kitchen. He raps on the glass, but she doesn't hear him, doesn't look up. He fumbles with the latch, flings the window open wide, and leans out over the sill.

"Annie!" he calls. "Annie!"

She looks up, startled, trying to locate the shout, tipping her head, like a bird, towards the sound.

"Annie!" he calls again. "Over here."

She turns off the path, comes to stand near enough to hear him properly, his body arched over the window sill, anchored in the warm mustiness of his room, thrust forward into sunlight and the scent of roses.

"Yes, sir?"

"Could you come in here a minute, please." Eldon regains his dignity, heaves his body back into the room as though it is an empty net he has cast into the ocean and he is hauling it back in full of fish. He closes the window, stands by his map table, waiting for her small knock on the door. "Come in."

Annie is nervous to be in the library in daylight with Mr. Dashell. What if he has found her out? What if he knows that she has *David Copperfield* jammed under the mattress of the perambulator in the baby-carriage room?

The first thing Annie notices, once she has become accustomed to the dull light after the brightness of the glasshouse and the outdoors, is how dusty the room is. The stacks of papers, like gills, opening and closing in the breeze from the door when she entered the room, breathing in and out, dust.

"Yes, sir?" she says again. "Is there something you want me to do for you?" She is late getting back to the house, having helped Isabelle drape muslin from the roof of the studio all morning, and there is work she needs to help Cook with to get ready for dinner.

"No, I don't want you to do anything," says Eldon. "I just thought you might like to see this." He taps the topmost map on the table. "It's a map of Ireland. Where you're from," he says, chiding himself silently for a fool as he says this. Of course she knows that's where she's from. "Have you ever seen a map of Ireland?"

"No, sir." Annie catches her breath. It flutters free.

"Well, come here, then," says Eldon.

Annie stands beside him at the table. She has thought and dreamt so much about the road her parents worked on that she has only imagined Ireland in terms of that road. She looks down at the map and is surprised that Ireland is not long and thin, loping off the top of the page into distance. Instead the shape is squat and strong-looking, a little longer than it is wide, the coast chewed into bays and peninsulas by the Atlantic Ocean, calmer and smoother on the side of the Irish Sea.

"Here." Eldon puts his finger down on the left-hand side of the map. "This is where you're from. County Clare."

County Clare is coloured pink. It has a long bit of land trailing out into the ocean, and the rest of it is thicker, looks like a piece of paper that has been crumpled and tossed down onto the blue floor of the sea.

Ennis Killaloe Kilkee Rineanna

These are names that mean nothing to her now. But maybe one of them was where she lived. Annie puts her finger down, gently, on Kilkee and traces the jagged outline of the Loop Head.

Eldon watches her. He understands this, it is what he does as well. How he has to touch something to make it real, to really see it. "It's all right," he says. "You won't hurt it." Annie's hands aren't black with photographic chemicals like Isabelle's.

"It's so small," says Annie, slowly dragging her finger around all the indentations on the Atlantic side of the county. She wants to feel the sharpness of the rocks in the coves, the stringy flags of seaweed hanging from the walls of the low-tide caves.

"No," says Eldon. "Stop." He lightly touches her arm and she pauses her moving finger on a small nodule of land near Ennistown. "Each one of these little bumps is a vast headland, where you could stand and look out over a sea that goes on and on, that opens before you and is endless, so that you are the smallest possible point in the landscape." He lifts his hand from her arm and they both look up towards the window, as though beyond it is the flat blue of the Atlantic, stretching its fluid muscle across the garden. "Do you see?" says Eldon.

"Yes, sir." There is the bright blue flare of sky through the window. Surely, it is the same blue as the sea would be. A sea Annie has never seen.

They look out across the sea. Eldon can almost hear the murmur of the surf, feel the rough hand of the wind in his hair.

"Have you been there?" asks Annie, looking down at the map of Ireland again, trying to burn the shape of it into her mind.

"No," says Eldon softly. "I haven't been there. Or anywhere. This is how I travel." He puts his hand down on the map. It entirely covers County Mayo.

"Do you think," asks Annie, "that I'm less from there because I've never been?"

"Not at all," says Eldon. "Some of the early map-makers themselves were never there. Lied and said they'd surveyed Ireland. Produced maps that were mostly invention. One of them, Baptiste Boazio, wrote the name of one of his friends across most of County Down. As though he owned it." Eldon thinks of the map he is never to make, which would have included Boazio as a cautionary note in the margin. "People can believe something," he says. "It doesn't have to be true for that to happen."

He doesn't say *God*, but Annie is sure this is what he means.

"But it's ending," Eldon says. "I fear it is all ending."

"What is?"

"Journeys. Maps. The getting there. Isabelle is right. The future is the photograph. And a photograph is always a destination. It's not concerned with getting there, but being there." Eldon looks up at Annie, who is still looking out the window at the sea. "To look at a photograph," he says, "is to always have arrived."

Annie thinks of the glasshouse, of how sometimes she is standing so still that her very breath seems to race around her like a wild, dangerous thing. Her breath draws a ragged line around the shape of her. "Your map," she says, "is better than a photograph." But the moment she says this she feels guilty, as though she has betrayed Isabelle. "What I mean," she says quickly, "is that your map of Ireland is both far away and close by. It is something in my head, and there it is." She taps the page. "There. Looking like that."

After Annie has gone, Eldon sits down in front of the map of Ireland and looks at it carefully. There is such detail around each bay on the Atlantic side of the island. This map would have once been a chart. It would have been important to show the shape of the coastline. Where one could land a vessel. Where one should keep clear of the rocks. A lot of maps evolved from charts. But it's not the same, Eldon thinks for the first time. All the bearings taken from a rolling deck were supposed to be the same as the bearings taken from a hillside. But how could they be the same? Those at sea were using the land to know where they were. On land there wouldn't be the same sense of opposites. Far inland, in a vast country, where you are would depend, not on the sea at all, but on other land-forms, geography. One wouldn't be thinking about where they were in the same way, using the same set of relational codes.

Eldon imagines sailing past Ireland, watching each sharp intake of bay for danger or a safe mooring. It was all like that, that absolute — being wrecked upon the rocks, or find-ing a safe harbour. Always moving, with the heft of the sea, and trying to ascertain a bearing, a solid footing, from this constant shift beneath you. Sextants and celestial navigation. Taking bearings from the heavens, how odd that was, trying to position oneself in relation to the expanding, unending universe. An invisible line cast between the solid, known earth and the ethereal imagined stars. Tying oneself to the infinite skies. Using the unseen to locate oneself in a place we already are.

The bearing was latitude, a horizontal line. Longitude, the vertical line — an upright human being, a straight, tall tree — required an accurate clock so that it could be worked out from a comparison of local time with a solar-position observation. An accurate clock proved one of the hardest things of all to invent. The position of longitude attached to a precise notion of time. Lines and spaces. The sweep of the second hand. The ruling on the map.

Eldon runs his finger gently around the coastline of County Clare. How can a physical self be entrusted to the distant, shifting fathoms of the sky and to a time honed so fine that it cannot be sensed or felt?

Perhaps knowing where you are is less a science than an act of faith? A line. A space. Step forward. Tell yourself that this is where you are.

All day long Annie sees the shape of Ireland. It is in the ghosting coal smoke, and the shifting flames themselves. The dough that Cook rolls out for the pastry looks like County Clare. The attenuated flicker of the coast is there in each feather of Annie's duster. She bangs it against the outside wall of the house and a cloud of dust rises into the shape of Ireland, floats down, and is gone.

At night she lies in her bed and watches the moon glow behind the silver clouds outside her window. The shiny length of cloud looks like the headland she had imagined herself standing on.

"Have you ever seen the sea?" she whispers across to Tess. "Have you ever gone there?"

Tess is thinking about Wilks. She is planning their next meeting and can't decide if she is imagining what they will do or is merely remembering what they did the last time they met. What did happen? What will happen? "The sea," she says, vaguely.

"The sea," repeats Annie. "Have you ever been there?"

"I worked for a family in Hastings once."

"And?"

"It makes everything damp," says Tess. "It's hard to give things a proper airing out."

"But how does it look?" says Annie impatiently.

"It looks..." Tess is a little annoyed. She is losing the delicious feeling of Wilks pressing up against her. "It looks like the sea," she says.

Annie is quiet for a moment. She lights a candle, reaches under her pillow, and pulls out her Bible. The candle flame stutters as she crosses the room to Tess. She sits down on the edge of Tess's bed. "Look," she says, opening her Bible and tipping the candle's light down towards it.

"What?" Tess twists around in bed to be able to see Annie and her Bible.

"This." On the inside front cover of the book Annie has drawn the map of Ireland. She has put in all the detail she has remembered from the map in Mr. Dashell's library, carefully pulling her pencil around all the inlets on the Atlantic coast. "It's Ireland," she says. "Where I'm from." There's no response from Tess. "County Clare," says Annie helpfully. She tilts the candle down too far over the page and a drop of wax lands in the ocean just off Galway. "England is just over here," says Annie, tapping the edge of the book. She thinks of the long, gnarled shape of England lying next to Ireland on Mr. Dashell's map, a thick arm of water between the two of them. "I went across the sea to come here," explains Annie. "I was small and don't remember any of the journey. But surely I know it, somewhere inside me, as I was there, on the sea. I was here." She bends her head over her faint pencil drawing.

"It looks like a stain," says Tess rudely. She flops over, away from Annie. She has lost the warm sensation between her legs that is there whenever she thinks of Wilks for a time, and she is angry at Annie for this loss. She doesn't care a whit about the sea. The house at Hastings was always damp. Nothing dried properly. Nothing was ever really clean. The house always smelled musty, no matter how many fires were lit and how diligently she cleaned the rooms. And those are the things she can bear to think about from her time there.

Annie closes her Bible and walks back over to her bed. She blows out the candle and climbs in under the covers again. She places the book open, face down, on her chest. Maybe the shape of Ireland will melt down into her skin. The weight of it is comforting. Her body must remember the sea, the voyage to England. She must have seen the coast of Ireland receding as the ship pulled slowly away from the docks. A stretching and tearing loose. Waving hands and the pattern of faces left behind. Annie lies still, willing her body to remember how that felt. How leaving felt.

The moon has lit another cloud into the shape of another world.

"It's a series," says Isabelle. "On the virtues." Annie is seated on the studio bench. Isabelle stands behind her, looking up at the thin cream-coloured muslin, draped across the glass roof. The corners of it are clumsily wired onto the steel roof beams. It is not stretched tight, but sags from the ceiling, like the belly of the moon. The light, sieved through it, floats down, rests on Annie's hair.

"No more stories, ma'am?" Annie has begun to rely on Isabelle's brief passionate tales.

"Not now," says Isabelle. She turns Annie's shoulders to the right so the light will dribble down the left side of Annie's face. "I want to see what you can do." I want to see what I can do with you.

Annie feels instantly nervous. The bed sheet pinned around

her shoulders flutters as she moves a little, anxiously, on the bench. Isabelle corrects this with her hands. "Don't," she says.

Isabelle is pleased with this new idea. It has come to her, free from associations with great art. She does not have to look at her staged scene and imagine oil paintings or plays. She has not been passed a character, down through the halls of time, so that when it finally gets to her it is sullied and worn out with the journey. She is not dealing with a character, but rather *with* character, with the character of Annie's face. Isabelle had been thinking of Annie. She had been lying in her bed, awake just before dawn, watching the room grow paler by degrees, as though the night was constantly rinsing lighter and lighter, until she could see the familiar shapes around her. A washed-out, grey-stained room. The fireplace. The wardrobe. A jug of water on the washstand. And always, everywhere, the face of Annie Phelan. She has many faces, Isabelle thinks. Each one was different from the next. Each one conveyed something beyond her own emotions of the moment. Something huge. Isabelle is telling the truth to Annie. She wants to see what she can do. If she can make each expression of Annie's represent a quality, then all of humanity can recognize the still point from the shifting fathoms of a single face.

"Grace," says Isabelle.

"Who's Grace?"

"No, no. Not a person. The virtue of grace. The quality. Don't worry," says Isabelle, seeing the look of concern on her model's face. "You never get it wrong." She stands beside the camera and looks at the scene she has arranged. The light floats from the ceiling, settles on Annie's head like a halo. It is alchemy, she thinks. What happens between them when they make a photograph. It is as though she moves as far as she can towards an image, and, from the other side of it,

Annie moves the rest of the way, so that when they meet up, the result is magical, stronger than the both of them.

"We will make a series of virtues," says Isabelle, deciding that everything looks as full of grace as she can make it look. "Then I will have enough photographs to submit an entry to the Dublin exhibition. I have never had anything worthy to send out before now." Isabelle smiles at Annie. "Before you."

The light, drizzling down through the muslin, is as particulate as dust. Annie can see the specks of it hovering before her eyes.

Isabelle is struggling to get the stopper out of her bottle of collodion. "Stuck," she says. "The blasted liquid is just like glue. They used to use it for closing wounds. Before photography." She hands the bottle across to Annie. "You try," she says. "You have stronger hands than I do."

Annie, without moving her shoulders from the position Isabelle has arranged them in, easily twists the stopper out of the collodion bottle. "Here you are, ma'am," she says, passing it back to Isabelle. She likes that moment of feeling she is stronger than Isabelle, of feeling that Isabelle needs her strength.

"We're going to use your method, Annie," says Isabelle, resting the stopper lightly on the top of the bottle, so she can get access to the collodion easily, and when she needs it.

"What method, ma'am?"

"The new focusing technique," says Isabelle. What you used on me, is what she should say, but she feels suddenly wary in crediting Annie for the Sappho photograph. What if this maid suddenly had illusions about herself as a photographer? "The one that was used in that photograph of Sappho," is what she says instead. "The close lens. The blurriness." She is carefully shifting the camera nearer to Annie as she says this. The lens is now as far from Annie's face as a person would be if she was engaged in conversation with her. Isabelle remembers the

Sappho photograph and how she felt like flinching from the lens when it was that close to her. "Do you mind?" she says suddenly. She wants to make sure that Annie Phelan is thinking of herself as a model, not as an artist. "Do you mind that I take photographs of you?"

Annie doesn't think of it this way. She doesn't think of the photographs as being of her. They are of Guinevere and Ophelia. Even this *Grace*, although a quality, seems more to do with someone else. They are not about her. But there is something so pleasant about sitting on this bench in the glasshouse, with the light drifting down around her. She is here, on this soft morning, with Mrs. Isabelle Dashell, and that seems such a perfect thing. "I don't mind," she says.

Isabelle has already moved past her question. She is no longer hesitant or uncertain. That moment has passed. She has passed it. *Grace*, she thinks, looking through the lens at Annie's face filling the frame. Grace through divinity. Grace through love.

When she was trying to be a painter, Isabelle had grown frustrated with her subjects. They all seemed so stagnant. A bowl of fruit. A vase of flowers. Even painting outdoors, the trees and fields looked flat and devoid of feeling. Of course there was the light, always galloping away so she had to use quick hands to throw a bright line after it, try and drag it back to the fenced pasture of her canvas. But even that was a disappointment. Too much was left up to her. The subjects did nothing to help the effort, didn't in fact care whether there was a painting of them or not. The occasional time she had worked with a live model (mostly Eldon) the pose had to be held for so long that all feeling and expression drained completely out of the model. She was using her brush then to stop the holes where the subject's essence leaked out.

Photography was entirely different. Even when the models were largely uncooperative — Isabelle thinks of Tess and of her cousin's children — the poses were short enough in duration that the subjects retained their energy. This energy helped to make the photograph happen, to keep it faithful to the living thing it portrayed. She could control how this energy was used. Isabelle could control her models. She told them what to do and they followed her instruction. She could even control the light around them. Unlike painting, she wasn't merely recording what was there, but creating what was there.

Someone like Robert Hill could never understand what she did. He had been schooled in the masters, had himself apprenticed with the great painter, Edward Arlington. He was passed, hand to hand, from one great man to another. He never had to doubt his place among them. His confidence and sense of his own genius was so great that when he used live models he didn't need to feel their energy. He didn't need even to see them. What he saw was himself, painting them. He wouldn't understand that Isabelle needed Annie Phelan to look how she looked, to be herself, and also that Isabelle needed to be projecting a quality onto her. To control what was happening. To let it happen.

Because the photographing of Annie has been going so well Isabelle suddenly has the confidence to send her art out into the world, for the first time. She will be judged, no doubt, by men such as Robert Hill, but she will try anyhow. She feels that in taking these photographs of Annie Phelan she is finally doing something right and she wants a stranger to confirm that this is indeed so. She cannot imagine these new photographs as anything other than they appear. Surely this means she is getting it right?

And Annie Phelan? She makes it all possible. The more

Isabelle looks upon her, the more there is for her to see. Every room she enters, Isabelle can immediately imagine how she would photograph Annie there. That face opens and opens, just as Isabelle twists the lens open, the wide eye of it staring Annie down. The sun an open shutter poised above them.

"Don't move," says Isabelle.

Isabelle is in a bad humour. She sits in the parlour, squeezing her hands together in an effort to keep from throwing something at the vicar who sits opposite. His voice drones on and on. She isn't paying attention. His wheedling, reedy voice sounds as foreign to her as if it belonged to an animal, was the song of some plain, undistinguished sparrow.

There is nothing Isabelle detests more than this, losing a perfectly good morning's work to a local plea for money. That's all it ever comes down to — money. Never mind that it's the vicar, supposed agent for God in this small corner of Sussex. Isabelle is the daughter of gentry, will always be expected to furnish the small hopes of those who live nearby.

Isabelle has done her best to escape this fate. She purposefully married a man with few prospects, a dreamer whose father had squandered his fortune on some wild scheme to import curios from the East. But because Isabelle was an only child her father could not afford to disown her. He needed someone to leave his money to, and even if Isabelle was largely unsatisfactory in this regard, perhaps, even with the ne'er-do-well Eldon, she would produce a suitable heir. So Isabelle's father had bought her and Eldon this house as a wedding gift. Shrewd, thinks Isabelle, squirming in her chair across from the vicar. That way he kept her in the part of the country she belonged to. He kept her responsible to the duties she'd been born to.

The vicar clatters his teacup down nervously onto its companion saucer. He has cake crumbs stuck to his left cheek. "Steeple," he says.

"What?"

"The steeple is full of bats," he says, his voice shaking slightly with the effort of finally stating his case.

You're full of bats, thinks Isabelle. She stares hard at his puffy, pink face. Who would ever want to photograph that? Thank God she isn't forced to make a living taking those horrid *cartes de visite* of people like this village idiot. Vicar, she corrects herself. Idiot, she thinks again, and smiles.

The vicar, heartened by Mrs. Dashell's smile, by her obvious sympathy to his cause, presses forward. "We would just require enough to repair the damage," he says.

Here it is, thinks Isabelle. The inevitable grab for money. "And why," she says, "should I support a church that caters to a God I don't believe in?"

The vicar makes little popping sounds with his breath. Outside the room the clock runs down the hour, the whole notes of the bells dropping ripe into the silence.

The vicar recovers nicely. "Your father," he says, "always helped our cause. Your father understood his duty to the parishioners, to the people of this village."

Of course, thinks Isabelle. He is wily. He knows exactly what to say to make her comply with his request.

Being her father's daughter has been such a mixed blessing. If she'd been a man, she would not get away with all she did, would be that much more tied to obligation, to having some credible career and carrying on her father's good name in conduct and deed. As it is, she is able to live comfortably off his money, is able to do exactly what she pleases. Perhaps the inconvenience of village responsibility, manifested this morning by the puffing presence of the toady vicar, is small measure against what she has been allowed. She remembers when her father had told her he was buying this house for her and Eldon. So you'll be settled enough, he said, to give me an heir.

Isabelle remembers her babies less and less now. The pain of them ebbs away from her and it's as if they have drifted off, floating on the wide sea of her grief. Gone. Her body can't call them back as it could in the first days after they'd been born. Or even her heart. Even her heart. And she wants to forget them. She wants to cancel their image entirely. Each photograph she takes now, each time she imagines and sets up a scene, pushes the memory of them farther and farther back, layered deep under all these new pictures of Annie Phelan.

"How much?" she says. "How much is it that you want?"

Annie is in the kitchen, washing the stone floor. Today is market day and Cook has gone into Tunbridge Wells to buy and order food. On market days, when Cook no longer owns the space, Annie spends half a day in the kitchen — scrubbing the floor, polishing the pots and pans. She is down on her knees with the scrub-brush and pail when she hears the sound. A whispery, rustling sound, which she finally recognizes as someone crying. She gets up, goes to the window by the door, and peers outside. There, on the bench just under the window, are Tess and Wilks. Wilks is smoking. Tess has her head in her hands and Annie can see the tremor in her shoulders that is evidence of her tears. Carefully, softly, Annie opens the kitchen door a crack, and bends her head to the space.

"Why didn't you tell me?" says Wilks. His voice has the raspy edge of anger to it.

Silence. Tess snuffles loudly. "I didn't know," she says finally.

"Liar."

"I wasn't sure." She tries again. "I suspected, but I didn't know for certain until just recently."

Even to Annie, bent over the crack of the open kitchen door, this sounds like a lie. A rehearsed lie. There's a shifting noise on the bench. He's comforting her, thinks Annie. He has slid across and is comforting her now. But the sound was Wilks standing up.

"I have thinking to do," he says as he walks away.

Tess says nothing, cries harder after he has gone. Annie backs away from the door, picks up her pail, and empties the water in it down the drain. Then she takes the empty pail to the kitchen door. She makes a considerable noise walking the few feet to the bench outside, but Tess doesn't look up.

"What is it?" Annie says, standing by the end of the bench, swinging the empty wooden pail nervously. "What has upset you so?"

"It's not your business," says Tess fiercely. She looks up at Annie. Her eyes are red and there's a braid of snot hanging from her nostrils. "What are you spying on me for anyway?"

"I'm not spying," says Annie. A lie and a sin. Do unto others, she thinks bitterly.

"Oh, just be gone from me," says Tess, rising from the bench and running across the garden, away from Annie, after Wilks.

Annie stands by the bench and watches Tess go. It is the end of summer now. The sun is out. It hasn't rained for days. The grasses and flowers bend to earth in the guttering heat.

Go then, thinks Annie, to Tess, to the last threads of summer, tying them here, to this earth. Go then.

Come back.

Annie can't move. Her body is wrapped tightly in cloth. She struggles her arms and legs but they remain caught. Above her the sky twists and turns, seems to be moving so fast. But it is she who is moving. The pressure she feels on her body is the weight of herself being passed from hand to hand, person to person. All along the road people have stopped working, have laid down their tools on the hard earth. Dust smokes down. Everything so still, just this baby in motion, passed from person to person, along the length of road.

Annie can feel the hands, strong as wings beneath her body. She is being shifted down this line of workers to her mother who waits at the end, arms outstretched. The relief of this, of finally having her mother back, is such a huge feeling it bursts out of her body, out of her skin, makes Annie cry out loud when, at last, her mother takes her in her arms.

Annie wakes crying. Tears are running down her cheeks. The attic room is hot and musty. She was almost there. She had almost seen her mother's face. The dark quiets her. The room and Tess asleep in the other bed quiet her. But there is no going back to sleep after this. Her body is jangly with feeling. She takes her candle and begins the familiar journey downstairs to the baby-carriage room.

She doesn't feel like reading, sits on the floor, puts her head down on her knees.

Why did they let her go? To save her? Has her life in England really been an escape? The workhouse. The strict labours of Mrs. Gilbey's. Even God, whom she has been grateful for, is perhaps not the same God she would have known if she'd remained Irish. Not the same religion, so how could it be the same God?

With her head down on her knees Annie looks across the half darkness of the carriage room. She is so familiar with this place, knows the position of everything so well, that it takes her a moment to realize that something is different. One of the prams has been pushed out into the middle of the room. This place that Annie had thought was only ever visited by her has been visited by someone else.

It is an accident, really, how it happens. Annie is in the glasshouse, being photographed as Humility. She is standing against a wall, dressed in a grey cape, with the hood up. She bends her head over a small bouquet of field poppies in her clasped hands. The light from above strikes the back of her head, like a sword. She is bowed beneath the straight weight of it.

Isabelle is having a hard time deciding what Humility should look like. She has moved Annie from the doorway to the bench, and now to stand beside this wall. Cape on. Cape off. Cape on with the hood up. Flowers. No flowers.

The cape is hot. In the cave of her hood Annie is sweating. She can feel the prickle of sweat on the back of her neck. The flowers, picked over two hours ago now, are wilting in her humid grasp. She bends over as though she is coaxing the small flame of them into life.

Isabelle flits around beside the camera. Annie watches the piece of stone floor by her boots. There is moss growing in the cracks. Isabelle is saying something, but Annie has stopped listening. She lowers the flowers, rests them against her leg because her arms are cramping from holding them so still in front of her. The heads of the posy droop down towards the floor, spill their light.

"Well, if you think so," says Isabelle. She is back behind the camera again, looking through the sight at this new position Annie has taken.

The sun illuminates the moss. The bright green of it unearthly by her boots. Annie looks up at Isabelle. I have changed the picture, she thinks, realizing what Isabelle has said. I have made her change her mind. This knowledge shivers through her. It is a bright, glittering thing. It is hers. She reaches up and pulls the hood from her head. "I think this is better," she says, testing her new power.

Isabelle looks through the camera. Humility. She can see that it is a tenuous thing, that the submissive flowers contradict the haughty, bareheaded expression of Annie. Yes, perhaps Humility is that line, that moment before it becomes itself. She can see that Annie is right. "You're right," she says. "I can see what you mean."

Annie stares out, unblinking, at the camera lens. I have made you do this, she thinks. I can make you see what I want you to.

"She was lovely," says Tess. "Her dress the most beautiful green I've ever seen." She giggles at her accidental rhyme.

They've just had their evening meal—Tess, Annie, and Cook—and are now having tea in the kitchen. Tess is describing how Mrs. Dashell looked when she left the house with Mr. Dashell earlier this evening, on their way to supper at the Hills'.

"Lovely," says Tess, again. "A lovely Lady."

"Tom drove them?" asks Cook.

"Yes."

"Then he'll be wanting a bit of food when he gets back." Cook begins the slow business of rising from the table, but Tess puts out an arm to stop her.

"Don't bother yourself," she says. "He'll be visiting with the stable boy there. You know how he is," she adds, suddenly fearing she has displayed too intimate a knowledge of Wilks's habits.

Cook sinks back down again. "If you say so," she says, relieved not to have to be up on her feet again right away, heating up a plate of supper.

"If I could look like that," says Tess, turning back to the sight of Isabelle Dashell stepping up into the trap. "If I could be a real Lady."

"What would you do?" says Annie. She has been quietly listening to Tess talk and is getting bored with the endless descriptions of Isabelle's dress.

"What would I do?" Tess looks over at Annie.

"If you were a Lady," says Annie.

They turn the table into a stage. Cook, as the audience, sits on a chair by the range. Tess perches on a chair up on top of the table, as though it's a throne. Annie, out of the room, knocks on the kitchen door.

"Come in," says Cook.

Annie enters the kitchen.

"The Lady will see you now," says Cook.

Annie walks over to the table, careful not to turn her back on Cook and spoil her view. "You asked to see me, ma'am?" she says, and bows before Tess.

"I have heard from others in this house," says Tess, in the most imperious voice she can muster, "that you have not been mindful of your duties. That you have not been cleaning the rooms properly. At the proper time," she says pointedly.

Annie feels herself blush. "Yes, ma'am," she says.

"Well," says Tess, waving her hand in what she hopes is an intimidating manner. "What have you to say in defence of yourself?"

Annie looks up at Tess, sitting on the kitchen table. Her hands are red and coarse from the washing soda she uses in the laundry, from being wet most of the day, from rubbing up against fabric. Her voice is rough and her way of speaking is ill-mannered. She will never be a Lady, thinks Annie. She can play at this because it will never happen. No Lord will swoop down and carry Tess Fairley back to his castle to be his bride.

"Answer me," snaps Tess. "You wretched girl."

Annie thinks of Mrs. Gilbey, of all the times she listened to her mistress abuse her. The words that slapped against her as she kneeled on the floor. The feeling of the cold stone against her bones. Slut. Heathen. Slattern. Cur. "I was forever accused and condemned," she says.

"What?" Tess has that suspicious look on her face that signals she doesn't understand what Annie has said.

"It's from *Jane Eyre*."

"What?"

"A book," says Annie. "*Jane Eyre* is a book."

"That's not being fair," says Cook. "You know she can't read."

"Yes," says Tess, "that's not being fair."

Annie looks up at Tess on top of the table. What can she say in her defence? The truth is that at Mrs. Gilbey's she *was* accused and condemned, was constantly suffering, and the only way out of this was to imagine being someone else. "I can't do it," she says.

"Can't do what?" Tess is confused again.

"Oh, go on," says Cook. "Let her be the Lady then. She seems more inclined that way, with her books and all. Just get on with it." She pours a little whisky into her tea, something she allows herself only when the Dashells are gone for an evening, and there is a certain looseness to the household.

"Thanks for nothing," says Tess, climbing down awkwardly from her throne. "You're a good bit of no fun at all."

Annie ignores her, reluctantly takes up residence on the table. They are playing this entirely for Cook's benefit now.

Tess eagerly banishes herself outdoors.

What would I do? thinks Annie. If I could do things?

There's no knock on the kitchen door.

"Come in," says Cook anyway. To Annie she says, "I hope that wretched girl hasn't wandered off. Come in!" she says again, this time in a more commanding tone.

The door bursts open and Tess stumbles into the kitchen, followed immediately by Wilks. Tess's face is flushed.

Wilks is surprised to see everyone still in the kitchen. "What's this, then?" he says. "Why's she sitting up there on the table?"

"She's a Lady," says Tess, and giggles.

"She doesn't look no Lady to me," says Wilks. He turns his attention to Cook. "Any supper left for me, missus?" he asks.

"Yes, Tom. I'll fetch you some." Cook sighs, rises slowly out of her chair.

Annie climbs down, with relief, from the table. Wilks is like a stone, thrown into the calm waters of the kitchen. Now they are all rippling out, away from each other, to their own particular solitary shores.

*

Annie kneels at her bedroom window. Tess has gone out into the garden with Wilks. They are out there, somewhere, in this darkness thick as fog. She had wanted Tess to come to their room instead of going out with Wilks. Even though Tess is often a disappointment to talk to, at least she's company, and Annie feels the need of company tonight. The episode in the kitchen has made her remember, with particular dread, her life at Mrs. Gilbey's.

When Annie had been a young girl in Mrs. Gilbey's house, she would lie in her windowless room off the kitchen, in her cot. There was only the smallest rivulet of light from under the door to reassure her that she wasn't sealed away forever. In those early days, when she was a child, Mrs. Gilbey would lock her in at night, afraid Annie might wander, uncontrolled, all through the house. Taking things. Breaking things. The only way for Annie to muffle the terror of this entombment was to talk out loud to herself, pretending that her own voice was the voice of another, offering comfort to a frightened child. Tonight, now, she wants Tess to be that voice of comfort, wants words to be sparks and light the darkness of the room.

Annie can see a figure rushing out into the garden. It's not Tess. It's Isabelle, the dark stain of her dress washing out behind her as she runs to the glasshouse. They must be back from supper. Annie waits for the glow of a lamp to light up the studio, make the whole glasshouse itself seem like a lantern God swings across the darkness of the garden.

Eldon has followed his wife down the dark ocean of garden and into the glasshouse. "Don't go," he says, even though he is right behind her and she can't go any farther away from him.

Isabelle lights a lantern, swings it forward to set it on the bench, and the light flexes against the panes of glass, makes them glisten. "Why do we do it?" she says. "It's a sham. A pretence. Sitting there in their drawing room chattering politely about the cattle plague. What a shame not to have beef as often as we would like." She puts her hand on the top of her camera, takes it off again. "Sometimes I despise this world I was born to," she says.

"You don't mind the privilege it affords you." Eldon steps forward. He has the sensation that he is receding out of this pool of light, floating right out of the glasshouse altogether. "Why did you marry me?" he says, and it's not what he wanted to say at all. What he wanted to say was, Why do you complain about what benefits you? Why do you pretend you could be different, that you could be someone other than who you are? But no, instead he says, Why did you marry me? Although they might be the same question after all.

Isabelle looks across the studio at Eldon. He is blurry with shadow. He is the place where the light ends, where it bumps up against darkness like a boat nudging the shallows. Because you didn't get in my way is what she wants to say. Instead she says, "Because I was expected to be a certain kind of person, to behave in a certain way, and you didn't expect that from me. You didn't expect anything from me."

"And is that what happened?" asks Eldon. "I didn't expect anything from you?"

"Isn't it a good arrangement?" says Isabelle. "Doesn't it suit us both?"

"We do our work. Your father bought us this house. We have his money. A good *arrangement*." Eldon stretches the last word out. He thinks of all the Arctic expeditions, of the months and months of preparation required before the first step was ever taken on the ice. This is what his marriage to Isabelle feels like, preparation. But what's it all for? What is the place that pulls them forward over the polar floes, over the ground cold with stone? "What if the children had lived?" he says.

Isabelle can't think of this. She goes through each day never allowing herself to think this. Instead she concentrates on the photograph she is taking, the one she hauls from the developing bath. What she can create. What she can control. Life is accidental. Art is thick with purpose. "Would I have loved you?" she says, because this is the real question.

The garden outside the glasshouse is a tangle of moonlight. Leaves and vines, the angles of branches. The relentless intent of the natural world both reassures and frightens Isabelle. What if art is not the greater power? What if art is an excuse to hide from life? What if her babies had lived? Would she have been able to love them? "We'll never know," she says, "will we."

The sun makes Isabelle drowsy as a flower. Her head droops forward, snaps back on its stalk as she tries to keep herself awake. Her photograph cooks on the path in front of her. If she falls asleep, it will burn away to black. She rises from the bench and walks briskly up and down in front of it. Her feet sound petulant on the stones.

All around Isabelle the garden opens its arms to the last traces of summer. *I'm here! I'm here!* Heat is a wish in the bones of all living things. A wish ached out through the skin. Isabelle stops walking. The flowers around her are open lenses, wide, wide open. It is the time of year, the moment even, when the garden is most fully alive. It is the moment right next to the one where everything begins to die. Flowers lose their hold on the air, curl inward, hold their small, dry, rattling thoughts to themselves. *Don't forget me. Don't forget me.* They stiffen and then collapse their shape entirely, as though the cost of remaining themselves for a motion longer is complete obliteration. Oblivion. A garden in winter is a state of oblivion.

Isabelle stretches her arms out, reaching with her fingers up towards the sun. It is as if she is the darkened window of the negative, the one through which the sun must pour to make the shape of her, to let her live.

In her studio Isabelle pushes the flimsy albumen positive under the surface of the fixative bath. The paper shudders with the motion of her hand and the liquid. The image blurs and then rolls back towards clarity, blurs again. The movement making it seem as though the photograph is breathing underwater.

This is where Isabelle likes to be, this moment when an image is swimming up towards her. When she is the light. This is the part of the photographic process that is the companion to the moment when the model is posed and the scene is set and hope is high that the photograph will look the way it is meant to look. It is the image finding its way back to the image.

Isabelle doesn't care for the transition phase. She doesn't like the tension and worry of it all, having to hurry the exposed plate to the darkroom before the collodion dries and the effort is ruined. Crouched on the cold floor of the coal cellar, her breathing loud in the darkness, from running through the garden with the exposed glass plate. Isabelle feels only anxiety as she plunges the plate into the developing bath. It is at this moment that the image is truly gone. She cannot make it stay. She has to let it go back into darkness and then she has to believe that it will return. It takes so much strength from her, to believe this. To believe that it still lives, that it will flutter towards her, like a thought not yet articulated, beating against a fluid darkness.

Now it is here again, the image. Isabelle has pulled it back to her, from the mouth of darkness. It swims under the light in the glasshouse, limpid, the dull colour of blood seen through water. When Isabelle hauls it up into the air the colour has shushed to a red the shade of bricks. She pulls it into the air, like something she has conjured up. She pulls it up and then plunges it down into a water bath, to clean all the fixative chemicals from its surface. Her hands are puckered from the liquid, blackened from the silver nitrate of the developer. Her hands are in worse shape than a maid's. When Isabelle is forced to attend social functions she tries always to wear gloves, or keep her hands crawled into the cave of each other, out of sight on her lap. Last night at the party, she had had a moment of forgetfulness. She had held her hands up to explain something and her hands had jumped like black fish under the light of the dining-room chandelier. Mercurial and slippery with light. She had seen the dismay on Robert Hill's face when this happened, the disgust on Letitia's.

Now, the black fish are where they live, swimming in the small tank of the water bath, bumping the albumen paper up and down. The black fish flex their tails and lift the print right up out of the water. Isabelle shakes the loose drops from it and then carefully lays it into the final bath. This is the toning bath, where Isabelle adds gold chloride to the water to cool the red colour of the print and to intensify the shadow areas. It is a constant experiment, the toning bath. How much gold chloride to use? Too much and the shadows will stiffen to black, lose definition. Too little and there will be no noticeable distinction, not enough contrast between different areas in the photograph. Isabelle tries a varying amount of gold chloride each time. She records it carefully in a little book. Which photograph. How much toner. How long in the toning bath.

Isabelle bends over the toning bath. The light from the roof of the glasshouse distorts her view of the photograph in the gold chloride, makes it seem lighter in shading than it really is. Sometimes it is more a matter of feeling than of knowing. When the rush of anxiety runs into her, Isabelle pulls the photograph from the bath by its corner. Liquid runs down it like rain on a window. She carries it before her, arm outstretched, carries it over to the line that bisects the end of the glasshouse, and pins the photograph up with a clothespin. It drifts on the line, moving a little from the motion of it being pinned, from the act of it drying, curling inward, stiffening.

The line is full of photographs. Annie as Humility. Annie as Grace. Each photograph slightly lighter or darker than the one beside it. Every one the same and different. They stutter towards the blank eye of light. They stutter towards the closed fist of darkness. Each one a word said a different way. The emphasis in a different place.

Isabelle stands in front of the row of photographs. Which is the one that is the closest to the image she saw in her mind before she created the image in the flesh? Which is the artic-ulation of her soul?

Sometimes it feels to Isabelle, at the end of the two hours it takes to wash, tone, and dry a print, that she is the thing being made. The black fish of her hands have swum through fixa-tive, through water, through gold chloride. They have breathed underwater. They have twisted their way up to the light, and here she is, standing now on the shore where they have pushed her, looking at the world anew. The wet heat of them flopping in her breast, turning inside her like a wish.

Member of the Expedition

As Christmas approaches it becomes obvious that Tess is
pregnant. In their attic bedroom she removes her dress and
Annie can see the flesh pulled tight across her belly, the circle
of baby under the skin.

"I could pray for you," says Annie, from her bed. "I could
pray for you and the bastard child."

"Oh, shut up." Tess pulls on her nightshirt and plunks
down angrily on the edge of her bed. Being pregnant hasn't
improved her mood any. "You're not allowed to have God in
this house. Don't you listen to rules?"

"But it's helpful," says Annie, meaning, really, that she is
trying to be helpful.

Tess just snorts with contempt. "Where was your God in
the beginning?" she says. "Before this happened. When he
could have been helpful." She gets into bed and kicks under
the covers for a few minutes to warm up the sheets. "Don't be
praying for me in your head," she says, which is just what
Annie is doing. "I don't want none of it."

It is chilly in their bedroom. They lie on their backs in
their beds and their breath smokes in the cold air. The
sheets are damp, and although Annie has piled extra
bedclothes on, to the extent that the weight of them actually
bends her toes, it is still impossible to feel warm. There is no

fire in their attic. In the mornings the windows are laced with frost.

There has been a lot of work in the Dashell house to prepare for winter. All fall Annie has helped Cook pit fruit for jam, the juice of damsons inking her fingers, the smell of gooseberries sweet in the kitchen. Now the jars are carefully lined up in the larder, plush with fruit. The kitchen garden has been harvested, vegetables lumped in burlap sacks into the root cellar so that in the middle of January there will still be carrots, potatoes, the hard, bitter truth of an onion. They have prepared for winter as though it is an expedition, as though they must have enough supplies to cross the cold, barren stretch of it before arriving on the warm shore of another year.

Annie yearns for spring already, lying in her damp bed with the suffocating bedclothes heavy on her body. Tess's baby is to be born in the early spring. It seems that it was no surprise to the rest of the house, that only Annie didn't know of it before now. She feels foolish in her ignorance, foolish when Cook says, I guessed, didn't I; foolish when Isabelle dismisses it so easily — it was to be expected, really. No one says what is to happen after the baby is born. Will it be sent away? Will it stay here with them in the house? Tess herself seems only angry at her pregnancy, ignores it as much as possible, even though, physically at least, this is becoming more and more difficult to do.

Annie wants to know what Tess really feels about the baby. If she is pleased at all, because Annie can imagine how she could be, how this baby, growing inside of Tess, will know her completely, will know her better than anyone. Right now, Tess is the baby's entire world. "Tess?" says Annie, over the cold darkness of the room, but Tess doesn't answer.

*

Early one morning, before the household is awake, Annie is in Eldon's library looking for a book to borrow. The feeling of reading burns through her like a kind of restlessness. She walks up and down the shelves, trolling her hand along the leather spines, but nothing seems perfectly, exactly right for this cold, dreary day.

As she's walking by Eldon's desk she sees something that makes her stop. A sheet of photographic paper lying on top of its envelope. The sheet is divided into a dozen small photographs, each one the same image, each one showing Eldon Dashell standing on a strip of carpet in front of a bare wall, his right hand resting on the top of a globe. Annie bends down to get a closer look. A *carte*. Mr. Dashell has had a *carte* made of himself. He has that stiff, awkward stance she recognizes from Cook's collection of *cartes*, but his expression is in complete contradiction to this. His expression is almost gleeful.

"Yes," says Eldon's voice from behind Annie, making her jump. "I succumbed to the fashion of the studio fantasy."

Annie turns and looks at him. She doesn't have a bucket or duster, no equipment to prove her reason for being in this room. But he doesn't ask why she's here, seems embarrassed that she has seen the photograph of him. Annie wants to ask if Isabelle knows about these *cartes*. She is certain that Isabelle would consider this as a betrayal, to be photographed by someone else, to be posed in a studio by another photographer. But she doesn't say this. "You look happy," is what she says instead, desperately thinking of an excuse to offer for her presence here.

Eldon puts a hand out and holds on to the back of a chair to steady himself. "I am a foolish man," he says.

"Why?"

"Have you ever wanted anything, Annie Phelan?"

"To be a good person, sir," says Annie.

"Not like that," says Eldon. "Not that general. Something specific, small and hot, that burns through you. And the longer it's not satisfied, the hotter it burns." Eldon picks up the sheet of photographs, puts them down again. "Did you ever hear of the Franklin Expedition?" he says.

"The man who went to the North Pole?"

"Not the Pole, but to find the Northwest Passage across the Arctic ice."

"And they died, sir?"

"They died."

"I recall hearing of it." Annie remembers the reverend from Portman Square talking about it once, praying that some recovery expedition would discover the final fate of Franklin and his crew. But what does this have to do with Eldon and the photographs of Eldon with his hand on a globe? "I'm not sure that I know what you're meaning," she finally says.

"Sit down." Eldon taps the chair back and Annie settles there.

The fire pulls in the hearth, sends a steady pulse of light into the room.

"I was a young man when Franklin left England in 1845," says Eldon. "It was the most exciting thing to me. I was sick at the time, confined to bed for days on end, and all I thought about was John Franklin and the voyage of the *Terror* and *Erebus*. I followed all reports of the expedition in the papers." Eldon walks over to the window and looks outside. A wind moves the branches of the rose bush on the other side of the glass, a slow wave, the rise and fall of words in his head.

"You wanted to be Franklin?" asks Annie. "Or go with him to the Arctic?"

"No, no." Eldon can remember, with particular intensity, the cool chamber of his sickroom, the summer that Franklin left England. There had been ivy outside his window and all August, while his body burned with fever and his mind floated serene on the icy waters of the Barrow Strait, the rustling of the summer wind in the leaves had sounded like people whispering in another room.

"It saved me," says Eldon. "Imagining Franklin. It possessed me entirely and I recovered because of that, because I didn't dwell on my illness, on being ill."

"And then they died," says Annie.

"Disappeared." Eldon leaves the window and comes back over to Annie. "Yes. Two years later, in forty-seven, they disappeared. And do you know that every year since then, up until McClintock came back in fifty-nine, there has been an expedition sent out to discover what happened to Franklin's expedition. They have mapped more of Canada's Arctic in looking for Franklin than was ever mapped by Franklin himself. And he was on a mapping expedition." Eldon looks down at the photograph of himself again. How foolish he felt when he climbed the studio stairs. How foolish, and how desirable, to stand there with one hand balanced on the top of the world. "That's what I wanted, Annie," he says. "To go in search of Franklin. To be part of an expedition that went looking for him."

"And you couldn't do that, sir?"

"No. I am the man who copies out the journeys of other men. I am of no use to an expedition."

Annie thinks that she would never have set sail in a ship called *Terror*. Was this not asking for trouble? Did Franklin never think of this himself?

"They found out what happened, didn't they?" she says.

"Not really," says Eldon. "Lady Franklin sponsored McClintock in fifty-seven and he found more than most.

Some physical evidence—bodies, the only written record—but it's still not clear if there were survivors and how long they lasted. Where Franklin is buried. What happened to the ships." Eldon touches Annie lightly on the shoulder. "I'm sorry," he says. "I'm keeping you from your duties."

But I'm interested, thinks Annie. Interested in this story of the men who froze to death on the ice and the men who went to find them.

"But perhaps you'd like to borrow McClintock's account of his search for Franklin? It's quite fascinating." Eldon goes to his bookshelves, takes the volume down, comes back, and hands *The Voyage of the 'Fox' in the Arctic Seas* to Annie. "You'll find it more interesting than the Johnson dictionary."

Annie weighs the book in her hand, the solid, smooth heft of it. "You know, then?" she says.

"I know."

"Because of the dictionary? I put it back in the wrong place?"

"You did."

Annie is on the verge of apologizing, but Eldon doesn't seem the least bit angry. In fact, he smiles at her and goes to his shelves, returns with another book. "Take this, too," he says. "It's Franklin's account of his first two voyages. Harrowing. It has always made me wonder why he wanted to go on a third expedition. Had to, I suppose." Eldon smiles again. "Just as you had to have books to read. Isn't that right?"

"That's right." Annie looks down at the books in her hands. They are cooling in her grasp already, setting her skin ashiver. Had to. It is just like that, reading as necessary to her now as breathing. Or so it feels. "Thank you," she says.

"Annie." Eldon waves his hand towards his shelves and accidentally sets a lamp staggering on its base. "I am honoured that you would like to use my library. It is yours any time you desire. And perhaps," he says excitedly, "we could talk about the books when you finish reading them? Wouldn't that be good?" He flails out with his arms again, and this time succeeds in knocking over the lamp entirely.

Annie spends her next afternoon off lying on her bed reading the books Eldon has loaned her. She opens the book by Franklin and reads of his first two journeys to Canada's Arctic. In his first expedition, from 1819–1822, travelling by canoe to explore the coast from the mouth of the Coppermine River to the Kent Peninsula, Franklin and his men were trapped by ice, went overland to hunt, split up into smaller groups. They were starving to death most of the time, boiled old hides to eat, ate their shoes, fried up old bones. There were instances of cannibalism among the men. It seemed a supreme act of luck that they managed to get out, any of them, alive. Not only alive, but intent to return.

The reader will probably be desirous to know how we passed our time in such a comfortless situation: the first operation after encamping was to thaw our frozen shoes.

Annie is desirous to know why Franklin went back to the Arctic after almost dying the first time. She hunches down into the blankets on her bed. The wind outside her attic bedroom creaks against the window glass. A cold expanse of desolation is easy to imagine up here.

...we went to bed, and kept up a cheerful conversation until our blankets were thawed by the heat of our bodies...

What could they possibly have talked about that was cheerful when they were freezing and starving to death? Their families? The summer in England they had sailed from, warm nights and days fragrant with flowers, the scent of new-mown hay in the fields. If they had allowed themselves just to be where they were and not to remember or wish, how could it have been stood? Annie is certain that they must have spent a lot of their cheerful conversation in either memory or wish. How else to survive a present that is unforgiving and unrelenting.

Franklin fared a lot better on his second expedition, exploring by ship the westward coast from the Mackenzie Delta. Everything went smoothly on this trip and, on the two expeditions, Franklin and his men mapped over seventeen hundred miles of Arctic coastline in the name of the British Empire.

Annie leaves John Franklin, happy and alive at the end of his book, and switches over to McClintock's account of his search for the truth about what happened to the ill-fated third expedition to the Arctic.

The year Annie was born. The year Eldon Dashell lay feverish in his sick room, fifty-nine-year-old John Franklin left England to try and find a passage through the Polar Sea that would join the Atlantic to the Pacific. Franklin was actually the second choice of the admiralty to lead the expedition. The first choice, Sir James Ross, had promised his bride not to undertake any more voyages of exploration. He must have been grateful to his bride for this for the rest of his life, thinks Annie.

The two ships commissioned for Franklin's use, the *Erebus* and the *Terror*, were fitted with railway steam engines and the bows plated with sheets of iron to break through the ice floes. They were provisioned for three years at sea with an astonishing amount of food that included forty-eight tons of canned and salted meat, and 3,684 gallons of liquor. The ships were to sail west through Lancaster Sound and the Barrow Strait as far as Cape Walker, and then proceed south towards the Bering Strait. If this way proved blocked by ice, it was possible to try a northward approach through the Wellington Channel, between Devon and Cornwallis islands.

Everything named for England. Why, thinks Annie, looking at the map in McClintock's book. Why call a chunk of barren, icy land *North Somerset*? Was it merely a way to reassure themselves that they would be returning to England, that England was, in fact, still near at hand? *North Cornwall, Cambridge Bay, Lands End.* And then the names that made sense to Annie—*Whale Sounds, Fury Point, Cape Farewell, Point Turnagain*, the Esquimaux-named *Upernavik*. And then the name that made no sense, *Cape Bunny*. Not *Cape Rabbit*, but *Bunny*, as though the person who named it were five years old.

Annie runs her finger around the coast of Beechey Island, where Franklin and his men spent the first winter locked in ice with no sun for four months and temperatures dropping to a cold that killed in a matter of hours. What did they do during those long months of darkness? Read perhaps, from a library of twenty-nine hundred books, administered by a shipboard librarian. Wrote letters home, in the hopes that there'd be a whaling ship to pass them on to, that the letters would make it back to England before the expedition did. Named things, she thinks. Connected themselves to where they were, tamed the wild, unforgiving landscape into something as harmless and friendly as a bunny.

Two years passed and nothing was heard from the expedition. Lady Franklin began agitating for a rescue expedition, and in 1848 Sir James Ross, the man who had turned down the leadership of the original expedition, commanded a search along the Arctic coast. He found nothing. After Ross, there were searches every year, sometimes more than one at a time, sponsored either by the navy, or the government, or by Lady Franklin. But it wasn't until McClintock's expedition in 1858 that there were real answers as to what had happened to the souls aboard the *Erebus* and the *Terror*.

Annie is surprised by McClintock's book. She had thought that an expedition that had set off in search of Franklin would spend the time sailing towards the Arctic pondering what might have happened to Franklin and his men, imagining their possible fate. But McClintock doesn't even mention Franklin for the first half of the book. Instead, he talks about what he's seeing and experiencing, as though he's on his own scientific survey of the Arctic.

The glacier serves to remind one at once of Time and of Eternity. Surely all who gaze upon this ice-overwhelmed region, this wide expanse of "terrestrial wreck," must be similarly assured that here "we have no abiding place."

Annie gets up and walks around the bedroom. Her arm has gone numb from where she was lying on it. She shakes it out in front of her body. From Tess's side of the room Annie's bed looks adrift, a raft of shadow snugged up against the sheer wall.

McClintock finally starting talking about Franklin when his ship, the *Fox*, reached Beechey Island. There they erected a tablet from Lady Franklin.

This tablet is erected near the spot where they passed their first Arctic winter, and whence they issued forth to conquer difficulties or to die.

They established a winter base near Bellot Strait and, from there, ventured forth by sled on a series of journeys to determine where Franklin's men had gone after their first winter. Some of the Esquimaux they met on these forays had relics from the Franklin Expedition — silver cutlery, buttons, bits of lead from the ships — these were bought or bartered back by McClintock and his crew. From interviews with the Esquimaux, McClintock found out the fate of the ships. One had sunk. The other had been forced up onto the ice and crushed to bits. The men had left for the "large river," taking a lifeboat or two with them. The following winter their bones were found there. One old woman told McClintock, "They fell down and died as they walked along."

Annie tries to imagine how strength could just flutter out of a body, softly, like a moth rising in the dusk. It is what happened to her own family. *They fell down and died as they walked along.* On a road, in Ireland. On the shifting, unsteady pans of ice in northern Canada. At almost the same time. And Annie is the record of her family. She is the cairn they left, what remained for the world to see after they had gone. Franklin's men left a note under rocks at Point Victory. A few lines on an admiralty report form to say that they'd wintered on Beechey Island, to say that all was well. And then, around the sides of the paper, a report from the second year saying that the ships were deserted, that men had died, including Franklin, that the remaining souls were heading out on April 26, 1848, for the Fish River.

Annie leans up against the wall by her bed, the strict flat of it hard against her spine. Were there people who saw her family die? Were there those who would remember her as belonging to them?

McClintock and his crew found one of the twenty-eight-foot boats Franklin's men had been pushing over the ice towards Fish River. It was lashed onto a crudely fashioned sledge, the whole contraption, according to McClintock's estimation, in excess of fourteen hundred pounds. Inside the boat were two skeletons, one of a young person, the other of a middle-aged man. The latter was perhaps an officer. The bodies had been obviously disturbed by animals. The sledge, loaded down with many unnecessary items such as silk handkerchiefs, teaspoons, dinner knives, needle-and-thread cases, would have required about seven men to move it over the ice. Had the others gone for help and left these two men, perhaps sick or too weak to come along? The only food in the boat was forty pounds of chocolate and some tea. There was a Bible, a prayer book, and the novel, *The Vicar of Wakefield*.

McClintock's search ended with his placing his own record under the cairn at Point Victory, a record stating all the explorations and discoveries his party had made. Because it was his voyage, thinks Annie, closing the book. John Franklin was just as much a place as Cape Farewell or Point Victory, something to head towards, something to take bearings from, but truly, the journey was McClintock's.

All the dead weren't found. Even with McClintock's new evidence, there still could have been survivors. And why, thinks Annie, holding *The Voyage of the 'Fox' in the Arctic Seas* against her chest, why have I never questioned Mrs. Cullen's account of my family's death? Why could I not believe, as Jane Franklin believed and kept believing, that out there, against all odds, there was perhaps one who had made it through alive. One person. One soul.

"The boots," says Annie, when she returns the books on Franklin to Eldon. "The boots are barely imaginable, and they're perhaps the easiest thing to imagine."

"What boots?" Eldon has made their book discussion a formal arrangement. He sits opposite Annie in front of the fire. He has poured them tea.

"The frozen boots." Annie notes that there's not quite enough milk in the pitcher for a second cup of tea. "Franklin and his men had to put on frozen boots every morning and walk across the ice. It is hard enough to have cold feet, but to put cold feet into boots of ice." She sips her tea. It is a bit odd to be here, in the library with Mr. Dashell, talking about books. They are both nervous. But, she thinks, putting her teacup back onto the saucer, they are both enjoying this, too.

"Frozen boots," says Eldon. He looks across at Annie, suddenly so grateful that she knows this about Franklin, that she knows some of what he knows of the expeditions. Isabelle, in all their married life, has never once read the same books as he has, has never shown the slightest interest in doing so. "Did you know that when Franklin returned to London after that disastrous first expedition, he was known as the man who had eaten his boots. That's what was said about him on the streets — 'There goes the man who ate his boots.'"

"Really?" says Annie. She feels a bit like giggling, but suppresses this urge. Mr. Dashell is eager to please. He is altogether easy. All Annie has to do is to sip her tea and say *frozen boots* and he will get wiggly with delight.

Isabelle is not easy. Later, when Annie is helping her pin up prints in the glasshouse, she thinks of this. Isabelle fusses and gets impatient. Isabelle is always convinced she is right. Isabelle is often short with Annie. "Oh, get out of my way," she'll say, even though it is she who has bumped into Annie. If that had been Mr. Dashell, he would have apologized and then, in his nervous regret, would have knocked something over.

But it is to Isabelle that Annie is drawn. Despite Eldon's kindness, it is Isabelle that Annie truly admires, wants to be like. Isabelle can take charge of the world more capably than any novel's heroine. Even being next to her in the glasshouse is happiness. Even when Isabelle bosses her around or complains about something, Annie can think of nowhere else she'd rather be. And when Isabelle holds up a print of Annie as Faith to the light, stammering through the glass window pane, and says, "Just look at you," with real feeling in her voice, Annie can forgive her anything.

Just before Christmas, Cook decides, finally, to have her *carte de visite* done. Wilks is to drive her to a photographer in Tunbridge Wells. She models, one last time, for Annie and Tess in the kitchen as she waits for Wilks to hook up the fly and bring it round to the kitchen door.

In the end Cook has chosen to go as her Sunday-best self. It's funny, thinks Annie, watching Cook adjust her bonnet for the umpteenth time, but what we think makes us more who we are sometimes makes us less. Cook is cautious in her good clothes, moves around the kitchen carefully, afraid to brush against something that will leave a mark on her.

"How do I look?" she asks one last time.

"Very good, missus," says Tess. But Annie can only nod in agreement. Sadness has closed her throat. Cook has thought about this moment all summer and fall. She has prepared in a hundred different ways. And this ordinary, nervous, frumpy woman in good clothes that have been her good clothes for so long that they're now out of fashion, this woman is not who she really wants to be. Annie thinks of the photograph in the Bible under her pillow upstairs. Isabelle as Sappho. That look on Isabelle's face, that knowing, that certainty in the moment. This is what she wishes, standing by the table in the kitchen, this is what she wishes for Cook with all her heart.

There's the sound of the horse and cart on the loose stones outside. Cook gives them a last nervous wave. "Well, I'm off, then," she says, and opens the door.

When she comes back from town, Cook doesn't talk much about the experience of having her likeness taken. "It was smooth enough," she says of the process, and hurries off to change out of her good clothes.

Later, over a cup of tea in the kitchen, she confesses to Annie how disappointing it was at the photographer's. "There was a queue," she says. "Right out into the hall. I had to stand in the landing for ever so long."

"Christmas," says Annie. "It must be the most popular time for likenesses."

"Well, I was almost there until Christmas," says Cook. "And what's worse is that once I finally made it into the studio, I was rushed through. The whole thing took only a few minutes from start to finish. He didn't care how I posed. Wouldn't advise me. He just wanted to get me out of there and be on to the next hapless soul in line."

Not like Isabelle, thinks Annie. Perhaps Cook, although she's always derisive about what takes place in the glasshouse, perhaps she had imagined that her likeness would be taken with as much care and attention as Isabelle lavishes on her models. As Isabelle lavishes on Annie.

Annie tilts her head up towards the kitchen ceiling. She can almost feel Isabelle's hands on her chin, carefully moving her head into position. She has never felt rushed or abandoned. In the glasshouse it seems that time sways and stops.

When Cook gets the photographs back of herself she dutifully gives one to Tess and one to Annie as Christmas presents. But she is disappointed with her *carte*, disappointed with the stiff, sharp image of herself sitting straight-backed in the leather studio chair. "I look like an old fool," she says when she hands Annie the *carte*. "But I have nothing else to give you for Christmas."

"It's beautiful, missus," says Annie. This isn't what she'd meant to say, but she feels badly for Cook and wants to help.

"It's bad enough without you lying," says Cook.

Annie doesn't know what to do with the *carte*. It makes her feel sad to look at it. She takes it up to her room and buries it in the bottom of her drawer of underthings. She can always pretend it's there for safe keeping.

For Christmas Annie gives Cook some sweets. She doesn't know what to give Tess, wants to make something for the baby, but thinks that Tess would be annoyed by this. Finally, out of desperation, she offers to help Tess with some of the laundry work for the remainder of her pregnancy, as bending over the mangle is work that Tess is finding it hard to do with her increasing girth.

She says this to Tess when they're in their beds on Christmas Eve. At first she doesn't think Tess has heard her, and clears her throat to say it again, more loudly. But Tess has heard. "Well," she says, her voice light with surprise. "That is a gift I can use, Annie Phelan."

Annie does not expect anything in return from Tess, knows that Tess doesn't really like her. So it's a sweet surprise to wake up Christmas morning and see that Tess has hung a wreath of holly at the foot of Annie's bed.

On Christmas morning, after Tess has dressed and left the bedroom, Annie says hurried, furtive prayers in her night-gown, then dresses and goes down to the kitchen.

The Christmas box from the Dashells consists of material for a new morning dress, two shillings, and some sweets. Isabelle and Eldon have gone to the Hills' for Christmas dinner so the servants have the day off. Cook roasts a small turkey and they have dinner in the kitchen, complete with gooseberry wine.

Wilks is there for dinner, and Annie notices that he and Tess aren't really speaking. Tess looks miserable, keeps her head bent down over her plate throughout the meal. Once she tentatively lays her hand on top of Wilks's but he shakes it off. Wilks bolts his food, takes an extra bottle of wine with him from the table, and leaves. Shortly afterwards Tess goes upstairs, saying she's tired out and needs to rest.

When Annie comes to their room, after washing up for Cook, she can hear the snuffled sounds of Tess crying.

Annie undresses without a word, climbs into bed, and pulls the covers up to her chin. She can see the holly wreath, dimly, hanging from the foot of her bed. She thinks of the oily green of the leaves, the dark berries like drops of blood. "Thank you for the wreath," she says. "It's the best present."

There's a gulp as Tess tries to switch from crying to talking. "I pricked my fingers getting it," she says. "It wasn't easy." She's quiet for a moment. "I thought you might like it because it's sort of holy. Isn't it?" Her voice is small.

Annie imagines Tess cutting her fingers as she forced the sprigs of holly into a clumsy circle. The sharpness of the leaves sticking like the fine points of loss into her skin. Holy. "Yes," says Annie. "I think it is."

Annie borrows *The Vicar of Wakefield* from Eldon.

She is not expecting it to be such a catalogue of disaster. She had thought that because it was found in the boat with the two dead members of Franklin's crew, it would be a complement to the Bible also found there. But no, it is not that at all.

The vicar himself is a rather pleasant man who lives, with his family, in a village in England. The family name is Primrose.

The vicar is an ardent supporter of the institution of marriage. He is very encouraging towards those who are considering it, but he also believes that a man must never marry after his wife dies, that there are to be no second marriages. He publishes huge tracts concerning this. Many people don't agree with him, and are annoyed by his constant reiteration of this subject.

Life seems good for the vicar, his wife, and their six children, until they suddenly fall upon hard times and have to move from their comfortable home into a small, cramped cottage.

Calamities always happen suddenly in *The Vicar of Wakefield*. The novel is like a bad storm and, at the end of it, Annie feels that she has been battered by the wind and rain, beaten down by all the disasters in the story, as sudden as weather. What were they thinking, those dying men on the ice, what were they thinking taking this book with them? Annie imagines them, hunkered down amidst their cargo of silver teaspoons and chocolate, reading to each other from *The Vicar of Wakefield*. Perhaps they would have marvelled at the terrible events that befell the Primrose family—*two* daughters stolen, all fortune lost—perhaps they would have, for a while anyway, felt lucky compared to them. For wouldn't England exist for them as a safe, secure paradise? To imagine something happening there, something of the magnitude of their situation on the ice, would be to acknowledge that there was no safe place, that home was not a carefully preserved idyll, free from danger. And then perhaps, as they grew weaker, and their situation more obviously hopeless, then perhaps they would have relied a little on the innate cheerfulness and optimism of the vicar—how he always tried to turn misfortune into reason for hope—how he forgave his enemies, forgave the cause of his troubles. He was an example of faith. And although, to Annie, he appeared a trifle foolish and pompous, and she skipped over most of his tedious sermons in the book, perhaps to these dying men his example provided comfort. And perhaps, too, they would not have thought the suddenness of the events in the book unlikely, for is that not what happened to them? A ship sunk, another crushed by ice, a journey across the ice, ice that was never solid ground, that shifted, that was unpredictable so that the very act of walking was dangerous. And now, huddled in the ribs of this boat, they were the living thing, the heartbeat. Around them all the comforts of an English parlour — silver service, a supply of tea that would outlast their lives here. Waiting to die or to be rescued. Were they able to do as the line in *The Vicar of Wakefield* said, the line that Annie stumbled over and then went back to again. *Read our anguish into patience.*

They fastened their dying breath to words.

On Annie's first day off in the new year she wakes before anyone in the house, lies in bed looking at the scratchings of frost on her attic window. She has slept well, the cold of the room stalling her usual dream of her parents on the road. She has woken with only the faintest sliver of that story in her head. Were there mornings as cold as this one where she came from?

Annie gets quietly out of bed and goes to the window to see if it has snowed during the night. Outside the world is still as held breath. Snow dusts the trees, the stone wall. Even the distant glasshouse looks suddenly white. And then, from the side of the house, a figure staggers down the garden path, staggers as though injured or dying.

Eldon Dashell.

Annie dresses quickly, careful not to wake Tess. Downstairs the house is cold. Her footsteps echo behind her as she crosses the stone floor of the kitchen, opens the door, and steps outside. Frost has sharpened the grass into small silver knives. Mist webs in the trees.

There is nothing to indicate that Mr. Dashell walked down the path. Perhaps Annie has imagined it? Perhaps it was a trick of the window frost and the light? Angles and shadows. She knows the power that light has. What it can make you see.

Annie hurries along the path towards the glasshouse. She thinks she sees the flash of a figure moving in the orchard, but by the time she catches up, it is gone.

She finally sees him at the far edge of the field behind the orchard. He is stumbling down the stream bank. She has to run to catch him up. "Sir," she cries, as she hurries after him. But that seems wrong, is a word for indoors and her life there as his maid. She is closer now. "Mr. Dashell," she cries, and he turns around and sees her, waits for her to reach him. He sways on his feet, reaches out to steady himself on her arm.

"Are you hurt?" asks Annie. Are you drunk? she thinks.

"First they burn, then they tingle, then they become blocks of stone," says Eldon slowly.

"What do?"

"Feet. My feet." They both look down at his feet, at the drops of water sponging out of his leather boots.

Annie suddenly understands what he is doing. "You froze your boots," she says. "Just like Franklin."

"I soaked them at the pump and left them there all night."

"And what does it feel like?" asks Annie. She has imagined this so fully that she needs to know how right she has been about it.

Eldon is freezing. His lungs burn with the cold fog of morning. His feet are completely without sensation. He thinks that he has never felt happier than now, than this moment of walking across the frozen ground towards the river. "Phelan," he says. "I'd call you Phelan if you were a member of the expedition. You would have to have been a man, then. There were no women on Franklin's ships."

"What is it like?" Annie has to know.

Eldon sways a little. "It is exactly," he says, "as you would imagine." And they both smile at this.

They walk together down towards the stream. The world shimmers through the trees. Their footsteps fasten the grass to the ground.

"Remember those two men in the boat," says Eldon. "The boat McClintock found. The silver service. The tea and chocolate. If we were those men in the boat, if that was us, what would we have done?"

Annie has thought about those two men in the boat a great deal. All through the reading of *The Vicar of Wakefield* she imagined them in the boat, crouched down out of the wind with a candle flickering on the thwart, reading the very page she was reading, seeing the same things in their minds as she was seeing. "At first there would have been others," she says. "To push the boat over the ice, all loaded down like that. But they would have gone on ahead to find shelter and food, or back to the ship for help."

"Ahead, I think," says Eldon. "That always seems like the action of possibility, to move ahead."

"The two men," says Annie. "Were they left to guard the things? Or was one of them sick? Or were they both sick?"

"McClintock said that judging by what was left of the clothes, one was probably an officer and one was a crew member," says Eldon. "My guess is that the officer was sick and the other man was left there to look out for him."

They have reached the bank of the stream and begin their awkward stumble down the slope. Ice has made a lace on the edges of the streambed.

"I was the officer," says Eldon. "I was sick." He looks down at the water, trying to make his shaky legs move towards it down the arch of stream bank. "That would have been who I was there. And you," he says, "would have hated me because I made you stay behind."

"Perhaps I volunteered," says Annie. She slides a little down the slope, catches her foot in a root, and manages to struggle upright again. "I don't think I would have minded at first. I would have thought that the others would be back soon enough, back with food or help of some sort."

"And then what?" Eldon collapses by the stream and Annie drops down beside him. Mist stands in needles above the moving water in front of them. Their breath reels out, reels in.

"And then," says Annie, "I would try and remain hopeful."

"You wouldn't go for help?"

"I would pray to the Lord for guidance and strength," says Annie. It is easy now that she is so cold, that her words are sticking a little in her head, coming out slow and slurry, it is easy to imagine this. Here they are, sheltered in this boat on the ice, this boat full of useless English things, nothing to save them, and she would fasten her breath to words, to prayer. "And we would die," she says. Because that is what happened. God did not reward their faith, their reckless perseverance of hope. They prayed and they died and it was painful and lonely and terrifying.

Annie lies back against the cold bolster of earth. She has

prayed all her life and it has always seemed like the right thing to do, has always seemed as if it was an action in itself. But now, here, she thinks that praying is perhaps merely a form of waiting. Praying is waiting for something better to happen. Salvation means rescue. "I should have gone for help," she says. "In the beginning when I still had some strength in my bones. I made a mistake in not doing that."

"It's all right, Phelan." Eldon's speech is slow and sticky, too. "Perhaps I wasn't brave enough to stay by myself, afraid of animals or something. Perhaps I begged you to stay."

But Annie cannot believe this. "No, sir," she says. "I should have gone back to the ship. I should have tried to save you."

This early in the morning, no sounds, the thin light of day winding round the bases of the trees near the stream, it seems as though the vapour above the water, over the grass, is from the world breathing out and then in again. A living creature, near to them. Everything so still, as though the world has emptied out. No birdsong. Only the occasional crack of a branch creaking with the cold.

"In the end," says Annie, "we read *The Vicar of Wakefield* out loud."

"Oh, God," says Eldon slowly. "I never liked that book. The vicar was such an idiot."

"Really, it's not so bad," says Annie. "You get used to him."

"Weren't the women all stolen?"

"By ruffians," says Annie. The word cracks and splits in the cold air, rolls away from her. "I'm cold, too," she says. "Even without frozen boots." She has hurried out without her cloak, has only her thin cotton dress covering her skin.

"Perhaps we really are freezing to death," says Eldon. "We should walk again." He kicks at his heavy feet, tries to launch himself upon them, but they won't hold his weight and he slides back down again. "Phelan," he says, in a small panic. "I can't seem to get up."

Annie grabs Eldon's cold, stiff hands and they are able, with a combined lurch, to set him on his feet.

Eldon feels the residue of panic still in his limbs. This is real now. "We have to get inside," he says. "We have to warm up."

They stumble along the side of the stream, climb on their hands and knees up the slope near the back field. Annie is half pulling Eldon along.

It's true, he thinks. I would have been that man in the boat. I would have been the sick one. The one who caused them both to die.

"Leave me," he says, suddenly both brave and reckless. "Leave me to die here." He doesn't mind just lying down in this field of frozen earth, letting the life ebb out of him, fall away into darkness. It is what he deserves for causing Phelan to remain behind with him.

"But there's the house," says Annie, pointing ahead. It looms in front of them on the horizon.

"Leave me," says Eldon, throwing off her arm. "Save yourself."

Annie hauls him onwards by the sleeve of his coat. "Sir," she says. "I think your brain is beginning to freeze up. I am taking charge of this expedition." She heaves him forward again, most of his weight leaning mightily into her. Halfway up the field she props him up against a fencepost while she recovers her breath, flaps her arms around to try and get feeling back into her fingers. She looks ahead as she walks, towards the grey, misted silhouette of the distant house. The ship, she thinks.

Eldon is draped over the fencepost, muttering something.

"What?" says Annie.

"I hated that book," he says. "I wouldn't have listened to it in the boat."

"Well, you did," she says firmly. "Really, you did."

Stacked against the fencepost is a small pile of stones, cleared from the field and placed safely outside its perimeter. They remind Annie of something. "Sir," she says. "Do you have paper and pen?"

Annie makes a cairn, puts the bit of paper securely on the bottom, piles rocks on top. She has used Eldon's back as a makeshift table, has written with frozen hand onto the envelope Eldon has in his pocket.

January 3, 1866. Expedition under the command of Captain Eldon Dashell, and with Annie Phelan as Ship's Company, set out to retrace the last known moments of two of John Franklin's crew.

By the time they get back to the house Eldon has regained some of his composure. It is now late enough that Cook will be up and so they cannot risk going through the kitchen, or through the front entrance. They walk around to Eldon's library and he pries open the window with an iron stake from the garden. Then he dives over the sill and Annie hears the crash of him hitting the floor.

"Careful," she says.

Eldon resurfaces, rubbing his head, offers her his hand, and she half jumps and he half pulls her into the room.

They sit right at the fire, trying to warm up. Annie is so cold that her skin hurts. She is wrapped in a rug from Eldon's divan. He has wrapped himself in a curtain. They pass the brandy decanter back and forth. Eldon had tried to pour the brandy into snifters but his cold hands couldn't negotiate the finer points of this civilized action.

Annie stretches out her feet into the hearth. Smoke is rising from her damp boots. She coughs as a hot knot of brandy uncurls in her stomach, passes the decanter over to Eldon.

"Phelan," says Eldon, "I lost control. I'm sorry. I'm glad you didn't take me on my word and leave me to die in the field."

"You were just cold, sir."

"Well, I thank you nonetheless."

"It was my pleasure."

They pass the brandy back and forth. Annie starts to shiver and then, finally, stops. Her fingers feel like her fingers again. Her boots continue to hiss and smoke.

"It's strange, sir," she says. "There were those men pushing their silver over the ice in that boat at about the same time my family were dying in Ireland. Both sets of people starving to death."

Eldon swirls brandy around inside his mouth. He feels quite drunk and has only heard part of what Annie said. "We think we're gods," he says. "Going all over the world. Exploring. Discovering. And there we are, appearing to the native people, either lost or staggering down to die. What pathetic souls they must think us." He passes the bottle back to Annie. "Gods," he says. "Gods."

God, thinks Annie. I have forsaken you. Or you have forsaken me. She isn't sure which it is any more. "I never thought to look for my family," she says. "I believed that story of their death. But what if they didn't all die as Mrs. Cullen said? What if there were survivors, or even people who lived where they had lived and knew more of what happened to them?" Annie puts the brandy down on the floor between them. Her head feels fiery and she wants it to stop.

Eldon has, by accident really, heard what it is that Annie has said. "I could write some letters for you," he says. "To the county clerk. See what's registered under your family name in that part of Ireland." He doesn't reach for the brandy. He suddenly feels exhausted, tilts his head back in the chair. "I'll do that, Phelan," he says. And then he's asleep.

Annie pulls Eldon's shroud of curtain well back out of the fire, replaces the brandy decanter on his table, and makes her way, unsteadily, back upstairs. Does she even dare to think of what he might find of her family? If she lets herself hope and then finds out that her family are all indeed dead, will this not be more painful than if she had just continued to believe the story of their death?

Some relics brought from the boat found in Lat. 69 08' 43" N., Long. 99 24' 42" N., upon the West Coast of King William Island, May 30, 1859:

The Vicar of Wakefield;

Two table knives with white handles — one is marked "W.R.",

26 pieces of silver plate — 11 spoons, 11 forks, and 4 teaspoons;

fragment of a silk handkerchief

piece of scented soap

two small glass-stoppered bottles (full);

a pair of silver forceps, such as a naturalist might use for holding or seizing small insects, etc.;

a small bead purse, piece of red sealing-wax, stopper of a pocket flask

Five watches.

Some relics seen in Lat. 69 09' N., Long. 99 24' W., not brought away, 30th of May, 1859: —

A large boat, measuring 28 feet in extreme length, 7 feet 3 inches in breadth, 2 feet 4 inches in depth

4 cakes of navy chocolate, shoemaker's box with implements complete,
carpet boots, sea boots and shoes — in all seven or eight pairs;
towels, sponge, tooth-brush, hair comb, a mackintosh
part of a boat's sail of No. 8 canvas, whale-line rope with yellow
*   mark, and white line with red mark;*
a great quantity of clothing

Madonna (mortal)

It's Annie's hands that first give Isabelle the idea. The sight of them, red and cracked, split from scrubbing floors. How different they look from Annie's sweet face, her fine features. If dressed differently, more like a Lady, Annie could pass in the world of gentility. It is her hands that would give her away, just as it's Isabelle's hands that she feels ashamed of when she's out in society, that she's made to feel ashamed of.

Annie's hands tell the entire history of her working life. There's no escaping what she has done. If Isabelle wants to show the essence of Annie Phelan in her photographs, how can she ignore the hands? What is beauty without suffering?

Isabelle holds her own black hands up to the window light. They keep the record of all the photographs she has taken. They are a logbook of the flesh, each voyage into light written onto them as darkness. They are the true negative of what she does. Who she is.

"The Madonna?" Annie is on her hands and knees, scrubbing the front steps and walk, when Isabelle comes to tell her of her new idea. Annie rests back on her knees, pushes a stray bit of hair off her forehead with the back of her hand.

Isabelle crouches down beside Annie, takes her hand in hers. "She was a woman much like yourself," she says, bending over Annie's hand to inspect each nick, each smooth rind of scar.

"I don't think so, ma'am."

Isabelle looks up at Annie. "You know the story, then?"

"Yes, ma'am." Annie likes the feeling of her hand in Isabelle's. Isabelle's skin is soft, warm. "This is a story that I am particularly familiar with."

"She was an ordinary, working woman," says Isabelle, still thinking that she must explain the Madonna to her maid.

Annie stares incredulously at Isabelle. "Ma'am," she says. "She was the mother of the Lord." She falls hard into the last word, a place to land, a place to push off from.

"Not yet," promises Isabelle. "Right now she's just an ordinary woman who makes a living from her hands."

"I don't know," says Annie. She doesn't feel right about this. I will not take the Lord's name in vain. What about his image?

Isabelle's knees are wet from the stoop. "Please," she says. The stone against her flesh, her bone, as unyielding as Annie. "Trust me," she says.

Annie sits back. She still holds her scrubbing brush in one hand, lays it down on the steps. Isabelle looks scared, she thinks. No, perhaps it's sadness. Isabelle spends so long studying Annie's face she must be able to read it perfectly by now, all the emotions and subtlety. Annie wishes she knew what Isabelle was feeling. She takes her hand gently away from Isabelle's. Her skin stings from this loss. "Ma'am," she says. "I'm not sure that you completely understand the story of the Lord." It would help Annie if she could read Isabelle's face, help her to know what she might and might not say. Instead of being angry, Isabelle seems relieved at Annie's words.

"Well," she says. "You can explain it to me while we're photographing."

*

"The Madonna?" Eldon turns from his library window where he has been looking out at the frosted garden and thinking of the sea. "But you're not a believer."

"It's not about believing," says Isabelle, exasperated. Doesn't anyone understand the notion of artistic freedom? "The Madonna is a symbol."

"Of Christianity," says Eldon, not convinced. "I thought you were with me on Charles's new theory. You seemed just as excited by an idea of evolution. Don't tell me you have succumbed to the allure of an all-knowing being."

"All I'm trying to do," says Isabelle, "is to traffic more in what is there."

"The Madonna?"

"A mortal woman at the point before she is the mother of the Saviour. A working woman."

"Working?"

"An ordinary woman," says Isabelle, wishing she'd never bothered to tell him of her new idea, to tell him anything of what she thought.

Eldon crosses his arms over his chest. "What do you know of an ordinary woman, Isabelle?" he says.

"Annie Phelan."

"As Mary?"

"Of course. She is my..." Isabelle wants to say *model*, but instead says the obvious, "servant."

It irks Eldon precisely because he can see the fit. He truly believes in his friend, Charles Darwin, and his theory of a slow progression of sea creatures to ape to man, a long parade towards walking upright. Yet he can perfectly believe that Annie Phelan could be a Madonna. There is still something achingly desirable in the notion of the Lord's will, of things just appearing on the earth. A flash of lightning and Eve tumbles from Adam's chest. A nod and the Red Sea splits down the middle. All the absolutes in religion seem preferable to the tentative steps of science. A long, slow, tedious journey to the upright man. Or, a wave of the hand and it's done. Believe and anything is possible. A woman as a pillar of salt. A child called to heaven.

"You don't need my approval, Isabelle," he says. "You do things your way."

Isabelle looks at the wall of him, in front of the window, arms crossed to ward her off. "Eldon," she says. "I didn't come here for your approval."

"What then?" He feels a wave of jealousy. He doesn't like to think of Annie Phelan as the Madonna. She had been a much better member of the expedition. Isabelle was wrong about her maid, about who she was, about who she should be. There was a strength in Annie that deserved better than this religious symbolism. "What then?" he says again, with real anger in his voice.

"Nothing," says Isabelle, turning to leave. "There is nothing I came here to say to you."

Annie thinks of her family all the time now. The sudden possibility of a new story of them. All this thought has somehow washed them up from the great ocean of the past onto the shores of the living world.

Annie has not seen Eldon Dashell since the day he set off after Franklin. She does not know if he remembered what he'd promised her, if he remembered to write letters on her behalf. He has been sick this past week, hidden away in his bedroom. She can hear him coughing sometimes when she's passing by in the hallway. But this morning she was required to light the fire in the library, so she knows he must be well enough to be considering working again.

Annie has thought of telling Isabelle about this new idea of hers, this decision to find out what happened to her family. But Isabelle has never expressed an interest in Annie's life outside the moments of her modelling, and Annie is not sure how to go about explaining everything, like Franklin and the march with Eldon in his frozen boots over the back field.

All day Annie has tried to go to Eldon in his library, but her work has been at the other end of the house and there hasn't been a moment to squeeze away for herself. Added to this Isabelle wanted to sit on the outside steps and talk about Annie's hands. Finally, though, she has managed to run down the hallway and is hurrying along to Eldon's library.

"Annie!" The call skids her to a stop. She spins around and sees Cook at the end of the hall.

"Yes, missus?" It takes all her self-control not to keep running, not to open the door to Eldon's library and fling herself inside. She has no doubt he would give her safe harbour.

"Mrs. Dashell wants you in the studio," says Cook. "She's been looking for you," she adds, which means that on not finding Annie she has sent Cook out in search and Cook is not pleased to be taken away from her kitchen.

"Yes, missus." Annie walks back up the hall towards Cook. "Sorry."

"You must be where you're supposed to be," says Cook. "I don't have the patience to be chasing you all through the house. Nor the inclination," she says.

"Yes," says Annie. She is more sorry that she wasn't able to get in to see Eldon. She considers pleading with Cook, but the stern look on Cook's face makes her change her mind.

When Annie gets to the studio, Isabelle is sitting on the bench, staring at the camera. "Ma'am?" says Annie, after she's entered the room but Isabelle hasn't seemed to notice this. "Ma'am, I'm here."

"I was imagining being you," says Isabelle. She says it with such sincerity that Annie feels tears start to her eyes. It touches her that Isabelle would want to do this, even if Isabelle is imagining being Annie while sitting in the studio, and not on her hands and knees scrubbing the floor.

Isabelle sees the tears in Annie's eyes. I did that, she thinks. I can do that. She had been sitting here, in the sunny studio, thinking of Annie Phelan, thinking that Annie reminded her both of what she'd lost and what she'd never had. Ellen. Her children.

The afternoon light gentles Isabelle. She lifts her face and the sun cups her chin in golden hands. Her sharp cheekbones soften, and she looks beautiful.

Annie sits down on the bench beside her. Isabelle takes her hand and Annie looks down at their entwined hands, the ugly red of hers, the ugly black of Isabelle's. She feels as if she is floating away, as if the only thing tethering her to earth is the pressure of Isabelle's hand in her own. "How do you imagine being me?" she asks.

"What do you mean?"

"What do you think of?" says Annie. "That makes it about me?"

Isabelle is quiet for a moment. She can feel the strength of sun through the glass. Spring's slow returning. "I was thinking of you sitting here and looking up at me." She waves her hand at the camera, the solitary stillness of it like a heron standing stiffly in a marsh. "How I would seem to you. From here. How I would look."

Annie thinks of the photograph of Sappho that she took in Isabelle's bedroom. How even as the model, Isabelle controlled the scene. How even when Annie was looking at her through the camera Annie wasn't sure how much Isabelle was allowing her to see. Isabelle could never be Annie. To be me, thinks Annie, to really be me, is to not be in control of the moment. I don't know what is going to happen. She does.

Mary Madonna wears the grey cloak with the hood up. She doesn't hold flowers or feathers. She has no children — yet. Unadorned and unaccompanied, she faces her world. Too humble to look straight at the camera, she is in profile, her working hands clutching the cloak around her as though she is out in a bitter north wind.

The Madonna has no idea what lies in wait for her. She does not see herself as special in any way, certainly not as an exalted figure. She does not know she has been born free of original sin, that she has been the immaculate conception. She will treat the baby Jesus in exactly the same manner as she would any child of hers. This is how great a goodness she possesses. How humble she is, how much a creature of the Lord's will.

Mary Madonna sits at first, but because there's no child to bend over, to tend to, she looks too lonely like that, the sculpting of her cloak a hollowed-out tree, the husk of it hunched forward around the part of it that is missing. No. Mary Madonna stands by the wall of glass with a curtain of muslin pinned across it. She stands in profile, head slightly bent forward. She would never look directly at the camera, that is too challenging, too intimate, that makes the assertion that she is entirely present. Also, her overt beauty might detract from her religious virtue. Better to stand in profile in front of diffuse light, light that is spongy and vague. Better to look down to show natural humility, but not at any specific object, that would indicate too much focus on one thing which would close down a general openness to the wonders and sorrows of the world. Mary Madonna can look down at her hands, but not to examine the intricate petals of a flower, not to have scientific, or even undue, curiosity about the natural world as that would imply a lack of faith in God's grand design and plan for all living things.

The hands.

The gaze downwards to the hands will pull the viewer's eyes down as well, down to the thick, strong fingers of the Madonna's hands. She scrubs floors and blackens grates. Hers are working hands. They indicate an ordinary woman. The mother of the Lord could be anyone. No, the mother of the Lord has to be someone like this Mary Madonna, someone whose sense of her own greatness, her own self, won't conflict with the greatness of her son. She is there for the Lord to make use of, but she cannot get in his way.

"Ma'am?" says Annie, looking up from the contemplation of her hands and these thoughts of what she is doing, standing by the soft filter of window light. "Is this a graven image?" She has remembered the companion order not to take the Lord's name in vain.

"No," says Isabelle quickly. "*Graven* means to engrave. This is not engraving."

"Yes, but," says Annie, doubting that the Bible advocates complete fidelity to the wording of the command.

"No," says Isabelle, before Annie can finish her sentence. "It's the Lord himself that shouldn't be graven, and this is only Mary. It's not the same."

Annie can see the weak logic in this. She looks down at her hands again, and then back up at Isabelle. Sometimes she thinks the perfect photograph is Isabelle standing beside her camera, as she is now.

This is the perfect image, Isabelle thinks. Annie Phelan as Mary Madonna. The softness of Annie's face, sharpened a little by the intelligence in her eyes. How her strong body looks ready to bear the Christ child, to carry that burden, that expectation. She can be an ordinary working woman, and yet she is so thoroughly herself as well. And she is destined for greatness, by association, but greatness just the same. She is destined to become the mother of the Saviour and she has no knowledge of this whatsoever. She is oblivious to her destiny.

It suits you, thinks Isabelle. Because Annie is familiar with the story of Mary there is an ease to her portrayal. She isn't straining hard to get the right sense. She knows what to do. She's also wary of playing the mother of Jesus, and this hesitancy comes over as humility and makes the portrayal that much more convincing.

"Did Mary fall in love with Joseph, or did God select him to be her husband?" asks Isabelle, moving the camera back so she can get the full sculptural effect of the cloak.

"I'm sure she was in love with him," says Annie, though she really has no idea and has never thought much about it, but she feels a certain responsibility towards this story, towards knowing it, lapsed as she has been lately about believing as thoroughly as she used to.

"I mean," says Isabelle, looking through the viewfinder, "would Mary have been the mother of Christ if there had been no Joseph?"

"Joseph was the father, ma'am."

"Wasn't God the father?"

"Perhaps there had to be two fathers."

"Why? So the child is of the Lord, but the act of making the child is still mortal?"

Annie wipes her forehead. It's getting hot inside the cloak. It seems as though any time she feels certain, Isabelle says something else to confuse her. "I don't know," she says, finally.

"Every child is divine. I suppose that's it. We all have the chance to make a little Jesus." Isabelle stands back. There's something wrong with the light. It's making everything too blurry, as if it's formed from smoke. "I couldn't bear to think like that," she says with bitterness. "Step back. The light's not good where you are."

"What were your children called, ma'am?" Annie has obediently moved back a few steps. The light is not so strong here. She feels the relief of shadow on the side of her head. The coolness of it like a hand.

"How did you know I had children?" Isabelle stiffens. She puts out a hand and touches the top of her camera. The wood is reassuringly smooth, warm from the air.

"Mr. Dashell told me."

"What was he doing telling you that?"

"I don't know. He just told me."

Isabelle goes back behind the camera. "He has no business telling you that, Annie. You must not speak of it again. Do you understand?"

"Yes, ma'am." Annie looks down at her hands, pushes them together into a peak, as if she's praying. She wishes she hadn't asked Isabelle about her children. "I didn't mean any harm by it," she says.

Isabelle likes the way the praying hands look on the Madonna. It makes them even more the focus of the photograph. Such a lovely contrast between the act of prayer and the physical state of the hands doing the praying. "I know," she says. The half light at the side of Annie stiffens the cloak into a geographic landform — a cliff, a bluff. "Only the first one," she says.

"What?"

"Only the first one had a name." Isabelle looks through the camera at Mary Madonna, her cloak in shadow, her praying hands tented under the light. "Rose," she says. "My first baby was called Rose."

Eldon is reading when Isabelle flings open his bedroom door. He sits propped up against a wall of pillows, book in hand. Isabelle's sudden entrance startles him. He jerks his head up in alarm when she comes into the room and his reading glasses fall onto the eiderdown.

"Isabelle," he announces needlessly.

She comes straight over to the bed, moves to sit down and Eldon quickly grabs his glasses before she squashes them. He feels slightly guilty, as though he's been caught out at something. "I was reading," he says.

"I can see that." Isabelle taps his open book with her forefinger. "Do I need permission to enter your room?"

"No, of course not." But Eldon does feel he has wanted some warning of her arrival. He carefully puts his glasses down on the nightstand by his bed and pulls himself higher up on the pillows to give his wife more room.

"You haven't been in to see me for a long time," says Isabelle. "Why not?"

"I've been busy," says Eldon quickly.

"Reading?"

"No." Eldon looks down at his book. "Yes." He closes it and puts it on the nightstand next to his glasses. "Reading, and other things."

"Ah," says Isabelle. "Other things. Like telling my maid about the babies." She looks hard at him. "Why would you do that? Is that not our private business?"

Eldon feels like a cornered animal. Annie Phelan. He's been thinking of her. Reading this logbook of a whaling captain and thinking of their voyage over the frozen grounds of this house.

"You have no answer?" Isabelle is angrier than she thought she was. She is not sure if she is angry because Annie knows this about her, or because she suspects that if Eldon told Annie such a thing he has more of a relationship with her than Isabelle had supposed. "Why are you telling my maid such a confidence?"

"Your maid." Eldon sees the flush on Isabelle's face. "I thought she was *our* maid. Yes," he says. "I did tell her about the babies. We were having a conversation." He doesn't mention the walk, or that Annie has been borrowing books from him. Or the brandy by the fire while they were recovering from freezing to death. "She was telling me about her family, how they all died in the famine, and I mentioned our children." He has a sudden recollection of the last baby being hurried from the birthing room, the small covered bundle of it, taken from Isabelle before she'd even seen its face. "I'm sorry," he says. "Sometimes I cannot help but think what they might have been like. How our lives would have been different." He means better, and Isabelle knows this. She knows, too, that Eldon's regret for the dead children is for the selves they might have become. He has probably already imagined them as adults and misses the conversations they might have had with him.

Isabelle reaches behind her neck and undoes the clasp of her dress. She stands up and steps out of it. "Move over," she says, and slips down beside her husband in the bed. His body is surprisingly cool. He slides down the pillows and they lie side by side. "You could touch me," says Isabelle, but the moment she says it, half plea, half order, Eldon loses all inclination to do this.

The flame from the oil lamp beside the bed casts a moving shadow on the ceiling above them. It nods and dances, nods and dances. Isabelle waits for Eldon to move his hand the few inches it would take to touch her. He used to trace the contours of her body as though she was a shore, his hands the waves, the moving line, as though he could not help himself, the constant toppling joy he felt at finding himself where she was.

Eldon does not move. His body feels shipwrecked, heavy and immobile, grinding to bits on the rocks. "I'm sorry," he says.

"Is it anybody's fault?" Isabelle rolls onto her side. "Look at me." She puts a hand against his cheek, pushes it down so his face is next to hers, so his eyes stare into her own. "Is it mine?"

"No."

"Is it?" Isabelle has never imagined conversations with her dead children, never saw them married or with children of their own. She has never even thought of them as children, really. Babies. They were babies. She made room for them. They took up space inside her and she gave them this space willingly. She felt them there and then they were gone before she could make room for them in other parts of her life, before she could know what she would feel for them when they were outside of her body, when they were not her.

"No," says Eldon again, but this time weaker than the first, and neither of them is convinced by it.

Isabelle gets out of the bed. The oil lamp flickers as regular as breathing. Her dress is a pool of fabric on the floor. She steps into it.

"I didn't mean to say anything," says Eldon.

Isabelle doesn't turn around. He has drifted so quickly away from her and back to Annie Phelan. She notices this and hates it. "Keep away from Annie Phelan," she says.

"What?"

Isabelle puts her hands behind her neck and fumbles the clasp of her dress into place. "I want you to stay away from her entirely." She stares at him, still huddled down in the bed. "You are a weak and pathetic man, Eldon Dashell," she says. "I can't think why I married you."

Because you needed me once, he thinks, but that seems so far away now that to bring it up would be almost inconsequential, wouldn't be a real reason at all. He says nothing.

"Right," says Isabelle. "Don't let me interrupt." She walks across the room, stops when she reaches the door. "Your reading," she says derisively, opens the door, and is gone.

Eldon has behaved badly, he knows this. He should have thought of something more reassuring to say to Isabelle. He should have touched her. But if he has to think first every time before he speaks to her or caresses her, then what does this mean? If intimacy is premeditated, can it still be genuine? Is it still wanted?

Eldon, with relief, goes back to reading the diary of the whaling captain from 1840. He is reading it for details of the voyage of the whaling party, but he finds that the character of the captain is far more interesting than his cartographic concerns. The captain, sailing from Nova Scotia, kept the diary so he could share it with his new wife when he returned from sea. Indeed, the captain starts out by addressing his wife, as though each entry were a letter. *Dear Alice.* This soon stops as he becomes increasingly obsessed with finding whales. He starts complaining about his sailors, how some of them are *pretending* they have scurvy. He stops complaining after several of them jump overboard and commit suicide. Gradually his entries get shorter and shorter, until they are the briefest description of the weather and whale sightings.

> *24th — Cloudy. No whales.*
> *26th — Fresh breeze from the SW. Nothing like a whale.*
> *27th — Rain. I really would like to see a whale.*
> *29th — Rain. No whales.*

When the party finally does start to catch some whales, his entries change again. Now he dispenses with the weather entirely and concentrates only on the state of the whales.

> *12th — Cut the whale.*
> *13th — Began boiling.*

The whales get scarce. He begins to write poems about killing whales, then sentimental poems from the dying whales' point of view. He begins to address himself in the third person, and seems to have forgotten completely that he ever was possessed of such a thing as a wife.

He circumnavigates the world twice.

His fourth year at sea he decides to head for home. He stops referring to himself in the third person and gets a little more optimistic.

No whales *yet*, he now writes, after the line about the weather, keeping up this newfound joviality all the way home, back to a woman whom he had known for just two weeks before putting to sea.

A woman who was still waiting for him.

It's a long way home to someone.

Eldon tries to imagine what it would have been like to be that woman, what it would have been like to live in the shadow of waiting. How would you remember anything about the person returning to you? Physical presence matters. A body standing in your room. Someone there to defy your imaginings of them, to stop you making them up.

Who would wait for him, he thinks, if he were gone a long, long time? Who would remember anything about him? What is there to remember? Eldon puts his book down. Can he find his way back to Isabelle? Does he even want to?

Isabelle is awake the next morning when Annie comes with the hot water for washing. Often Isabelle is still asleep and Annie has to haul back the curtains dramatically and flood the room with light in order to wake her up. This morning Isabelle is sitting up in bed, not reading, just sitting there, wide awake, hands clasped together overtop of the sheet.

"Good morning, Annie," she says. Her voice is low, melodious with sorrow. When Annie gets nearer she sees that Isabelle has been crying.

"Morning, ma'am." She pours some water into the basin and sets the jug down beside it. Should she just leave? Should she ask what is wrong?

"Why are you just standing there?"

"No reason, ma'am."

"Well, light me a fire, then. It's cold in here this morning. I'm cold," says Isabelle.

Annie welcomes the task, having something to do. She brushes out the ashes and coal dust with vigour. She banks the coal, lights the fire, all the time hearing the sniffles of Isabelle behind her. I won't ask, I will just leave, she thinks. It is no business of mine. She collects her pan of ashes and makes to exit the room.

"Don't go," says Isabelle, as Annie is crossing the floor. "I hate crying. Annie."

Annie turns and walks back to the bed, carrying the pan of ashes before her like a coveted prize, an offering.

"What would you like me to do, ma'am?" she asks.

"Make me stop crying," says Isabelle. She rubs the back of her hand across her red eyes. "Can't you do that?"

Annie waves her hand with the dustpan in it and a small pillow of ash rises into the air, scatters and falls like fine, grey rain. "I order you to stop crying, ma'am," she says. She carefully lays the dustpan down on top of the wash jug. "Did it work?"

"No," Isabelle says. She pulls the covers back and swings her legs over the side of the bed. "Perhaps I should be you."

"Me?"

Isabelle stands up. "Everything would be easier if I were you," she says.

Hardly, thinks Annie, but she gives in to Isabelle's wish. "Come here, then," she says.

Isabelle obediently follows Annie to the fireplace. Annie presses a cloth into Isabelle's hand. "Dust the mantel," she says. "And the paintings. And the various ornaments. And mind you put them back where they were, ma'am."

"It would be a bit more convincing if you didn't say 'ma'am,'" says Isabelle.

"Yes, ma'am," says Annie, and they both smile.

Isabelle dusts the room while Annie pulls the curtains and strips the sheets from the bed. They work in silence, the only sounds being the small noise of vases being lifted and then lowered back into place, the whisper of the sheets being slipped from the mattress. Annie stops once, standing by the window, through which grey clouds roll out across the sky, and she watches Isabelle work. Mrs. Dashell is careful with the dusting. She is not hurrying in her usual way, or missing the dusting of certain things. She is methodical and thorough.

"You would make a good servant," says Annie.

Isabelle looks up from the surface of her dressing table and sees Annie backlit by the window, the stormy morning light. "You," she says. "Not just any servant, but you."

It has worked. She has stopped crying, has stopped thinking of Eldon and her visit to him last night, going over it in her mind, wishing it different, wishing him different. For a few moments she has thought only of dusting under the hand mirror and hairbrushes, replacing them exactly where they had been. That relief had felt like a gift.

"There's nothing like work, ma'am, to make you forget your troubles." Annie says this and Isabelle immediately remembers her troubles again, thinks of Eldon and how he blames her for the dead babies, as though the fault is her body, her faulty body.

Isabelle puts her dusting cloth down. She leans against the mantel, the coal fire warm through her nightdress. "Annie."

"Yes?"

"Don't leave me."

Annie looks up. Isabelle seems about to cry again, hunched against the mantel, too close to the fire. Out the window the storm rolls towards them. There's the sound of thunder in the distance. "You're too near to the fire, ma'am," she says. "You should step aside."

Isabelle doesn't move. "Don't leave me," she says again.

"No. I won't."

Isabelle moves away from the fireplace.

The rain starts.

*

Isabelle photographs the Madonna through the rainy light of the afternoon. Posed against the glass wall of the studio, the grey rain coursing down outside, making streaks of smoky light inside the room. Long exposures. The Madonna leaning her head on the glass. On her knees, praying before the watery veil. Each pose adds an understanding to the overall concept of goodness and virtue, all that the Madonna represents and Annie personifies, as if each pose were a word in a sentence and the sentence, when revealed, would explain all the sorrow of life to Isabelle.

It is amazing how cold it becomes in the glasshouse when there is no sun to cover it. There are draughts under the door and from between the panes of glass. The air is damp and stirs the cold about so that it coats everything inside the studio. Annie huddles into the cave of her cloak, glad, for once, of the heavy wool it's made from.

"That's good," says Isabelle. "Trepidation. A little nervousness. The humility of servitude."

Annie knows better than to correct her. She burrows deeper into the folds of the cloak, into humility, thinks only of the hot cup of tea she will be able to have when this modelling session is over.

When Cook comes into the studio Annie thinks that perhaps Cook has realized how damp and cold she must be, and has thoughtfully brought her a cup of tea out to the glasshouse. But Cook ignores Annie, slouched against the studio wall, instead goes directly to Isabelle.

"Mrs. Dashell," she says. "The letter you bade me watch out for has come." She hands over a thick brown envelope.

"Thank you, Gertie." Isabelle takes the envelope, and then, as though she can't bear to touch it, she puts it down on top of the camera. "Sorry you had to come all the way out here to deliver it to me."

"No trouble, ma'am. Glad to do it."

Annie notices how different Cook sounds when she talks to Isabelle. Her voice is light and giving, nothing shuts down inside it. *Gertie.* Annie has never heard Cook's name spoken before.

Cook leaves the studio without so much as a glance at Annie. She does not approve of the modelling, Annie knows this. A housemaid should only do the duties of a housemaid. Posing as the Madonna is not a suitable thing for a housemaid to do.

"What is it?" asks Annie when Cook has gone. Isabelle is just staring at the letter on top of the camera, making no move to open the envelope.

"You do it," says Isabelle. "You open it. And don't read it out. Just tell me what it says."

Annie takes the letter. It is heavy. There's something inside it. She carefully slits along the top edge with her finger and tips the envelope. A round metal disc falls into her palm. She unfolds the letter and reads it over to herself. When she looks up, Isabelle is standing by the camera, one hand on the top of it. She has her eyes closed.

Annie holds the medal out in her hand. It flashes bright even in the dull light of the studio. "Ma'am," she says. "Look. It's from the Dublin Exposition. Your photographs have won the gold medal."

Isabelle opens her eyes.

Isabelle decides to have a party in order to celebrate her victory. A dinner party.

"I will invite both those who have encouraged and those

who have maligned me," she says to Annie. "I will reward and punish, all with the same event."

They are in Isabelle's bedroom, sifting through her closet, picking out dresses for Annie to try on. Isabelle has insisted that Annie attend the party as a guest, not as a servant. "After all," she said, "it's the photographs of you that won the prize. This is all because of you." It is the series on the virtues that has taken the gold medal. Annie as Grace, as Humility, as Faith.

"Try this on," says Isabelle, hauling from the wardrobe the dress she wore to supper at the Hills'. "I think green would go nicely with your natural colouring."

"I don't know, ma'am. It's so fancy. I might ruin it."

"How could you ruin it by wearing it?" Isabelle holds the dress in front of Annie. "You would do it an honour by wearing it. Here. Let me help you." She puts the dress down, moves behind Annie, and unfastens her black dress. "And take off that infernal cap. I think they are the most ugly things imaginable." She taps the white maid's cap with her finger. "It really is your gold medal, you know. I will have you come to this party as the guest of honour. As a Lady."

Annie unpins her cap and hands it to Isabelle, who tosses it in the direction of a chair. Annie steps out of her uniform, struggles into the corset Isabelle proffers, and then carefully steps into the circle of the green dress. She stands motionless as Isabelle does up the hooks in the back and then steps round in front of Annie to assess her.

"Lovely!" she says. "You look lovely."

Annie walks over to the looking-glass and surveys herself. She seems nothing like the self she used to be. A dress instead of a uniform. A colour instead of the washed-out lilac morning dress and the black afternoon dress. She doesn't look like herself at all and it unsettles her a little.

Annie is still not sure how she feels about the photographs of her winning the medal at the Dublin Exposition. She finds it hard to imagine them as a public thing, they seemed so much to be something she and Mrs. Dashell did, something private just between themselves. Scores of people will have seen the photographs of her in Dublin. They will have walked right up to the images, studying her as though she were a specimen of a butterfly, pinned out on the wall with an explanatory label attached.

"What if," she says, "I can't do things properly?"

"What things?"

Annie turns in front of the mirror to get a better look at the back of the dress and stumbles on the hem. "Walking," she says. "And talking. Knowing what to say."

"You always know what to say."

"Well, how to say it, then." Annie looks beseechingly at Isabelle. "I am scared to death at the thought of this."

Isabelle takes Annie's hand. "Could you not have been me?" she asks. "If our lives were different, could I not have been you?" For this is what she has always believed about Ellen, that they were the same.

No, thinks Annie. You could not have been me. Isabelle squeezes her hand and then drops it. Annie practises walking, over to the window and back again. The dress makes soft scratchy noises as she walks, like someone whispering to her. Don't forget me. Don't forget me.

"Everything looks right on you," says Isabelle, watching Annie move across the room, the dress gliding along with her. "You can be anyone."

At that moment Annie turns from the window. The sun,

cast out from the clouds, hooks a finger into the room, creates a thin band of light for her to walk through. The room seems suspended in this light, floats here before her. She lifts her arm and twirls around in the sunlight. Isabelle's laughter from across the room is warm and buoyant.

I can be anyone.

Annie walks up and down in the hallway outside Isabelle's room in the green dress, to practise for the party. Isabelle has left for the studio, to print out the photographs she took yesterday of the Madonna.

Annie walks up and down the hallway, turning hard at the end so that the dress spins out from her body. She enjoys the sound of it, the weight of it, the way it reaches out and then slithers down, heavy against her legs.

Tess comes puffing up the stairs with an armload of clean linen.

"Hello," says Annie, performing one of her twirls for Tess's benefit.

"I heard there's to be a party," says Tess. She's still panting a little from her climb up the stairs. "I've always loved that dress," she says. She remembers how she had seen herself in that dress, being helped down from her carriage by Wilks. The casual wave of her hand as the driver is dismissed for the evening and she and Wilks walk up the front steps of the Hill house, to be announced to all at the party there. She slumps against the banister, the bundle of linen resting on her huge, pregnant stomach. "I would look such a fat cow in that dress," she says.

Annie turns again, slowly, and the dress sparkles in the sunlight, like a piece of glass underwater. The glittering green of it. "Don't say that," she says. "It could just as easily be you wearing this, going to the dinner."

Tess smiles sadly at Annie. "No," she says. "It could never

be me." She hugs the linen tighter to her chest, brushes past Annie and continues on down the hall.

A few days later Annie steps from the shadows of Isabelle's room and begins her slow descent down the main staircase into the uncertain world of the dinner party. Isabelle, who has dressed Annie and done her hair, and who was supposed to wait and escort her downstairs, has instead flown on ahead and is lost down there somewhere amidst the tangle of guests in the front hall.

Annie walks slowly in her borrowed dress. It is heavier than the thin cotton she is used to, makes her feel as though she is being dragged to earth. It is an effort to walk, to keep her head up and not worry about tripping over her hem. She is barely down the stairs and already she feels defeated.

Cook, Wilks, and Tess have been hard at work all day, preparing the house for visitors. Annie had been undertaking the lengthy business of getting dressed as a Lady, all the time hearing footsteps up and down the staircase, the opening and closing of the kitchen door. This constant activity had made her feel guilty for not being able to help set the table or polish the silver.

The guests have been ushered into the drawing room for a glass of claret before dinner is served. When Annie walks into the room, a dozen people look up. She hears someone say, "That's her. That's the maid." The talk stops. People lean forward, staring at Annie over their glasses of wine. She backs herself into a corner by the piano.

"Miss?" Tess is in front of her with a tray of drinks. Annie takes one and Tess does a curtsy.

"Don't," says Annie.

Tess gives her a half smirk, half smile as she moves away.

Annie drinks her wine too fast and then doesn't know what to do with the empty glass. Around her the buzz of voices lifts and falls. Every time she looks up, someone else is staring straight at her, unabashedly, as though she herself was a photograph, a portrait and not a living person at all.

"We have been offered a proposal of marriage," whispers Isabelle. She is suddenly beside Annie, leans into her.

"We have?" says Annie, so grateful Isabelle has finally rescued her that she almost doesn't pay attention to what she is saying.

"Shhh," whispers Isabelle, her voice close to Annie's ear. "He's over there. See. Between Letitia Hill and that man with the gold watch-chain."

Annie sees an elderly man with curly white hair and an unusually large head. He has his hands on his knees and is staring intently at Annie and Isabelle.

"He's staring at me," Annie says. "And he must be ninety years old."

"Well, he probably can't even see you then."

"Are you serious?" says Annie. Surely Isabelle wouldn't marry her off to that old man? He looks as if he can barely stand. "Did he actually propose?"

"What would you like to say in response?"

"No," says Annie, a bit too loudly. A woman to the left of her turns her head at the sound of Annie's vehement refusal.

"Shhh," whispers Isabelle again. Her breath is warm on Annie's cheek. "Of course it's no. I'll go and tell him. He's Archibald Stanford. One of *the* Stanfords. He collects portraits. He says he saw your image in the photograph of Humility and he fell in love with you, right then." Isabelle looks across at Archibald Stanford, who is winking at Annie Phelan from the other side of the room. "It will give me great pleasure to kindly, but firmly, decline his generous offer of marriage. He has never thought me worth collecting before."

"Don't leave me," says Annie, in a panic. "Don't go. They're all staring at me."

Isabelle puts her arm around Annie's shoulders. "Well, then," she says. "Don't take your eyes from me."

Annie watches Isabelle cross the room to Mr. Stanford. She walks slowly, has such poise doing something as simple as moving across a room. That is part of being a Lady, thinks Annie. The luxury of moving slowly. A Lady is not meant to have any worries, none that require her to hurry. It doesn't matter if the beds need changing or Cook wants help. A Lady always leaves these small concerns to others. That's what servants are for, the small concerns.

Isabelle is talking to Archibald Stanford. Annie watches the graceful nod of Isabelle's head. She sees Mr. Stanford slap the arm of his chair, as if he's killing an insect. Then Isabelle lifts her head and stares straight at Annie. Don't take your eyes from me. She's making sure, thinks Annie, that this is what I'm doing, that I'm watching her.

At dinner Annie finds herself seated between Robert Hill and a Mr. Drake. This is even worse than drinks in the drawing room. Now she is trapped, wedged in on either side, facing a confusing puzzle of cutlery.

There are eight courses to dinner and Annie feels full right at the beginning, after the clear soup. She pokes at the main dish of roast pork, occasionally pops a boiled carrot into her mouth to keep up the pretence of eating.

Cook serves the dinner. She is wearing a maid's uniform for this duty, something Annie has never seen before. Tess is too pregnant to help serve. Annie can imagine Isabelle thinking that the puffy, stumbling pregnant figure of Tess would put everyone off their food.

When Cook leans in to ladle Annie the turnips, she accidentally knocks Annie's plate and sends a small rivulet of gravy down Annie's borrowed dress. "Sorry Miss," she says, her voice hard and flat. When Annie looks into her eyes she sees that Cook is closed to her. It is as if they've never known each other. It is as if Cook hates her now.

"The Irish," says a voice beside her. "It's all the fault of the Irish."

Annie looks over at Robert Hill. What is he talking about? Luckily Eldon asks the question she is thinking.

"What is the fault of the Irish?"

"Everything," says Robert Hill. "The great mass of them coming here and taking the jobs of Englishmen, relying on our benevolence. Even the cattle plague."

"What about the cattle plague?" says Eldon, his voice low and quiet.

"I think the cows caught that plague from the Irish."

"The Irish died of starvation."

"How do we know that?" Robert Hill leans forward over his dinner plate. "Perhaps their sickness wasn't caused by hunger, but was an epidemic. We were told it was hunger so we wouldn't worry. And now the cows have caught it."

"What nonsense," says Eldon. He looks at Annie and she stares back at him.

"And who's to say," says Robert, getting carried away with his enthusiasm for his theory of the rinderpest, "that as many Irish died as we were told. Perhaps hardly any died. Perhaps none at all."

"My family died," says Annie. She hadn't meant to speak

at all during this dinner, had meant to sit and be the living photograph Isabelle wanted her to be. But Isabelle, despite all her earlier promises never to leave Annie's side during the evening, seems to have abandoned her completely during dinner. Robert Hill's remark is the last thing she can bear. "My family died building a road for your government," she says. "A road that went nowhere. A useless scheme for which they weren't even paid."

The dinner guests are suddenly silent. Annie can hear the loud sounds of her own breathing, reeling in, reeling out. "Excuse me," she says, and rising from her chair with some dignity, rushes from the dining room with none.

She runs through the drawing room and out the doors to the garden. The cold air is balm to her nerves as she hurries round the side of the house. Laughter rises, like the scent of flowers, from the sunken windows of the dining room. How could she have agreed to attend the dinner? How could she have let herself be put on display like that? Did Isabelle really have the right to expect such things from her?

"Phelan." It is Eldon, rushing after her. "Phelan." He is slightly out of breath when he catches her up.

"Sir," says Annie, "you didn't have to leave the party on my account."

"I know," he says.

They're standing by the lit window of the dining room. Outside their breath is cloudy in the cold night air. Inside, the charlotte russe is being served. Isabelle waves her arms, conducting the tempo of her dinner party.

"Sometimes I think I married Isabelle because I wanted to be her." Eldon watches the ease with which his wife draws all the attention to herself, sews up the space around her, the absence of himself and Annie. "Do you want that? To be like her?"

Does she? Annie watches Isabelle through the window. She thinks of the glasshouse, how sometimes all she wants is for Isabelle to be looking at her in the way she does when she has all the hope in the world that whatever photograph she's taking of Annie at the moment will be the answer that she wants. *Don't take your eyes from me.* "That's not it," she says.

They stand at the window, watching the dinner party go on without them. Eldon is glad to be away from the dinner. It is not that he doesn't feel proud of Isabelle for her unexpected success. But her success makes him think about his own failures. In the drawing room, before dinner, when he'd been standing with Isabelle and Mr. Drake had come over and exclaimed about the photographs, he'd felt glad for his wife, glad to see how pleased the praise made her. But when Mr. Drake had offered to exhibit all of Isabelle's new work, without even seeing it beforehand, Eldon had felt the sharp teeth of envy at his throat. She was being rewarded for doing what she wanted to do. He was being stopped from doing what he had waited his whole life to do. There was no escaping the dismal comparison. And he has wanted so little in his life. He has wanted to travel and then to be able to record where he has been. To go away. To come back. He has wanted to turn his face to the stars. To draw the line of his breath across a blank piece of paper. *I was here.*

"You should go back in," he says. "Phelan, they'll miss you." He puts a hand on Annie's shoulder, squeezes it gently. "Isabelle will mind that you're gone," he says, and starts off down the path, away from the house, leaving Annie standing by the window.

*

The dinner party that Isabelle has meticulously planned and anticipated is not going very well at all. First Annie Phelan has bolted from the room, and now Robert Hill is holding forth on the limits of the photographic arts. Why has everything gone so horribly wrong? Isabelle looks around the table at her guests. Perhaps the sad truth is that she is only accepted within this society because she is the daughter of a Lord. They don't care a whit about her identity as an artist. They are moved only by the status of the peerage. Why did she imagine that they would care about her gold medal from Dublin? And is that why Robert Hill went on about Ireland and drove Annie Phelan from the room? Because Isabelle's award was from Dublin?

"I fear that photography will be the death of painting," Robert Hill is saying, loudly, to the dinner guests. "An art that depends so largely on technical skill and craft, on God-given talent, will be subsumed by a machine that practically anyone can operate with a little instruction. We are entering a new and dangerous age when being an artist will not mean what it does now, when an image is quick and temporary, casual even, not something to be invested with meaning, to be laboured over and appreciated partly as a result of that labour. What will art mean," he says, dramatically waving his cheese knife in the air, "when it is the property of anyone? When it is even the property of those so obviously beneath us? Of course, my dear Isabelle, you cannot help this. You aren't responsible for what is to come."

Isabelle raises an eyebrow. "Am I not?" she says. What a pompous idiot he is. Afraid, she thinks. He is so afraid that she is at the beginning of what he is at the end of, that her success will ultimately mean his failure. "Am I not the future, Robert?" she says. "Isn't that what you were saying?"

Letitia Hill clasps a napkin to her mouth. She is either coughing or laughing.

Robert hesitates for only a moment. He raises his glass of wine to the assembled guests, nods deferentially to Isabelle. "To the future, then," he says, and drinks.

As Annie slips back around the side of the house, back through the drawing-room doors, ready to go upstairs and hide in her room to avoid rejoining the dinner party, she hears voices. Crying. Wilks is trying to walk out into the hallway, but Tess has both her hands around his arm, holding on. Neither of them has seen Annie. She stops just inside the garden doors. Beyond Tess and Wilks are the closed doors of the dining room, the sounds of the dinner guests. The loud booming voice of Robert Hill.

"Get off me," hisses Wilks, shaking his arm, trying to dislodge Tess. "Get away from me, you fat cow."

"But you love me. I love you." Tess's second declaration comes out softer, like a whisper.

"Won't change anything. It's not my child. I don't have duties to you. If you hadn't gone slutting after your last master, you wouldn't be with child at all."

"He forced me," says Tess, her voice a real whisper now. "You know that. I told you that."

"Could have been lies. It all could be lies. Everything you say. In any case, I want nought to do with you now." Wilks uses his hands to firmly pry Tess's fingers from his sleeve. He turns to walk out of the room.

"I thought you cared for me?" says Tess. "Don't leave me," she cries, and throws herself onto the ground, grabs onto

Wilks's leg to stop him from walking out of the room.

Annie has recognized the scene, the pose, this vocabulary for love and loss. Guinevere. It frightens her. It is powerful, what happens in the glasshouse. Isabelle is powerful, perhaps more powerful than Annie had thought.

Wilks has surged free of Tess's desperate grasp, and is out into the hall, is gone. Annie crouches down beside Tess, tries to haul her up, but Tess collapses into Annie's arms instead, cries onto her shoulder.

The baby is not Wilks's after all. The real father is the master of the last house Tess worked in. Probably this is what made her leave that employ. Annie suddenly feels sorry for the baby, sorry for Tess. Annie rocks Tess slowly. "Hush," she says. "Hush, now. Don't cry. I'm here."

Eldon sits at his desk. When he was a boy, confined mostly to bed, coughing into a handkerchief and having to drink great steaming mixtures of foul-tasting liquids, he'd dreamed of travel. It was foolishness, he thinks now, nothing but romantic nonsense. He has read the field journal of a surveyor in the Canadian wilderness. He knows that the reality of that man's life was nothing even close to the heroicism Eldon had imagined for him. Canadian survey parties were given rations unsuitable to the harshness of the northern bush where they worked. Flour would become saturated with water from an overturned canoe. Butter would go rancid in the heat. Half the time the survey party was starving. The other half they were so badly besieged by mosquitoes and blackflies that it was, as the surveyor had recorded, *an agony of which leads men to madness.* No matter how they smeared tar and paint on their bodies or swathed their heads in cloth, the insects crawled into their noses and ears, swarmed about their heads. It was impossible to breathe without swallowing them and the faces of the men would have been constantly swollen beyond recognition.

If Eldon had been there, he would have wanted to get out. Never being able to see more than a few feet in front of him for the tangle of branches and swamp alders. Laying the heavy survey chain down across the forest floor, one sixty-six foot length at a time. The thick, thick heat of the summer pressing at him like so many hands. The flies. The rations spoiled and the men in the survey party restless with hardship. He would want to get away from that. The long climb alone with his clothes humid and filthy on his body, loose rocks of the screes skittering out from under his feet like nervous laughter. And perhaps there was one moment, near the top of the cliff, one moment before he fell from the sky. When he could see. For miles.

Eldon gets up and goes over to his map table, flips through the stack of maps until he finds the one he wants. It's the last map that this surveyor made. He finally was able to leave the closeness of the northern bush and was given the task of mapping the Great Lakes. The relief he felt at this change is evident everywhere on this map. Eldon lays a finger down and runs it slowly over the faint lines of ink. The compass rose is a spiky chrysanthemum. There are coastlines scalloped like holly leaves, islands as chiselled arrowheads. Lakes are river-tentacled, covered in grey spots and floating unattached to land, like large, bulbous soft-bag jellyfish. The scale is draped with a garland of flowers and vines. Lake Huron is called *the Grand Lake of the Sweet Sea*. This map makes Eldon's breath burn in his throat. The cartographer loved this map, not as a record or a guide or a deed of ownership, but as a landscape itself. To shift the pen so carefully around the indentations of a bay. To draw the mountain ranges as thick lengths of rope. To have no explanations. To list *latitudes observed* as though they were migrating ducks, something seen overhead and fleeting, on wing. To say on the edge of the map, *From this place to the fiery nation is forty-three days' Journey.* This map-maker felt the geography as a runner feels speed, a solid, tangible thing, bridged by the mind and crossed by the body.

When the map-maker made this map he had no idea that it might be used, years later, as a guide to the area's minerals, so they might be exploited for profit.

Terra cognito. The known world. Eldon stares down at his hand on the sheet of paper in front of him. It is a dangerous thing, making a map. If there is a pure curiosity, an authentic urge for discovery and knowledge, why is it that every map seems a precursor to some form of exploitation? Settlement or battle. When the cartographer stands on a high place and draws lines radiating out like spokes, like the rays of the sun, how can he doubt that where he is, is not the centre of the world?

I am here.

This is mine.

And whether the idea of a New World is land, or love, the map is often the first step towards colonization. The voyage motivated by the desire for discovery. The map the proof of the voyage. Settlement or battle, the proof of the map.

Eldon sits at the pivot point of an imaginary compass and wonders how straight it is in human beings, this line between discovery and conquest. How direct. The bearings of the compass. The compass of the heart.

*

Annie is hiding in her reading room, crouched down on the floor between the carriages, head resting on her knees, crying. She is still wearing Isabelle's dress, couldn't bear to face Isabelle to return it, as she is certain Isabelle will be angry that she bolted from the dinner party and never returned.

It is late at night. All the dinner guests have gone. Tess is sleeping fitfully in their attic bedroom. The house creaks with night sounds, but is quiet of human noises.

Annie doesn't know what to do about Isabelle. She can't hide here forever, will have to, at some point, go up to Isabelle's room and present herself in order to return the dress. She'll have to accept whatever blame or punishment Isabelle has decided to give to her. But it seems so unfair. Annie hugs her knees. If her family had lived, if she'd never had to leave Ireland, would she have ended up as a maid? It is as though another life has grown quietly beside her all the while she has been living this life, another life that might have been hers. In that life she might have been working on a farm, or even as a schoolteacher. She would have been Catholic, would have had a different God, or the same God approached from a different direction, up a different set of steps.

There's a sudden scrabbling noise. Mouse, thinks Annie, but it's louder than that. Rat. It's the sound of the door to the room being opened. Annie chokes back her tears, holds her breath. Someone is here in this room with her. There's the sound of the door being closed, the flicker of a candle as the person moves further into the room. Annie presses back against a carriage wheel, trying to make herself invisible. The carriage squeaks, not a small noise that could have perhaps been caused by a mouse, or by gravity working the rusted springs to earth, but a noise that could only have been caused by another person in the room.

The candle swings round towards Annie.

"Who's here?" It is Isabelle. The person in the room is Isabelle.

For a moment Annie thinks that Isabelle has followed her here, is angry enough that she can't wait for Annie to come to her. But why then would she ask, in a nervous-sounding voice, who it was who was crouched here in the dark? No, Isabelle doesn't know who it is. Annie remembers the time she was in this room before and saw that a carriage had been moved. She had thought that she was the only one to visit this room, but Isabelle must come here as well. Those carriages and prams, which Annie has thought of as belonging to this room, really belong to Isabelle. They belong to the children who died.

"Who's here?"

The voice is closer now. Annie must say something or be discovered. She stands up. "It is I," she says.

"Annie?"

"Yes, Annie."

Isabelle steps right up to her, waves the candle in her face, almost setting her hair on fire. "What in God's name are you doing here?"

Annie can't think of a good way to tell Isabelle. "This is where I come when I want to be alone." She can see the look of shock on Isabelle's face. "I know I shouldn't," she says.

Isabelle looks caught between exploding into anger or collapsing into tears. She lowers the candle. "What else," she says. "What else can happen this evening that I didn't expect." She sounds utterly defeated.

"I'm sorry about the dinner," says Annie. "I know how you wanted it to be special."

Isabelle sighs. "I'm sorry, too," she says. "Sorry that arrogant man tried to suggest the Irish gave a disease to the English cattle. How ridiculous." She touches the handle of a pram, pushes it gently so the body of the pram rocks up and down on the wheels. "I thought they would be happy for me," she says. "But they don't even like me. They certainly don't care about the photographs. All they care about is that I'm my father's daughter." Isabelle continues rocking the pram, as carefully as one would rock it if there was a baby lying asleep inside the cave of it. "What do you do here?" she asks.

Annie isn't sure if she should confess her arrangement with Mr. Dashell, how he operates a library service for her. "Think mostly," she says. "It's quiet. I like that."

"What do you think about?"

"My life."

"What about your life?" Isabelle jigs the pram up and down.

"How it might have been different," says Annie. "Sometimes I think about that."

They look at one another.

"Yes," says Isabelle. "I think about that too."

The springs of the pram make sharp squeaks. If Annie closes her eyes she can hear it as birdsong, imagine it is a summer's day and she and Isabelle are walking in the square in London.

The moving springs of the pram remind Isabelle of birdsong. It could be dusk on a summer's day. She could be rushing out to meet Ellen in the woods behind the house. "Sometimes," she says, "I think that you're the only person in the world who truly cares for me." She stops pushing the pram.

Annie doesn't know why she does what she does next. Later, when she is lying in her bed in the attic room, she tries to locate the exact point at which she decided something that she didn't even tell herself at the time. The exact moment her body acted by itself. All she can think, lying on her back in the dark, listening to Tess snore from across the room, is that it was the words. The words slid under her skin so surely and cleanly that she didn't even feel them until they'd lodged in her heart.

You're the only person in the world who truly cares for me.

It is easier than Annie would have ever imagined. Easy to lean into Isabelle, put an arm around her. Easy to kiss her. And there is that one moment when Isabelle kisses her back that Annie feels an overwhelming sense of arrival, feels that there is nothing else to want. Time, the room, her life, all of it still and stop in this kiss that takes as long as a full breathing moment.

And then the candle sets Annie's hair on fire.

There is the acrid stink of it burning. Isabelle pulls away quickly, watches Annie swat the singe out. The sound of their breathing, the overlap of it, fills the room.

"This didn't happen," says Isabelle. "Remember that."

Madonna (divine)

&

The moon shakes light through the trees outside the window and into the small attic room. The shadows of branches sway against the wall.

Annie lies awake. The branches bow and glide across the wall opposite the window.

When is the moment she crossed over and became, not someone who took orders, who reacted to what was happening, but someone who acted? Why did she do it, and why, even with that admonishment from Isabelle to undo the entire event, is Annie not sorry about that kiss?

Because she acted entirely on feeling.

Because the words loosened her skin.

Because she was not afraid, was not behaving as a servant, but as an equal.

Because she and Eldon had stood outside the house together, looking into the lit dining room, watching Isabelle cloak their absence with her voice, the fluid way she gestured, an arc of description; because, despite her anger with Robert Hill, Annie had been so taken with Isabelle's beauty that she had forgotten her reason for standing there watching the dinner go on without her.

Because God was gone from her.

Because God was suddenly back.

Because she had no past, no history, and every day Isabelle Dashell gave her a new story to believe in.

Because the body doesn't lie.

Because it was her body.

Because she has wanted to live and not known what it was she even meant by that.

Because no one has looked at her as Isabelle does.

Because it was what she wanted to happen.

Because Isabelle Dashell kissed her back.

"We have children," says Isabelle the next morning. "Real children. Not those annoying sons of my cousin. A baby and a boy. I've hired them from the bell-ringer and his wife. We'll pay them a crown a day. Baby this week. Boy the next."

"I thought I wasn't to have a child?" says Annie uneasily. "I thought we were concentrating on the state of my hands?"

"Oh, we're long finished with that." Isabelle rushes round the studio, in great spirits. She is spreading straw on the floor to simulate the stable where the baby Jesus was born. She kicks it around with her feet, as though she's playing football. "I woke up so invigorated this morning," she says. "It was such a good idea I had about the children. Doesn't it fill you with happiness, Annie?" She drop kicks a chunk of straw into the corner. It scatters into the air and floats down.

Happy isn't the word that springs foremost to Annie's mind today. She is tired from lying awake rethinking the kiss all last night. She can't believe that Isabelle has slept, that Isabelle has woken up invigorated. That Isabelle really is pretending the kiss between them never happened. And now Annie is being expected to mother a living Christ, something she swore Isabelle had promised she would not have to do.

"About last night," she says. She can't help herself.

"Stop," says Isabelle. "I thought you understood what I said." She's down on her hands and knees now, spreading the straw around. "Go and wait for the baby. The bell-ringer is meant to deliver it any minute now. And put on the cloak. You might as well be the Madonna from the moment it arrives."

Annie pulls on the heavy grey cloak and reluctantly trudges out to the front of the house to wait for the baby Jesus.

The baby Jesus is a girl. Her name is Adeline. The bell-ringer, whose name is William, hands her over hesitantly to Annie.

"She will not meet with any harm?" he says.

"She is only being photographed," says Annie.

"And that will not harm her?"

"No, no. It is as if she were being painted," explains Annie, realizing that he has no clear notion of what it means to be photographed. "She will be lying peacefully in my arms and Mrs. Dashell will be taking our photograph. Like a *carte*," she says.

"Well, I'll be back for her at teatime," says the bell-ringer, leaning over to kiss his daughter on the forehead. "Mind you take good care of her, miss."

"I will," promises Annie. The weight of Adeline is a pleasant one in her arms. She walks slowly away with the baby, feeling the father watch them until they turn past the kitchen door.

"The bell-ringer's nervous," says Annie, when she's back in the studio. "He thinks you're using his daughter as a sacrifice or something."

"Well, I'll give him an extra crown, then." Isabelle is still on her hands and knees, shaping the straw. She has made quite a pleasing hillock by the glass wall. "It will be easier when Tess has her baby. We won't have to pay her. What do you think?"

"Very nice, ma'am. A very nice stable."

"Don't mock me, Annie. We'll put the muslin on the wall so the light from the side is soft and the light from above is strong and direct," says Isabelle. "Like God. The light from above will look like God. That holy light that happens sometimes at sunset." She leans back on her heels and surveys her handiwork with satisfaction. "Yes, this will do nicely."

"This is the baby," says Annie, kneeling down beside Isabelle in the straw and passing over Adeline.

Isabelle holds the baby awkwardly. It looks up at her and gurgles approvingly. Isabelle hands Adeline quickly back to Annie. "Swaddle it," she says. "There's an old sheet over there by the camera."

Adeline doesn't like being swaddled. She cries when Annie wraps the sheet tightly around her body. "Shhh," says Annie. She rocks the baby close in her arms, whispering to it reassuringly. "You're fine. I've got you."

Isabelle watches Annie calm the baby. She does it so effortlessly. It looks as if she has always had the baby. She is the perfect Madonna. This is all she must think. The perfect Madonna. She mustn't dwell at all on what happened last night. What didn't happen last night.

"Kneel down with Rose and let me have a look at that," she says.

"Pardon?" Annie looks up at Isabelle. "What did you say?"

"I need to get a look at the scene," says Isabelle, moving over to her camera.

"You said *Rose*."

"No, I didn't."

Annie kneels down with the hot cocoon of Adeline in her

arms. The sun is strong from above. The baby closes her eyes.

Isabelle looks through the camera at Mary and the baby Jesus. Rose. "Did I really say 'Rose'?" she asks, from behind her camera.

"Yes."

Isabelle is quiet for a moment. The baby looks so peaceful sleeping. The Madonna looks wise and forgiving. "When Rose was born," she says finally, "there was so much blood. I just kept bleeding. They couldn't get it to stop. And the strange thing was that I couldn't feel it coming out of me. That scared me more than anything. There was no pain. It was my body and it was as if I was just tethered to it and it floated free of me." Isabelle remembers the terrible panic when she'd raised herself up on the pillows and was able to see down the length of her body, see that the bed sheets were drenched in her blood. "At that moment," she says, "I didn't care about the baby. I was afraid for my life. I cared only that I would not lose it. I cared only for myself. Maybe that is why she died."

Annie sees the unfamiliar look of despair on Isabelle's face. "It's all right," she says. "Look." She raises the baby gently in her arms and it's as though it's being lifted by the sun itself, up from the straw into the pure rain of light from heaven. "The baby's fine."

Isabelle finds it easier than she'd thought to persuade herself that she never kissed Annie Phelan. There are a lot of reasons for why it happened, each one strong enough to cancel the actuality of it, make it shift from light to shadow in her mind.

Because I was upset by the earlier events of the evening.

Because I was in the room with the carriages and that always unsettles me.

Because, when I first saw her, there in the dark, she looked like Ellen. It seemed like all those years ago and I stumbled into that old moment without thinking. She stepped out from the trees, and I had arrived.

Because I didn't plan for it to happen.

Because Annie Phelan is my maid.

Because it could easily have been a dream, could have been some imagined continuation of my act as Sappho.

Because I would never allow myself to want that. Again.

Because I am dead inside now.

Because I am dead inside.

Adeline is a good baby Jesus. As long as she is well-fed she doesn't mind lying in the straw, or being coddled by Annie. She seems to like the glasshouse, the bits of sun that circle around her head like bright planets. She bats her hands at them and makes noises like a bird.

Baby Jesus lies in Mary's lap. She gazes down at him in wonder. No, in shock. No, with love. She cups one hand behind his tiny head and turns it slightly towards the camera. Her other hand she tucks in against his ribs, each one as slender and small as a chicken bone.

Mary has the hood of the cloak up so that her body and the cloak are a cave for her infant son to shelter in. Mary has the hood of the cloak folded down so that her hair spills out, partially covers the baby Jesus, reminding the viewer that they were once of the same flesh. He did come from her. He is not just the child of the Lord.

Baby Jesus lies on the straw and Mary kneels beside him, an open hand at each end of his body, so that he is the base of a visual triangle that ends in the peak of her hood.

"This looks as if I just dropped him," says Annie. "As if I dropped him on the ground and now he's dead." She feels faint, she is that undone by the posing and the heat inside the glasshouse.

Isabelle looks at the scene through the camera. "You're exclaiming in wonder at the Christ child," she says.

"Yes," says Annie. "Because I dropped him and now his neck's broken. I'm sorry." She sits back on her heels and the laughter she's been suppressing bubbles out of her. Adeline wakes up and starts to cry.

"All right, all right," says Isabelle. "We'll have a little break then." She reluctantly steps back from the camera.

Annie pulls the hood from her head. She is baking inside her cloak. "Let's go outside," she says.

They walk down to the coolness of the orchard, baby Adeline held up against Annie's shoulder so that she has a perfect view of where they've come from.

The dead apples smell like melancholy — sweet, with a hint of decay under the sweetness. Isabelle puts out her hands and touches each tree as they pass. She remembers how she hurried down here to collect the fruit for a still life that was, well, lifeless. That seems to have taken place in another life altogether. A still life.

They walk through the orchard, not speaking, breathing in the scent of the aging apples. Annie watches Isabelle stretch her arms between two apple trees, like some graceful, slender bird. She shifts the warm weight of Adeline to her other shoulder. The Lord. Do I still love the Lord? What does she, Annie Phelan, know of love anyway? Does Tess truly love Wilks?

Those stopped stolen nights rocking against his body, standing up at the laundry wall. Is all love merely a hunger of the flesh?

Annie gently squeezes the baby Jesus and she lets out a little pop of air.

Do I love you? Annie stands under an apple tree and watches Isabelle walk on ahead. What is gratitude? What is love? Is love just a willingness to call feelings back by that name?

Isabelle is walking back towards Annie and Adeline. "What's the matter?" she says. "Why did you stop?"

"The baby's heavy. I want you to take her." Annie holds out the bundle of Adeline.

"No," says Isabelle. "I can't do that."

A single frozen apple falls from a tree beside them, the thunk of it hitting the ground exactly like the sound of Annie's heart in her chest.

Perhaps she could be the mother of the Lord. Perhaps part of faith is being able to become what you believe in. What you love.

"Ma'am," she says. "I want you to take the baby." She feels such poise in this moment, such a still point of certainty that this is the right thing to do.

The Lord's Will. My Will.

Without a word, Isabelle takes the small weight of the child into her arms.

Eldon watches Annie and Isabelle walk down the path from the studio to the orchard. Annie is wearing the grey cloak of the Madonna and carries a baby.

Eldon watches his wife and his housemaid enter the orchard. The last he sees, before they pass from view into the trees, is the small blank face of the baby over Annie's shoulder. He turns from the window, goes back to his desk and a stack of letters that all begin the same way.

I am writing to you concerning a young woman in my employ. Her name is Annie Phelan.

"I will miss Adeline," says Annie, in the afternoon when the baby is to be returned to her rightful parents.

"Yes, so will I." Isabelle unwinds the sheet from the small body and, when Adeline is naked, Isabelle wiggles the baby's fat arms and legs until she makes what they have come to recognize as her sounds of profound happiness. "You are a perfect creature," says Isabelle to the baby.

"A creature of the Lord," says Annie.

"A creature of the bell-ringer," says Isabelle. "You take her out to the father. I have said my goodbyes."

Annie takes the baby and dresses her in the clothes of Adeline, instead of the swaddling sheet of the Lord.

"Here," says Isabelle, when all is in order and Annie is about to leave the studio with the baby. "Take this to William." She hands Annie a photograph. It's the baby Jesus lying on the straw in the manger, with his mother leaning dutifully over him. The baby looks particularly holy as he is lying in a shaft of sunlight. "And this." Isabelle drops the coins for Adeline's hire into Annie's cloak pocket. "With our thanks."

At the end of the hire of Adeline, her father, William, has become a devotee of photography. He takes the coins. He studies the photograph with a sort of strained earnestness. "I have a cow," he says. "If you're wanting that."

"Why would we be wanting a cow?" says Annie.

"Well, you're after making a stable, are you not?" says William, pointing to the straw in the photograph. "Every good stable has at least one cow in it."

"The boy will be fine," says Annie. "Just the boy will be fine. We'll be expecting him tomorrow morning. Thank you. Goodbye." She says this last word more to Adeline than to the bell-ringer.

"Wait," William calls after her. "What about a goat? Or a nice suckling pig? I could get you a good price on a pair of geese."

The bell-ringer's son is five years old. His name is Gus, a strong name for such a delicate boy.

"He's never been a well lad," says William apologetically, when he hands him over to Annie. "You mind her, now," he says to Gus, and leaves abruptly. There are no affectionate farewells as there were with the baby Adeline. Annie already feels sorry for Gus. It's clear his father hasn't explained properly why he's here and he looks afraid and confused. Isabelle won't like it if he appears too timid.

"Are you hungry?" she asks him. "Would you like a bit of cake and some tea before we start?"

Gus nods his head and Annie takes him by the hand into the kitchen.

Isabelle is not happy this morning. It is a good idea to delay the walk to the glasshouse. She was crashing around there when Annie left her, trying to decide how to stage the child Jesus. "Boys," she'd said, thinking of the difficulty of posing her cousin's children. "Boys are always hard."

Cook is in the kitchen making stock.

"Could I have a piece of seed cake and mug of tea for the boy," says Annie. Things have not been the same between her and Cook in the fortnight since the dinner party. The friendliness between them has come apart in their hands. She swings Gus up onto the tabletop. He kicks his legs out, and back, looks around the kitchen with interest.

"Do you know what it is you're doing here?" asks Annie.

The boy shakes his head.

"Do you have a voice in your head?"

He nods.

Annie smiles. "All right," she says. "You don't have to talk if you don't wish."

Cook slaps a plate of cake and a mug of tea down next to Gus. "There you are," she says.

"Thank you," says Annie. "Eat," she says to the boy. "Then you and I will walk down the garden to Mrs. Dashell's studio. It's a house made entirely of glass. Have you ever seen one like that before?"

The boy, his mouth crammed with cake, shakes his head.

"You will be the boy you are," says Annie. "And I will be your mother, and Mrs. Dashell will take photographs of us in different poses. Then we'll have lunch. All right?"

"All right," says Gus.

"Good," says Annie, pleased that he seems to understand, even vaguely, his reason for being here.

Isabelle has regained none of her good temper by the time they get to the studio.

"What took you so long?" she says when they arrive. "I've been ready for ages." She stares at the boy. "What's your name, lad?"

"Gus, ma'am," he says, in a thin, reedy voice.

Isabelle pulls Annie aside. "What's the matter with him?" she asks. "He looks ill."

"I think he's just a little shy," says Annie.

"Nonsense. He's frail. Look at him."

They both stare at the boy. He backs up nervously and almost knocks over the camera.

"Just go over there and sit on the bench," says Isabelle, after she has rushed forward and saved her teetering camera. She returns to Annie. "Perhaps we should get Adeline back," she says.

"I thought you wanted a boy?"

"I do. But he just looks so..."

"Sensitive?" suggests Annie. "Sensitive to the wrongs of the world." She likes the boy. It's not his fault he doesn't look the way Isabelle expected him to. "If he was sleeping, it would work better," she says. "All children look more like that when they're sleeping."

Isabelle stares at Gus again, but his countenance isn't changing, no matter how hard she wills it. In fact, he's becoming more nervous and darting his head about like a startled animal. "It's too bad you won't age," she says to Annie. "I could have a whole succession of boys, all ascending in age to a man Christ. But, at a certain point, you'll stop looking like their mother and start looking like their lover. So now I'm stuck with a Christ who looks as if he's dying of a wasting disease."

"It will be fine," says Annie. "Don't worry."

Isabelle photographs Annie and Gus in duplicate poses of those she used for Annie and Adeline. Gus, for all his physical faults, is very obedient. He understands what's required of him, and he does it without a fuss. Christ lying on the straw with Mary kneeling over him. Christ splayed out across his mother's lap. He sleeps in the scene on the straw. He has his eyes open when lying on Mary's lap, for fear he'll look dead if they're closed.

The perfect temperament for going into service, thinks Annie. The passivity that Isabelle finds so annoying in him could one day get him hired into her household.

While Annie takes Gus off to the kitchen for lunch, Isabelle prints up one of the photographs she took this morning, to see how Gus really performed. She would rather do this than face luncheon in the house. Eldon, for the last week or more, has been having lunch brought to his library, saying he is too busy with work to spare the time to lunch formally. Isabelle has, in fact, barely seen her husband at all in the last little while, and finds that, in some ways, it makes no difference to her. Still, she does not want to face the emptiness of a lonely lunch for one in the dining room, and prefers to have Cook bring her food out to the studio, where, invariably, it gets cold or she forgets to eat it.

Gus is surprisingly good as a young Jesus. His slightness, instead of making him look sickly, gives him a kind of grace. His eyes are soulful. He has a resolute chin.

"Good judgement, Mary," says Isabelle, showing Annie the photograph of her holding Gus across her lap. "You were right about him."

"You called me Mary," says Annie.

"I want you to stay in character," says Isabelle. "It's easier for me to construct the scenes if you remain as the Madonna. I want you to wear the cloak every day. And from now on I will be calling you Mary."

Mrs. Gilbey had said to Annie when she arrived at Portman Square, There are only Marys and Janes in this house. You will be a Mary.

"I don't want to," she says. The name shakes loose too many horrors in her.

"Please," says Isabelle. "It's just until this series is finished." She pats Annie distractedly on the shoulder, and heads outside to print another photograph.

The next day Isabelle asks Annie to lock Gus in a cupboard. "I want to have him as an angel," she says, "and that will give him a nice look of gentle despair."

"A cupboard?" Annie looks at the pale boy standing patiently by the mound of straw that is the holy stable.

"I've done it before. It works beautifully," says Isabelle.

"Well, I'm glad you never locked me in a cupboard."

"I didn't need to. That's the joy of you, Mary. I never have to resort to my desperate tactics."

Mary. Every time Annie hears that name she flinches as though she's been struck. "How long?" she asks. "How long is he supposed to be locked in a cupboard for?"

"Two hours."

"Two hours," repeats Annie doubtfully. She remembers the closet at Mrs. Gilbey's. When she was young and locked in there at night it felt as if she would be trapped inside forever.

"Trust me. It works," says Isabelle. "Gus!" She calls him over. "You go off with Mary to the house for a little while."

Annie steers Gus up the path. "Do you have a look of gentle despair?" she asks him.

"Pardon, miss?"

"Well," says Annie. "We're going to practise your look of gentle despair. Over here, where no one can watch us." She pulls him off the path and round the side of the dew pond. "We'll stay here until we get it right, and then we'll go back to the studio and you'll tell Mrs. Dashell that I locked you in a cupboard."

"Why would you do that, miss?" asks Gus, in his tentative voice.

"Why, indeed," says Annie.

Gus has a genuine look of gentle despair after an hour and ten minutes. It alternates with his look of profound boredom that is a result of his having to practise the look of gentle despair.

"Very nice," says Isabelle approvingly, when they go back to the glasshouse to show her. "I hope you aren't too upset with Mary for what she did."

"What *you* did," says Annie to Isabelle under her breath.

"No," says Gus. Annie has promised him some cake and jam when the session is over today. He is now only thinking forward to that moment. Everything before that is simply getting there.

"I know, I know," says Isabelle to Annie. She doesn't like it when Annie is annoyed with her. Can't she see that Isabelle needs to do these things to get the proper perspective to create? "Can't you just give yourself over to the work of art?" she says.

"I *am* the work of art," says Annie. She feels less afraid of Isabelle since the kiss, since that moment of feeling truly equal to her.

"On your lap or on the ground?" asks Gus, thinking only of his promised reward for this slow torture. Already he is forgetting his look of gentle despair. "I'm forgetting the look," he says, with real despair on his face. What if he won't get the cake now?

"Perfect," says Isabelle, rushing to the camera. "Just stay as you are."

Later, when Annie remembers this moment she will forget that she was angry with Isabelle for calling her Mary and for suggesting that she lock the boy in a cupboard. She will forget Gus's boredom. She will even forget the strength and quality of the sun as it made a bow through the window wall of the glasshouse. She will call this moment back as happiness, and what she will remember of it, only, is kneeling on the straw with the soft weight of a child in her arms. "Look up at me," Isabelle says. "As if you love me."

"An angel is a good thing," says Annie, carefully threading one of Gus's small arms through the leather straps on the underside of the goose wing.

"It doesn't mean I'm dead?"

"No, no." Annie pats his shoulder, reassuringly. "It means you're heavenly. A creature of the Lord. It's not about being dead. It's about being chosen to be special because you are full of kindness and mercy." She kneels down in front of him and guides his other arm into the wing harness.

"I look big," says Gus, peering over her shoulder into the looking-glass. With his outstretched winged arms he is as big as an eagle. Annie tightens the straps and then moves behind him. He stands with his arms stretched right out and they both look at the magnificence of this, of him, in the mirror.

They are in Eldon's bedroom because the looking-glass there is large enough to show Gus his reflection with his wings spread. He had expressed reluctance at being an angel, and Annie has brought him indoors to show him how wonderful he would look as a creature of heaven.

"Do angels have clothes?" asks Gus, looking in the mirror at his loose blouse and short pants.

"Good question." Could he just wear his blouse, like a nightshirt? Would they have to tailor a sheet to fit around him like a shift? He and Annie stare at each other in the mirror. "Why don't I run out and ask the photographer," she says. "You just stay where you are and admire yourself."

"All right," says Gus, perfectly happy to remain in attendance to his visually impressive bird self until she returns to him.

Annie walks out of Mr. Dashell's bedroom, along the upstairs hall, and down the main stairs. At the bottom she turns left into the drawing room. Tess is there, sweeping out the hearth. They stare at each other as Annie crosses the room, opens the French doors onto the terrace, and goes outside.

Isabelle is not in the studio. The bench has been moved onto the carpet of straw so that the boy angel can kneel on the straw and rest his elbows on the bench, hands pressed together in prayer.

It's a dull, cool day. The absence of sun makes the straw and the narrow bench look as if they really are inside a stable. Annie surveys the dark starkness of it. Perhaps the bell-ringer is right and they do need a cow or some sort of animal to fill out the scene. Without them, without Annie and Isabelle and Gus, the studio seems huge with loneliness. Funny that a photograph, which is a still thing like this room, depends so much on their living, moving selves.

Annie sits on the bench and tries to imagine how she looks from Isabelle's usual position at the camera. She tilts her head up. She turns to the right. That's your best side, Isabelle had said, although Annie, when she sees herself in a mirror, cannot deduce why this is.

After sitting on the bench for a while Annie goes to the

camera, stands behind it, and tries to imagine herself sitting on the bench. She swings up the tiny brass cover and peers through the lens. The perspective of the lens shrinks the world to only what is directly in front of it — the straw, the stone bench. The side walls of the studio are no longer there. Nor the cold day beyond the glass. It is a small enough world, thinks Annie, that it can be easily controlled. That is something to want.

The wind knocks softly against the studio. Annie straightens up. That is something, too, she thinks. None of the sounds of the world, the smells, the way things feel, make it to the photograph. The photograph is evidence of this world and yet it really doesn't come from this world at all.

Annie is not sure how long she stands behind the camera, listening to the weather and the creak of the building. Suddenly she remembers Gus waiting in Eldon's bedroom for her return. He will be getting worried.

Isabelle must be in the darkroom. Annie will walk over there and knock on the door, their signal for Isabelle to finish what she is doing and rejoin the above-ground world.

Tess is crying, down on her knees in front of the drawing-room fireplace. Her tears fall into the ash, become inky black drops on the stone. Tess has again tried to talk to Wilks, to plead for his understanding. All that has happened is that she has heard again how he doesn't love her, has heard again how he no longer wants to touch her now that she has grown so huge with the pregnancy. He avoids her when- and wherever possible. He has actually said the words, *Don't come near me*. She said, *I love you*, and he said, *You're a slut. How could anyone love you?*

Tess has been told by Cook to set fires in the drawing room and upstairs in the bedrooms because it is a cold day and the house, drained of heat, is chill and damp. Tess has trouble with the tinder. It's not catching. She takes some crumpled paper from the wastebasket and throws it on top of the coals. It licks into flame. In her distress Tess neglects to put the screen back in front of the fireplace. As she leaves the room and closes the door one of the fiery balls of paper rolls out onto the rug.

The fire chooses favourites. The tassels of the rug. A shawl draped over the back of a chair. The fire is quick-fingered, touching what it wants so gently at first, saying, Trust me, trust me.

Annie has knocked on the door of the coal cellar and is standing in the stone stairwell, waiting for Isabelle to come out. The entrance to the coal cellar is down a small flight of steps, so that where Annie is standing is partially underground. She can't see over the structure of the cellar. The rest of the house is far away and invisible. She doesn't see the fire, but she does hear Tess's screams, shrill and terrifying.

Annie scrambles up the steps and around the side of the coal cellar. Tess, tearing down the path from the house, runs right into her. She clutches Annie's cloak. "Help," she says. "Help."

"What? What is it?"

Tess's breath is threadbare. "Fire," she says, holding tight onto Annie. "The house is on fire."

"Tess," says Annie. "Calm down." She grabs Tess's face in her hands, so she's looking straight into Annie's eyes. "Is Cook out? Is Mr. Dashell?"

"Cook is getting Mr. Dashell. It's the main house. He's not in danger. Cook is *outside*," says Tess, fumbling for the right words to make Annie understand what is happening. "She's getting Mr. Dashell from outside."

"Go," says Annie. "Get Wilks to ride out to the Brooks' farm for help."

Tess stumbles off down the path.

"No, wait." Annie runs after her. "What about the boy? Did he get out?"

"What boy?" says Tess.

Isabelle thought she heard a knock on the darkroom door, but it didn't happen again, so she thinks she's mistaken. Then she thinks she hears a scream, but she's counting off the seconds that the negative needs to be under the developing liquid, and she is relieved when the scream doesn't recur and she doesn't have to rush outside to see what is happening. If it is urgent enough, Annie will come and bang on the door to let her know. She doesn't have to worry.

"Thirty-six, thirty-seven." She counts out loud and her voice fills the small brick chamber, seals her safely inside this pocket of darkness.

Cook stands in the roses outside Mr. Dashell's library, banging on the window with her fist. "Fire," she yells. And then, "Sir." The thorns are scratching at her legs. She turned her ankle rushing down the path and long needles of pain shoot up it as she stands in the flower bed.

Eldon, sitting at his desk, hears the shouts from far away, as though they're underwater. He looks up and sees a face at his library window, and then a fist raised and hammering on the leaded glass. It's Cook. Behind her, smoke trails in wisps above the hedge. His first thought is that the garden is on fire. He doesn't realize that the smoke has blown over from the main house until he has unlatched the window and sees where it is coming from.

"Quick," says Cook, not knowing how much longer she'll be able to remain on her painful ankle. "The house is on fire. Come out the window. Sir," she says, as an afterthought.

Eldon unlatches his window and swings his leg over the sill. He sees the smoke behind Cook gathering like a storm cloud. "Is everyone out?" he asks.

"Everyone's out, sir." Cook puts her hand out for him to grasp as he guides himself over the sill and out of the library, but at that moment Tess rushes round the side of the house.

"She's gone in," she says to Cook. "She says there's a boy in there."

"The bell-ringer's son," says Cook. "I thought they were all down the garden."

"Who's gone in?" says Eldon. He is perched on the window sill, one leg out against the wall of the house, one leg still anchored on the floor of the library.

"Annie, sir. Annie's gone back in," says Tess.

It is the easiest thing Eldon has ever done. He doesn't even think about it, just leans his weight back into the room and his leg clears the sill. He lets go of Cook's hand, and as he moves from the window, listening to their cries of protest, it's as if they're at sea, the great smoky spray behind their wrecked ship. It is their drowning cries he hears, as he sails safely past them.

*

Annie comes through the kitchen door. She wets a cloth in the pail of water by the sink and clamps it over her face. The kitchen is clear but there's a lot of smoke in the main hall, billowing out from the drawing room where the fire must have started. Annie sprints up the staircase, as fast as her heavy cloak will allow.

Gus is standing in the upstairs hall, pressed against a wall. He is not crying or screaming, doesn't say anything to Annie when she rushes out of the smoke towards him. There are flames trickling down the feathers on his wings. She removes the cloth from her mouth. They stare at each other for the briefest of moments. It is now that Annie feels afraid. When she ran into the house and up the stairs she was so intent on finding the boy that she wasn't aware of anything else. Now, when she sees how frightened Gus is, she thinks he must be recognizing the same fear in her eyes. He must know how afraid she is, and in that moment, with the smoke blurring around them, Gus reminds Annie of herself as a child in Mrs. Gilbey's home. How small and scared she must have been.

"Put your arms out," she says to Gus. He stretches his burning wings so that they stay clear of her clothes and she runs with him like this, down the hallway to Isabelle's bedroom. The bedroom is at the end of the house. The fire seems to be mainly in the central portion of the building, seems to have burnt through the drawing-room ceiling into part of the upstairs hall. It is not fanning out. They will be safer in Isabelle's bedroom.

There is smoke in the room, but the window is open. Annie sets Gus down by the door, closes it, then goes over to the bed and hauls the mattress off it. She struggles the mattress through the window and it somersaults to the earth below.

The wings on Gus's arms are burning. It is too late to try and fumble them off him. It will take too long to undo the leather straps. Annie grabs the boy under the arms again, rushes him over to the window, and then leans with him in her arms over the sill.

"I've got you," she says.

And then she lets him go.

The shape he makes as he's falling, his fiery wings spread and holding the air, is almost the shape of a country. All jagged on the edges, carved out by the punishing sea.

Annie leans out over the sill and watches the boy fall to safety. Michael, she thinks. Connor. He is her brother and she has saved him and now he can live, again. She has dropped him from the heavens and he flies down to his mortal life.

Angel of Mercy. I have set you down upon the earth.

Annie feels something around her ankles. It's like a tickle, like a feather that has worked loose from the wings and is brushing up against her legs. She looks down. Her cloak is on fire.

Eldon moves through the corridor outside his library towards the main part of the house. He is moving into the smoke and halfway down the hall his eyes are stinging too much and he can no longer see. He puts his arms out, feeling along the walls to find out where he is. He has never realized how thoroughly he knows this house, how every nick in the wallpaper, every texture of picture frame is a landmark detailing his position. His hands, he thinks, his hands have always made journeys. They have been to many wondrous places. They have traced the skin of Isabelle and felt along the walls of this darkened hallway. They have held the head of a flower filled with rain. If he had been a surveyor, walking through the wilderness, surely he would have been no different. He would have felt distance out, tree by tree, measuring the landscape by feel. Just as now his hands slide over walls, marry the shape of doorframe and lintel.

I am here.

The main staircase is burning. The banister a shivering ladder of flame. Eldon has pulled himself up the few stairs that are still safe. He is coughing now and having trouble breathing. There's a pain in his head. He sits down on the bottom stair. Perhaps the back staircase is still functional. He should go into the kitchen and check it. He could get out through the kitchen door if need be. Phelan is probably long gone by now. But he doesn't move. He has used all his strength to get here and now he's coughing too much to go any farther. But it is all right, he thinks, sitting on the stair. He has done his best. He has gone back for a member of the expedition. He has been his bravest self.

It has been a long journey. He is finally home.

And as Eldon sits there, for the few moments that he sits there, he feels the air cool around him, until his skin tingles with it. His breath is smoke, rising out of his body. Ash wafts down from the floor above, floats down the emptiness where the staircase used to be, as fine and particulate as snow falling to earth. He is snow, falling to earth.

When Isabelle finally opens the door of the coal cellar and climbs up the few stairs into the garden, it is as if she is climbing up into one of her own photographs. Everything is blurry, out of focus, soft and grey as the inside of a cloud. She walks through the smoke in the slow way one moves inside a dream, noticing things as though she's drugged or underwater. Smoke, she thinks. It is smoke after all.

When she gets round the side of the coal cellar and can see the burning house, she thinks, Who lived there? as though the fiery ruin is something she has stumbled across, accidentally, on a walk in the woods.

There are men with buckets, and Cook and Tess sitting on the ground by the rose bushes.

The kitchen is still intact. So is the wing with the library. Everything else is a smouldering wall of stone. Isabelle walks closer to the guttering main part of the house. She hears her formal name, distant, as if she is being called back from across a great stretch of water. This is where the stairs were, she thinks. This is where I lived.

She looks down. Her feet are hot from walking on the jumble of stones. There, by the toe of her left boot, is something familiar. She bends down and picks up the glass plate. It is smoky and the glass is warm like skin. When she holds it up to the light she can still make out the image. The head turned towards the camera. The beautiful, ordinary face of Annie Phelan, as Grace, looking out at her.

"Look!" cries a man's voice behind Isabelle. She turns to the voice. It's one of the men with the water buckets. He's pointing to the upstairs of the house. Isabelle looks up. She sees a slow blur riding down the smoke from an upstairs window. An angel. A child. It's the winged boy, floating down a ladder of air, drifting calmly down to earth.

Cosmographia universalis

Eldon is laid out in the library. It is one of the few parts of the house that has remained undamaged and it is the most dignified place to put him until the doctor can get there. He has been heaved up onto the big library table, right on top of a stack of his maps.

Isabelle stands in front of her husband. Most of his clothes have burnt off his body. He still wears the upper portion of his trousers, and one shoe. His hair and beard are gone. Mercifully, one of the men has shut his blackened eyes. The stench of his scorched flesh is so strong that Isabelle will wake for months afterward with the acrid smell of his burnt body occupying her like a ghost.

His skin is black and blistered. Most of his fingernails are missing. "From crawling," one of the men said. "We found him on his hands and knees. He must have been crawling to the kitchen to try and get out that way."

Cook has blamed herself. "I had him by the hand," she said. "I should have been quicker in getting him out that window."

Isabelle can't bring herself to touch her husband, to lay a hand on his flesh, black and bubbled like tar. She wants instead to remember the smooth slide of it from before. A long time before. Intact. Beautiful.

It must have hurt so much. She hopes he wasn't too afraid. She hopes he wasn't calling for her. If she'd known what was happening she would have gone in after him. But even as she thinks this she knows that this is not the truth.

"I'm sorry," she says.

They had moved away from each other slowly, almost imperceptibly, like the drift of the continents that he'd told her about once, each year a microscopic shift in attitude and distance. They had married for what they had pretended was love. They had lived in this house. They had buried three infants together, each one marked with a small white stone with a carving of an angel's wing on it. The unnamed graves said simply, *Infant Son* and *Infant Daughter of Isabelle and Eldon Dashell.* On Rose's small stone it said, *Our Baby Called Too Soon to Heaven.*

He was a shore her body had once sought. He was a place she had been that still glows dimly in the memory of her flesh. Now that he has died he has taken their whole shared past with him and she is left, here, in the ruin of their lives, to go on into a new world, without him. What is she to do with her understanding of him? She knows his history, the names of all his family, every piece of his clothing. All the details of Eldon that, when he lived, were just part of their life together. And what about her? Will anyone ever know Isabelle again, as long and as well as Eldon did? He has remembered her, so she doesn't have to. Wasn't this love? Not the bright flare of Isabelle's past, but the subtle, constant present of life with Eldon. The accumulation of small moments, wasn't that at least equivalent to an instant of profligate desire?

The truth is that Eldon's death means also that Isabelle will never be as she was, will not exist as strongly as before. She pushes her forehead against the hard edge of the library table. The truth is that Eldon has gone, and he has taken her with him.

Isabelle closes her eyes.

"Dear God," says the doctor, when he sees the condition of Eldon's body. He approaches it slowly, keeps raising his hand above it, but never setting it down on the burnt flesh.

Isabelle stands by her husband's desk and watches the village doctor, whom she and Eldon have known all their married life, the man who delivered her three dead children, struggle with accepting what has happened.

Isabelle sits down at the desk. "He was dead when they had controlled the fire enough to go inside. He was found like this. There is nothing you could have done for him, Russell."

The doctor bows his head over Eldon, says nothing.

Isabelle turns away and, in doing so, sees a letter on her husband's desk. She picks it up and slips it into the pocket of her dress.

When they carry Eldon from the library to the doctor's carriage, Isabelle stands by the table, watching as he is moved from the room. The smell of him is still in the air, the scorch of hair and flesh. When she looks down, after she has heard the clatter of the carriage wheels over the stones on the driveway, she sees the map he was lying on has become a blotter for the ink of his dissolving body. His flesh has divided counties and formed tiny islands in the sea. The seepage from his body has permanently altered the maps beneath him. New lines have been created. New bays and, further inland from the coast of Ireland, a darker shading to the landscape. On the map under that one, an early survey of the Great Lakes in the Dominion of Canada, Eldon's body has oozed plasma into the basin of Lake Superior, completely changing the course of the northern shore. And on the map under that, the Arctic Circle spreads out to join hands with Greenland. Like strata in a bluff, Isabelle peels the maps one from the other to see how they have changed, how they have revealed themselves. He has been granted his wish. Eldon Dashell has been on a journey. He has made his map of the world.

In the days after the fire they live in the parts of the house that have survived the flames. The several rooms in Eldon's wing have been turned into a bedroom for Isabelle, a bedroom for Annie and Tess. Eldon's library, aside from storing some of the wreckage from the fire, has been left as it was. The kitchen is functional, although now that there is no longer a main section to the house, it is only accessible from the garden. To get a cup of tea or to make supper, Isabelle has to walk around to the kitchen, which has become its own building now, and enter through the kitchen door. The part of the wing that used to be attached to the main house, and was just a jagged hole, has been partially bricked up to provide shelter from the elements, to make the wing a self-contained building. A heavy blanket serves as a door.

Isabelle can't decide what to do about the house. At first she wanted to leave it immediately, but there were too many things to think through, to consider, and so she just stayed, because really that seemed the easiest course of action. And now, there is something comforting about being there. The house is as

Isabelle feels. Parts of it are safe, parts of it are utterly ruined. She is constantly reminded, by everything around her, of what has been lost to her. And what has been saved.

Wilks has been let go. Cook has gone to her sister's in Chertsey to recuperate and rest. She says she wants to come back into the household, but Isabelle thinks this is only because she still feels guilty about Eldon. Isabelle is not sure she wants Cook back, and hopes that, in the end, Cook decides to move on. At the moment it feels as if the fewer people she is responsible for, the better.

Annie Phelan has burns on her hands from when her cloak was on fire and she turned back from the window after dropping Gus to safety, turned back and tore the burning cloth from her body. She is still bruised and sore from her own flight down, but otherwise, miraculously, unscathed. Gus, aside from some minor burns on his arms, is also fine.

Because Annie can't do much with her hands at the moment, and because Tess's baby is due soon, it is Isabelle who has to take care of their everyday survival. She is not used to this kind of work, this kind of responsibility. A week of cooking has put her into extremely bad humour.

"This has to stop," she says, slamming down two plates of fish pie in front of Tess and Annie. "I can't be expected to continue in this way."

Annie gingerly combs her fork through the mound of potatoes, looking for fish bones. Isabelle hasn't proved to be the most careful of cooks. Yesterday there were small stones in with the vegetables.

"I'm sorry, ma'am," says Tess. This is her response to Isabelle's frustration at her new household role, and it only seems to infuriate Isabelle further.

"You will just have to leave," says Isabelle. "I can't be

expected to keep you on. Not with the baby coming this month. You'll be of no use whatsoever."

There is silence. Annie can hear the wind fumbling the kitchen door. She watches the breath catch in Tess's throat, the way her hands flutter down to her sides and are still. She thinks of the Vicar of Wakefield, of how he would embrace this new misfortune, would be optimistic and generous in this moment. "You can't do that," she says to Isabelle. "You're in charge now. You have to look after us. All of us."

Isabelle is standing very still. "And why," she says, "do I have to do anything you say?" Her voice snaps shut on each word.

Tess is breathing hard with nerves. She keeps her head down, won't look up at Isabelle.

What would happen to Tess if she was forced to leave Middle Road Farm? Would the baby end up in an orphanage? Then a workhouse? Would the baby end up like Annie?

Annie stands up to face Isabelle. She hadn't realized it before but they are close to the same height. She wants to say, You have to think of someone other than yourself for once, but instead she says, "I thought you cared for me." The line, meant to be another line, meant to sound casual, comes out all shaky, the words rattling hollow in the stillness of the room.

Isabelle looks about to say something, but says nothing, and Annie turns from her, walks out of the kitchen.

Eldon's library smells of the fire. Annie stands by his desk and the charred rasp of the air in her lungs brings back the moment in Isabelle's bedroom when she leaped out the window. The stench of her own clothes burning on her body. The rush of air pushing at her like a soft choir of hands as she fell to earth.

What Annie wants from this room is right where she remembered it being. She tucks it inside her cloak and hurries from the house.

The winter is nearly over. Already, as Annie walks across the garden, there are snowdrops starting to inch up through the grass, the sudden sight of them so unexpected, like words you didn't mean to say that blossomed on your tongue and surprised you with their truth.

I thought you cared for me.

The trees are webbed in soft light. They are waiting for their green selves to begin. There are small fat robins on the grass, hopeful for worms. Everywhere the trust in spring, that what is here will be enough, will be all that there is to want.

The stones are still piled up by the fencepost. The note they left is still there. Annie unfolds it carefully, reads the simple words they left, again.

January 3, 1866. Expedition under the command of Captain Eldon Dashell, and with Annie Phelan as Ship's Company, set out to retrace the last known moments of two of John Franklin's crew.

Then she removes what she took from Eldon's library from under her cloak. The sheet of *cartes* he had made. The images of him standing very upright, one hand on the top of the world. With the pencil she also took she writes around the edges of their original note. *February 15, 1866. Captain Dashell died a week ago. I have...* There are really only two things to say now. *I have gone on.* Or, *I have gone back.* Annie leans against the fencepost, looks out across the empty field, looks back towards the bulk of the house. *I have gone on,* she writes.

And then she goes back.

*

The glasshouse wasn't touched by the fire. Some of the panes of glass cracked with the heat from across the garden and some of the panes are blurred with smoke stains. Isabelle hasn't been in here since the fire. Nothing has changed. The straw is still on the floor by one wall. The bench is arranged on the straw, all set for the angel that was Gus to kneel down beside it. Her camera stands patiently in front of the empty scene, waiting for it to arrive.

At first Isabelle doesn't see Annie Phelan standing against the far wall, so intent is she on surveying for damage. When she does finally notice her, she just stands and stares, puts her hand into her dress pocket, and runs her thumb along the edge of the letter there, the letter she took from Eldon's desk. *Miss Annie Phelan c/o Mr. Eldon Dashell* it says on the envelope. It's postmarked Country Clare, Ireland. On the overleaf the name of the sender, *Phelan*. Isabelle has steamed the letter open and read the contents, knows what they say so thoroughly that she could open her mouth and recite them.

> *Dear Sir,*
>
> *I was given your letter by the County Clerk to whom you wrote concerning a certain Annie Phelan with whom you are acquainted.*
>
> *My name is Michael Phelan. I have reason to believe that I am Annie's brother. I was told my entire family died in the famine, so you can imagine how happy your letter has made me for forging this new and unexpected hope.*
>
> *Please be so kind as to pass this along to my sister so she may write to me at the address below.*
>
> *Respectfully yours,*
> *Michael Phelan*

Isabelle wants to close her hand around this letter, draw it out, hand it to Annie, say—"Here, this is what you've been waiting for." But instead she says, "Tess doesn't have to go. I won't make her go."

Annie looks at the straw on the ground. The light coming through the roof makes the straw a tangle of gold at her feet.

She remembers the architecture of this scene they were preparing for. She remembers the moment she stood in the studio, looking at the straw and the dull light hefting through the window, the moment before she went out to the coal cellar in search of Isabelle. "Take my photograph," she says.

"As who?"

"As me." Annie tilts her head up, looks at Isabelle.

The light this afternoon is beautiful. Clean. Every object caught by it seems sharp and distinct. The spring sky, through the glass roof, is as blue as the sea.

Isabelle stands behind her camera. Don't leave me, she thinks. I can't lose you too. She moves the camera forward so that Annie's face fills the frame. She screws down the focus. It takes a few tries to get the stopper out of the collodion bottle, but she accomplishes this, coats the glass plate with the sticky liquid. She plunges it into the silver nitrate bath, slides the glass into the plate holder, and pops that into the back of the camera.

Annie holds her head up as straight as she can. Perhaps, for once, for the first time, the photograph of this moment will be the same image to her and Isabelle. They will see the identical thing. It will not be simply persuasion. It will not be one person describing and one person believing that story. It will be a place to start out from, a moment unclouded by desire. A clear, clear day. That is something to hope for. That is something to want.

Isabelle has her hand on the camera lens. "That's good,"

she says. "You look like a heroine. Like someone who has just saved a child. Don't move."

Annie thinks of the night she kissed Isabelle, how that moment when she felt fully alive she is not allowed to speak of again. How Isabelle kept a room full of carriages and toys that belonged to children she can't forget and won't remember. And that room, where they kissed, is gone now, destroyed by the fire. Nothing left of that evening. How here, in the studio, this place where they've been the most intimate, in front of the camera, Isabelle will let Annie be anyone, except herself. Annie has existed for Isabelle, not as who she is, but only as who Isabelle wanted her to be at a particular moment. Now, again, she is to be a heroine, a girl who has rescued a child from a deadly fire. Early on, when Annie was full of admiration for Isabelle's competent strength in the world, when Annie was grateful just to be noticed, it was enough just to be paid attention to. Now it is not. That kiss felt real, was real. She wants Isabelle to admit this, to admit that it was Annie she kissed. But Isabelle Dashell has looked so hard at Annie Phelan and has never once seen her at all.

Annie thinks of Eldon, of all the places he imagined going and never went to. Now he is buried beside his children in the small village cemetery. It rained on the day of his funeral. Annie had stood beside Isabelle while the coffin was lowered into the muddy grave. On the way down it bumped against the sides, against roots thick as fists, the dark eye of a stone embedded into the earth wall. Annie had cried. Isabelle had turned back for the carriage at the first shovel load of earth on the coffin. She had flinched at the sound of it.

Eldon would have been proud that Annie had rescued the boy from the fire. She had behaved in a loyal way to those in her charge. She had been a good member of the expedition.

What she thinks now is that she will go back to Ireland by herself, back to County Clare, to try and find out what happened to her family. Eldon would like that. And even though the letters he sent there were never answered, if she went herself and made enquiries, there might be someone who would recall the Phelans. Yes, this is what she will do.

Annie holds her head up as straight as she can. This photograph is all Isabelle will allow her to give. This is all Isabelle will have to remember her by. She wants it to be a good likeness. "I'm ready, Isabelle," she says.

~

The winged boy falls to earth. Isabelle watches his slow flight down, the streaks of smoke articulate from the trailing ends of his feathery arms. The knot his small body makes in the air.

It is the perfect photograph, and she has missed it.

This is what she has always feared. That she will not be able, no matter how she wills it or orchestrates it, to create an image as pure and true as this. That what she does is not really about life, about living. It is about holding on to something long after it has already left.

Like grief. Like hope.

Life is the unexpected generosity of a kiss.

It is the falling moment. Unrecorded.

Author's Note

The photographs described in *Afterimage* are loosely imagined renderings of a series of photographs taken by the Victorian photographer Julia Margaret Cameron of her housemaid, Mary Hillier.

The quotes from Sappho are taken from a translation by Mary Barnard.

The quoted passages of the whaling diary are from the *Journal of the Margaret Rait—1840–1844* by Captain James Doane Coffin.

The quoted passages and descriptions of McClintock's voyage in search of Franklin are from *The Voyage of the 'Fox' in the Arctic Seas: A Narrative of the Discovery of the Fate of Sir John Franklin and His Companions* by Captain Francis Leopold McClintock; London, 1859.

The quoted passages from John Franklin are taken from *Arctic Breakthrough: Franklin's Expeditions 1819–1847* by Paul Nanton.

Acknowledgements

I am indebted to the photographs of Julia Margaret Cameron for their haunting inspiration.

Thanks to the Corporation of Yaddo, where some of this book was written.

I would like to thank M. Lindsay Lambert for his expertise in Victorian photography, and my grandfather, Ronald Brett, for his imaginings of Sussex life in 1865.

Thanks, as always, to Frances Hanna.

In particular, I am grateful to my editor, Phyllis Bruce. Her kindness, thoroughness, and keen judgement have made me a better writer, and *Afterimage* a better book.